THE AUTHOR

Nick Cann was born in London in '
Since 1981 he has worked as a free
journalist and graphic designer.
In 1989 he moved to Northern Ireland
where he works as a design consultant.
Come Home, Harry String is his third
published novel.

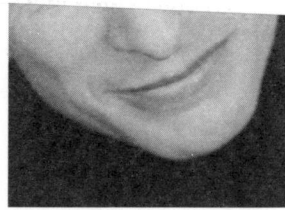

Come Home Harry String

BY NICK CANN

indiego.co.uk

FIRST PUBLISHED IN THE UK IN 2017 BY

indiego

HOLYWOOD, COUNTY DOWN

© indiego 2017

TEXT © NICK CANN

ALL RIGHTS RESERVED

Nick Cann is hereby identified as author of this work in accordance with section 77 of the copyright, designs & patents act 1988

ISBN 978-0-9549066-2-7

WRITTEN BY NICK CANN

FRONT COVER ILLUSTRATION BY NICK CANN SENIOR

EDITED & PROOFREAD BY VICTORIA WOODSIDE

PRINTED BY GRANGE PRINTING

BOUND BY ROFINSON MORNIN

All rights reserved.
No part of this publication may be reproduced, stored in a retrieval system or transmitted in any form or by any means – nor by way of trade or otherwise, be lent, resold, hired out or otherwise circulated – in any form binding or cover other than that in which it is published and without the publisher's prior permission in writing and without similar condition, including this condition being imposed on the subsequent purchaser.

FOR BRIAN AND SHEILA

ACKNOWLEDGEMENTS:

"Sorry Seems To Be The Hardest Word"

Words by Bernie Taupin
Music by Elton John
© Copyright 1976 Rouge Booze Incorporated/HST Publishing Limited.
Universal Music Publishing Limited.
All Rights Reserved. International Copyright Secured.
Used by permission of Music Sales Limited.

WITH THANKS TO:

Dawn, Sophie, Chloe, Jack and Poppy
Wendy and Judy

And special thanks to my good friend and illustrator,
Nick Cann from Napa, California for the front cover illustration

AND TO THOSE WHO HAVE HELPED, ADVISED & SUPPORTED:

Derek and Valerie Geddis
Terry McCracken, Al Cassels, John Wallace
Romas Foord, Simon Gough
and Robert Doherty

1

10pm. Tuesday, 20 May 2008.

Fifteen miles out of Enniskillen, on the main road to Belfast, the carriageway is empty. A shower lashes at the tarmac. It is a black night, and cold for the time of year.

Beyond the grass verge a Volvo Estate has careered off the road, ploughing a scar down the embankment and leaving clods of earth curling away from the furrow like ears of corn. The car has barrel rolled into the field, sliding the last few yards on its roof before coming to rest.

The Volvo's engine stalls and dies in a shudder. The key is still turned in the ignition, however; the electrics live. Andy Williams continues to sing "Music to Watch Girls By" on the car radio cassette mindless of the mayhem.

In his topsy-turvy world the driver dangles upside down suspended by his seat belt, limbs limp and eyes shut. Blood oozes from a cut above his eye and then drips onto the ceiling below staining the fabric a watery red.

There is little other sound to accompany Andy Williams save for the gusting wind and the whining of a wheel spinning as though determined to reach its destination come what may and screeching on its bearings like a badly worn stylus.

Meanwhile, the surviving headlamp fires its beam across the field to illuminate the copse on the far side as though there is to be a theatrical performance.

Caught in the glare, a figure bobbles through the mire towards the wreck: an old man towing a waterlogged collie on a length of string. Every time he runs into the lamplight the man jerks his hand to shield his eyes and half chokes the dog. His other hand waves a torch through the dark to dance a flickering light over the wreckage.

The man moves through the grass as fast as he can with legs swathed in a sodden overcoat. Silhouettes stretch far behind man and dog, distorted into the shadow puppets of a giant and its beast.

Though tired, the old man knows he has no option but to help, and on reaching the wreck kneels down beside the shattered windscreen, careless of the mud soaking into the knees of his trousers. The dog tugs to back away from the car, pulling and wriggling to free itself from its collar. The old man grips harder.

"You all right, son?"

No answer.

The old man removes his cap and, bending double, leans in through the small aperture to reach for the driver's wrist. The flesh is cold. He feels the pulse. It's weak. The old man smells diesel. He imagines the fuel seeping into the soil and the stain it will leave long after the wreckage is gone. The diesel has an overbearing stench.

Beside a puddle of fuel on what was once the car's ceiling but now is its floor, the old man finds a mobile phone that he lifts free from the nuggets of glass and splatters of blood. He doesn't own a mobile himself and has never used one, but taps in 999 and then presses the green telephone symbol whilst praying that he is not being as incompetent as he feels. He clasps the phone to his ear as if listening for the sea and sighs with relief when he hears ringing and then a voice:

"Emergency services—"

"There's a man trapped in a car. He's rolled it. He's still inside. I think he's in a bad way!"

"OK. Can you give me your exact location, please?"

"Er, the main road to Belfast, near Ballykeenan. About

fifteen miles out of Enniskillen. The field runs beside Moss Road on the Enniskillen side. They'll see the car lights."

"Can you tell me anything about the driver's condition, sir?"

"Not good. He's out cold and he's bleeding. So be quick. Please be quick ... I can smell diesel."

The old man steps back and stands beside the car's steaming carcass to wait for the din of the emergency services. And as the wind dies down and the rain eases and the offside wheel stops spinning, Andy Williams sings on oblivious to the chaos and of the commotion to come.

2

4pm. Monday, 24 November 2008.

*"What have I got to do to make you love me?
What have I got to do to make you care?"*

Radio 2. Elton John and Blue singing "Sorry Seems To Be The Hardest Word" – a reworking of the classic and, perhaps, not everybody's cup of tea. It brought a tear to Harry String's eye, though. The song sparked a memory of being at home with his mother, off school and confined to bed with tonsillitis. 1970-something; the original version was a big hit then.

At home in Portstewart on the North Antrim coast, Harry's head would have been fuzzy with fever. He'd be absent from school now for as long as he could be bothered to feign illness after the antibiotics had worked their magic. Since he was an only child, his mother would be wary of the slightest sign of infection, virus or cold. Couldn't afford to lose him. Couldn't afford to be overprotective either. But whilst he was laid up she would run around fetching glasses of Lucozade and mining jigsaws from the cupboard under the stairs. And there were crayons. Lots of crayons.

"What shall I draw?"

"Why don't you draw me a cat, Harry?"

To this day he could never understand: why always a cat? *She preferred dogs. Why always a frigging cat?*

But he'd give it a bash whilst listening to the radio.

This was the last time he could remember being mothered before the onset of puberty, teenage rebellion, a university education and the escape into adulthood. He didn't know it then but realised now that the song marked the ending of their special bond.

"And it always seems to me, that sorry seems to be—"
Harry reached forward and turned the radio off.
Thinking of his mother still brought a tear. The five years since her death seemed like a few months. And what had he left? Memories of being a small boy in her care and an art deco locket passed down to her by his grandmother. He felt its outline under his shirt. A woman's locket, but he always wore it. It carried his mother's photo. It was all he had; the only memento to survive his father's grief. The heartbreak had driven his dad to dump or burn the rest of her belongings, including her diaries.

If Billy String, Harry's father, noticed his son's distress, he didn't react. He was too busy steering clear of the other cars on the dual carriageway, their number growing in the rush hour. He was intent on driving his son home from the hospital without incident. But they'd be sure to be safe. The journey from Belfast was short; the traffic in a funeral crawl.
Within twenty minutes of leaving the hospital they were nearing Harry's terraced street in Holywood, County Down. From the top of the road there was a sea view that disappeared behind the rooftops as they drove down the hill to Harry's two-up two-down.
When he pulled up, his father's instinct was to race round to the passenger side to support his son, but he knew that he shouldn't. It was time to let Harry stand on his own feet and release him back into the urban jungle.
The father fought to hold his tongue.
"See you, then," he said casually, stretching behind to retrieve Harry's bag and pass it to him through the open door.
"Cheers. I'll call you later, Dad."

"No problem. You know where I am if you need me."

His father gave him a wink and a knowing smile then drove on without looking back. It was hard not to surrender to the temptation to run and hold his son up as he hobbled from the kerb to the doorstep.

And Harry String struggled. It was no more than ten yards but might have been a mile for all it took him to make the distance without tripping or dropping his bag. The effort took intense concentration, contorting Harry's face into a grimacing parody of its usual calm indifference. But the painful steps on frail legs, the fiddling about in his pockets to find the key, retrieve it and maintain his balance whilst locating the keyhole all played their part in distracting him from the main event: the dread of returning to an empty house.

Harry had no memory of living at 26 Vicarage Road, Holywood. He had bought the small property as an investment with a buy-to-let mortgage. It was odd to find his belongings dotted about the place as though he had been living there for years. He last remembered the house as a shell: surfaces covered in brick dust and plaster. No bathroom, no kitchen, no running water; nowhere to sleep, bathe or eat. But now he found it transformed with a new kitchen, new bathroom, hot water, a working heating system and fully furnished.

This was not home as he remembered it. Not *his* home. His home was eight hundred yards away on the next road over where he lived with a wife and two children. Not here. Not alone. Not in this tiny, compact space.

Harry hobbled from room to room and acquainted himself with the mystery house. The layout, the furnishings and furniture were all his taste, but he couldn't remember buying any of it; couldn't remember seeing any of it here before.

The framed photos of friends and family were his all right. The books, CDs, clothes and bric-a-brac were also his, but it was confusing to find them here. He tottered up the narrow staircase pulling on the handrail with one arm and dragging his holdall behind him with the other. Harry dumped his bag in the front bedroom and sat on the bed. Nope. No recollection here either. Strange bedclothes, strange decor, strange bed.

A deep sigh. He leaned back until he was staring up at the ceiling, closed his eyes and searched his memory for even the vaguest hint of having seen the house full of his clobber before. Nothing came. And before long Harry drifted off into a deep sleep.

At four in the morning he woke with a start. He'd been dreaming of people he didn't know. The lights were on and he was still dressed, so he got up, blinking into the brightness, and switched everything off, stripped and got under the covers trying to recount the dream. Who was the woman who'd been staring at him from the opposite pillow? Not his wife. And no one he could recall.

He rolled over to go back to sleep but couldn't get the woman out of his thoughts. Who was she? He'd had a clear view of her face but felt no spark of recognition.

Sleep wouldn't come. Not now he was distracted by the dull incessant nagging of loneliness, so haunting in this cold and quiet house. The din on the hospital ward at night had made sleep difficult at times, but this absolute silence seemed worse.

It felt unnatural to be alone. He missed his wife and children and was perplexed as to why he was not at home with them. He didn't like being on his own, never had. Come the desert island, he was confident he could build a shelter from flotsam and jetsam and maybe even whittle a canoe from a tree trunk, but survive the isolation without going round the twist? He doubted it.

First light. A good enough excuse to get up. Trying to sleep was getting him nowhere.

Tea. Yes, a pot of tea. His drug of choice. He thought himself lucky that having tried most artificial stimulants – some legal, some less so – it was tea that he found the most effective. He wasn't hooked, but what would it matter if he were? The effect of tea on his mood was startling. Calming.

At the top of the stairs he contemplated his descent. His instinct was to sit and then ease himself down on his backside, but he knew if he were to make the full recovery he coveted, he would have to exercise his legs as much as possible, so tottered forwards an inch or two. Since it had taken man millions of years to get up and walk, he, Harry String, couldn't shirk his responsibility and discontinue the practice now – even at dawn when no one was looking.

But then the tiled floor at the bottom of the staircase loomed threatening a hard landing. Harry shrugged, sat on his arse and slid.

The kitchen, refurbished in the clean, cream and clinical shaker style of the day, was cold and unwelcoming. Harry winced at the sterile aroma of bleach. His dad, however, had ensured that the fridge and cupboards were well stocked with the basics. Locating teabags and milk, he brewed up.

When he wandered back into the knock-through he was drawn to a cardboard box on the dining table, the kind used for transporting documents when moving office. It was sturdy with a snug fitting lid. On the side, a handwritten label:

Personal Effects: Henry String

There was a note beside it:

Harry,
The police returned this stuff to me a while ago. It's whatever was left in your car. If you think there's anything missing, please let me know.
Dad X.

How his father could expect him to remember whether there was anything missing was beyond him. His camera equipment had already been returned undamaged and functioning and that was all that mattered. The rest of the stuff was bound to be the usual kind of tat that gets dumped in any car boot. He'd leave this Pandora's box for another day.

The daylight was gaining in intensity. He'd shave and get dressed. Time to face the world.

3

10.55am. Tuesday, 25 November 2008.

Susan Heywood's office was grim. Synthetic. A patchwork of nylon and Formica. The carpet was Brillo-pad pink and threatened friction burns. The blinds, vertical slats swivelled shut, were a magnet for dust. They were once cream with flecks of oatmeal but were now enveloped in a coat of fluff. The view: brick; the side wall of an adjoining building.

The furniture was a mismatch of style and age. Susan's chair was standard office issue: black with gas-powered height adjustment and magenta fabric. Her desk: an orange Formica top on anonymous legs. The remainder comprised an A2 flip chart, a pair of navy plastic seats – conjoined in tubular steal – that faced her and a cottage-style chair crammed against the wall behind. The old wooden chair had become a dump for case histories that were too live to be consigned to the filing cabinet.

A calendar boasting a view of Coventry hung on the opposite wall. The hook was coming loose. The calendar was three years out of date, showing the wrong month and the wrong season.

Susan Heywood sat at her desk, head in hands, contemplating the day ahead and gathering her wits in anticipation of her eleven o'clock appointment. The Strings. First-timers.

She was staring through her fingers and focusing on the scratches scarring her desktop when she heard a knock.

Show time!

A head popped round the door. It smiled.

"Mr String?" Susan enquired in a friendly tone.

"Yes," the smiling head replied.

Susan Heywood clicked into professional mode.

"Come on in, Mr String. Is your partner with you?"

String shuffled through the doorway and crossed the Brillo-pad carpet towards Susan's desk. Though it was autumn, he was perspiring. That it was painful for him to walk showed in his gritted teeth and furrowed brow. He slumped onto one of the twin chairs opposite her.

Susan Heywood watched his progress in silence. She paused to allow her new client a moment to compose himself that, judging by the way his eyes darted about the room, was a state he would be slow in achieving.

"And where is your partner, Mr String?"

"Harry."

"Where is Harry, Mr String?"

"No, I am Harry, Susan," he said, reading her name from the Toblerone-shaped plate perched on the front of her desk and avoiding eye contact.

"It's *Mrs Heywood* here," she said, smiling for emphasis. "Now, where is your partner, Harry, er ... Mr String? Did she or he not wish to come with you today?" she continued, assuming a firm tone.

"I don't have a partner, Mrs Heywood."

"Oh."

Susan Heywood raised an eyebrow, easing off on the warm and friendly. This wasn't going to take long.

"So, what are you doing here, Mr String, if you don't have a partner?"

Harry String looked down into his lap. He gathered himself.

"I need ... Well, I *think* I need help."

The words were wrung out like the very last squeeze of toothpaste.

"OK. But are we really the right people to help you? If you had a partner, I think we could do something. But since you're on your own—"

"I've paid the fee."

"Yes, but without a partner, Mr—"

"No. It's not that simple. It's not easy ... You see, I did have one. It's just ... as I say ... Oh, it's so hard to explain."

Time to stand.

Susan had been a counsellor long enough to know a good time to stand, the right time to assert herself.

She stretched to her full height, folded her arms and edged around the desk. String's inarticulate mumblings had been enough to alert her. He was obviously "one of those" that the more experienced counsellors had warned her about. She might have to make a dash for the door if she couldn't subdue the anxious man through body language alone.

"Are you married, Mr String?"

"Er, no. Technically not."

"Are you in a long-term relationship? Cohabiting?"

"Not at the moment. No."

"Mr String," she said, continuing to use the formality of his surname to distance herself. "You are aware of the nature of the service we provide?"

"Of course."

"So, why do you think marriage guidance counselling might be suitable for you?"

"As I say, I *did* have a partner. And I'd like her back. The thing is, I don't think she'll have *me*. I'd like to try though."

"I don't think you get the point, Mr String."

"What?"

He looked blank.

"Well, here we offer advice to married couples, couples in a civil partnership or couples in a long-term relationship – you know, at least cohabiting – on how to resolve their relationship problems. Yes, we sometimes see just one partner – sometimes the other partner refuses to, or is reluctant to come, but I don't think I've ever helped someone who isn't actually *in* a relationship. That is to say, someone who doesn't have a partner and is on their own, i.e. *is single*."

"Oh."

Silence.

Susan Heywood had reached the door. She felt safer now that she had got between Mr String and the exit, and further reassured when she noticed she was about an inch or two taller than him, too.

"Well then?" she said testily then paused. "We can refund your fee, Mr String."

Susan placed her hand on the door handle.

"*Harry*," he urged.

"Harry."

"I was advised to come to you," he said in a quiet, almost childlike voice that prompted her to ask in a whisper:

"How old are you, Mr String?"

"Forty-four."

"So, who—"

"Who what?"

"Who on earth advised you to come here?"

"A psychologist. I told them the story I'd like to tell you. She told me I needed marriage guidance counselling."

"Well, that's as maybe. And a little unfortunate. But you do know that you really *are* in the wrong place, don't you?" Susan Heywood posed the question with a frown returning to her original argument at full volume.

She twisted the door handle.

He looked down into his lap.

"I am divorced," he said, looking mournful.

"Then marriage counselling *is* a bit late for you, isn't it?"

She allowed a little sarcasm to creep into her voice. She was past caring now. She opened the door.

"Well, it's quite—"

"Unpleasant, I'm sure, but I imagine you'll be able to come to terms with it in time."

"Yes, if I have to. But it's a bit more complicated than that. It's a bit of a nightmare, really."

She gulped.

"Divorce is never easy, Mr String."

"Moving on isn't easy either," he said, whilst raising his head to look up at her.

Then, for the first time, she noticed his eyes. They were bright, blue and quite disarming. A beautiful azure with a fine, dark, outer ring; almost hypnotic.

And in that moment she was slightly bedazzled, and, growing curious, felt compelled to grant him a reprieve: an opportunity to expand on his subject and explain a little further. She would give him a chance. A brief one.

Susan Heywood paused, sighed, shut the door, returned to her desk and sat down, thinking to study him a little; appraise his physical characteristics.

Though shorter than her, he wasn't *that* small. Average height, five eight maybe. And fair-haired. Hair shorn to stubble with a long winding scar that made the back of his head look like a tennis ball. The bright, blue eyes and smile lines intimated kindness. Perhaps not your average psychopath after all.

"Oh, you'll be all right, Mr String. You probably need a little confidence boost. Maybe you should join a single's club or try internet dating."

Susan knew she was being dismissive but ...

Harry String didn't respond. Sat silent. His chance ebbing.

"I don't think you understand. I don't want or need to meet anyone new!" he suddenly spurted out in a truculent spasm.

Susan Heywood looked over to the clock on her desk. No. Enough was enough. He'd had his chance and blown it. String was already five minutes into his first session and was in danger of becoming a client by default. Anyway, she had begun to relish the hour of free time the cancellation would bring and if she didn't usher him out soon, it would be too late.

"Good, because we're not a dating agency either. I really don't think we can help you, Mr String. So I'll ring through to reception and ask them to—"

"Look, I need help. I need to understand. I want to see if it could be possible to regain something of what I've lost."

"I'm not sure you know what it is you're saying or what you want, but you've got to be positive and look forward, Mr String."

"I know. You're right. Absolutely. But I feel I need to understand and become reconciled with my past first."

Susan Heywood looked at her watch. She felt like a fish being reeled in. She didn't want to be reeled in by anybody and certainly not by Mr String.

His blue eyes moved away from hers, his smile lines diminished. He sighed. Looked defeated.

"*Bloody hell!*" she swore to herself, veering back towards pity.

"Right, Mr String. Why don't you tell me a little more about what's bothering you and we'll see? I'm not promising that I can help you, but since you've paid for your first session, and since the first session is usually for assessment, we'll see what we can do. But, I must repeat, I doubt if I can help you."

"Thank you, Susan. Thank you very much."

"It's *Mrs Heywood!*"

As he spoke Harry String's eyes regained some of their sparkle.

"Look, Mrs Heywood, it's a complicated situation, but I can't just give up. You see, I really would like things to be back the way they were. I don't know if that's possible, but I'd like to give it a go." Harry String sighed again, now cupping his face in his hands.

"Mmm. How long have you been divorced, Mr String?"

"About a year. Or so I have been told."

"Don't you know?"

"Well, that's the problem. The crux of the problem, you might say."

"How come?"

"Because I don't actually remember."

"Surely you would remember getting divorced?"

"Oh, of course I would. Anyone would. *I would,* but I was involved in an accident—"

"Accident?"

"Yes. I was involved in a car accident. And, as I say, I've had problems. Problems remembering."

"Amnesia?"

"Severe. It's like my brain has been put through a salami slicer and then the whole lot thrown to the winds. I've been gathering up the slices ever since and been trying to put them back into some kind of order and shape that makes sense. Well, back into a salami, I suppose."

Susan Heywood raised her eyebrows.

"Oh, I see. And now?"

"My memory of everything that happened up to a year or so before the accident is perfectly clear, but my short-term memory has been compromised. It seems I have little or no memory of the year before the accident. It's as though everything that happened and everybody I met during that period has been wiped away. I know some of the history though. I've learnt it thoroughly. I've talked to friends and family. I've managed to piece together most of the story from what they've told me, but I don't remember anything of that time in the natural sense."

"So, you mean you remember being married but not divorced?"

"Exactly. I don't remember the divorce. I have no memory of getting divorced. Things apparently went downhill in the marriage about a year before my accident, but I don't know how or why. You see, as far as I was aware – when I regained consciousness in hospital, that is – I still had a wife and two kids and was living in the family home. I didn't even know that I'd moved out."

"Something of a shock, then?"

"Yes! And that's why I need your help. I need to understand the divorce. I need the counselling I might have had – should have had – before the divorce. Do you understand?"

"You want retrospective counselling because – as far as you are aware – you are still married, even though the facts would indicate otherwise? And you don't expect the counselling to save your marriage but to help salvage it?"

"Yes. Possibly. But obviously that's a tall order. Maybe I just want to understand how the divorce happened. To explore the background. Look at the symptoms. It might help me recover my memory. It certainly might help give that period a context so I can move forward."

"To be honest, Mr String, I don't know if I can help you, or whether I'm even *qualified* to help you."

"But you'll give it a go?"

"I can't say. I'll have to refer this to my superiors, and they may well recommend that you need another form of counselling – you know, another agency. You probably need specialist help."

"Oh, I'm getting plenty of that, believe me."

"Well, we'll see. Anyway, the accident, Mr String. Tell me about that."

Compared to the humdrum sessions that comprised her average working day – refereeing petty squabbles and handing out tissues with well-versed advice – Susan Heywood found, much to her annoyance, that she was growing interested in the enigmatic man with the vivid blue eyes.

Following years of exposure to pitiful stories of betrayal and failure, she rarely succumbed to pity. But, for the first time in a long time, she found herself teetering at the top of a slippery slope. She was intrigued now and wanted to know more.

"Tell me about the accident, Mr String. But, please ... Try to be brief."

4

4pm. Thursday, 26 June 2008.

The air hanging over the playing fields of Camberhill College was suffused with the scent of cut grass. The concrete track that wound a path between the rugby pitches and led towards the back gate was strewn with cuttings and deserted save for the beanpole of a man lolloping away from the school. The gangly man was hunched over a bundle of books clasped under one arm and a small bronze sculpture cupped in the other. He trod gingerly juggling stamina, common sense and the laws of gravity, careful lest he should slip on the loose grass that littered his way.

The rest of the staff were gathered in the chapel for the assembly that marked the end of the school year and the start of the long summer break.

The gangly man, Clive Heywood, winced when he heard the introductory bars of the school song drifting across the lawns followed by a chorus of male voices gelling in a low drone; the Latin indecipherable against the hum of traffic on the carriageway ahead. A short hymn, Heywood knew that following the last verse the boys would be dismissed and then come pouring down the path in a tsunami of mindless exuberance in a dash for the bus stop.

Latin!

Clive Heywood raised his eyebrows.

Bloody Latin!

Over thirty years of teaching Latin and he had lost faith in the classic's charm. Thirty years of arguing for its validity in the twentieth, and latterly twenty-first, century had exhausted his appetite for sharing the ancient language with a sceptical audience. Monday to Friday, week after week, year after year, he had faced a similar crop of young faces; few of whom shared his passion or even gave a damn. Civility in the classroom was rare, eagerness long extinct.

But now he need worry no longer. The last day of the last term was also Clive Heywood's final day as a teacher, his last day of incarceration, *his* last day of school.

As he struggled along, Heywood took stock of his mental state:

Relieved?
Yes.
Regretful?
A little.
Sad?
Maybe.
Anxious?
Definitely.
(Teaching was the only job listed on his CV.)

Heywood had spent a lifetime at Camberhill. He'd arrived aged nine as a prep school pupil and stayed until taking a four-year sabbatical to attend university and then teacher training college before returning as a member of staff. Then the long haul until now. Longer than the mandatory life sentence for murder.

That he had only achieved the position of head of department seemed a disappointment considering his length of service.

It amused him to remember his school days and early career and the punishments meted out to the boys on a daily basis. It seemed shocking now. Gratuitous intimidation of the unruly was still accepted back in the seventies: a cuff round the ear, the teacher's stock-in-trade; waking up snoozers with a well-aimed blackboard duster or piece of chalk was the norm. But both chalk and chalk dust were gone. In their place: whiteboards and water-soluble markers. And in the last ten years or so the physical intimidation was in-coming. No more cuffs or caning; now the staff were the prey.

At first Heywood's evangelism for his subject had burned brightly. Wednesday games, when he was press-ganged into refereeing the fifth fifteen rugby squad, was an unwanted distraction from his quest to breathe life into what most of his pupils believed to be a dead language.

Recently, however, the regular afternoons of sport had come as a blessed escape from the torture of the classroom and its inmates. As his love of his subject diminished and his dislike of teaching grew, so his interest in sport blossomed. Now he not only took games on Wednesday with enthusiasm, but also coached the Junior Colts every lunch hour, had discovered golf and founded the school's golf society.

Stopping to catch his breath, Heywood turned to take a last look at the school buildings. Gothic and red brick, it was a single-sex public school that shouted tradition, bearing all the characteristics of class, wealth and privilege. The rugby pitches, tennis courts, croquet green, chapel, founder's statue, school house and boat club were all obvious landmarks. Heywood felt elated to be escaping the regime to rejoin and play a part in the real world.

As he moved off to continue on his way he glanced down at the bronze sculpture. The arm cradling it was starved of blood. Pins and needles was setting in.

The small globe was an award for loyalty and service. A form of long-service medal that seemed more of a wooden spoon than a reward. Heywood had received this accolade at the beginning of the school assembly. The end of year ritual had started well enough and had held his attention for a while. He was happy to smile and indulge the headmaster's crass humour. A wide variety of awards were presented. The next year's prefects were announced, a new head and deputy head boy appointed and congratulations offered for exam successes, university entrances and team victories on the sports field, but then the headmaster's mood grew sterner as he started the main thrust of his address: a sermon of sorts.

Clive Heywood considered the lecture a brainwashing too far in support of a brand of schooling he no longer supported. An elite system skewed in favour of the rich and bent on populating the universities and feeding the political class whilst doing little or nothing of benefit for the local community. Heywood had heard enough, had heard it all before. He had lifted his globe and slipped away unnoticed.

Heywood jiggled the globe to get a better grip. He chuckled at the inadequacy of his prize when considering the years that he had given to the school, the bloody hard work and emotional strain. A little two-faced, he thought, that the head had been so lavish with praise for him and had whipped up such a clapping of hands and stamping of feet in his honour when previously he had been so keen to make Clive aware of the early retirement opportunities available to teachers of his age and experience:

"*Ah, Clive, let's take a minute or two to go over what's on offer here, shall we?*" the head had enthused.

"*Let's just float the idea. Nothing definite. Just wanted to let you know. You see, this offer won't be on the table for too long. Could just be a chance worth taking. That's all.*"

Clive knew that this really meant:

"*Fuck off, Clive. I want you out of here. The sooner the better. If you don't take this crummy offer, I'll be making you redundant anyway. So you might as well go now. And quietly. Better for us all, really.*"

Clive Heywood cursed under his breath, dropped the globe into one of the large wheelie bins loitering by the back entrance, slipped through the half-open gate, merged into the melee on the streets of South Belfast and headed for home. Free at last.

5

11.50am. Tuesday, 25 November 2008.

Outside the marriage counselling offices on the Donegall Road rain was drizzling over a herd of freshers processing from the university quarter towards Belfast's Royal Avenue, eager to blow their student loans on tat. Teenage-scruffy and self-conscious, the boys still looked like sixth-formers whilst the girls marched through the mizzle, muffin flesh bared, brash, blooming and self-confident.

"The accident, apparently – and I say apparently because I only heard the story secondhand – was due to an aneurysm."
 "And that's—"
 "A swelling of blood in an artery. It can occur anywhere in the body but commonly around the lungs, brain or heart. If the blood vessel haemorrhages, the consequences can be fatal. I've been told that my aneurysm may have been present for anything up to six months."
 "So you suffered a—"
 "A brain haemorrhage. Almost certainly." String paused. "Stress can be a contributory factor. And when I think back – and again, judging from what I've been told since – I'd been under a lot of pressure at around that time."
 She could see the stress in his fingernails.
 "What do you do, by the way?"
 "I'm a photographer. A professional photographer."
 "Oh, OK."
 "I'm told I'd been working long hours and was stressed out

by the divorce. Money was tight. Now that everybody's got a digital camera, smartphone or iPad or whatever, they all think they're bloody photographers. So to cut a long story short, I started having some terrible headaches. An early symptom. Then it happened. *Bang!* The brain haemorrhage caused a blackout. Unfortunately I was driving my car at the time."

"My goodness."

"I'd been on location in Sligo doing some food photography for a seaweed cookbook. You know, a heavy workload. Trying to keep on schedule. And I was driving back to Belfast. The weather was bad, visibility poor. Then I passed out at the wheel doing about seventy. The car flipped over into a field. It was a Volvo. Solid as a rock. Built like a tank. Even so, the impact was severe. I mean, on top of the haemorrhage I suffered multiple bone fractures ... broken legs, ribs—"

"And you remember ..."

"Nothing. I know nothing of the crash. Nothing except what I've been told since. So I'm rushed off to hospital in a coma. Once there they had to open up my skull. They removed a slice of it – you know – to help relieve the pressure from the brain swelling. And though my legs were in a bad way, they could only patch them up. They couldn't operate on them. Can't. Not till my neurological condition stabilises. Anyway, I was in a coma for weeks. Oh, and they didn't replace the bit of skull for nearly two months. Can you imagine? They implanted it in my abdomen to keep it viable until they were ready to pop it back into place."

"Sounds like you're lucky to be alive, Mr String."

"At this point I was on full life support. The hospital warned my father, God bless him, that the chances of me having brain damage were pretty high. They gave him the impression that I was probably going to end up either severely brain damaged or ... well ... just dead.

"Then came the next crisis. I got a blood infection. A massive setback. My body started to close down, organs failing. Apparently I was hours away from dying. The hospital phoned Dad and told him I had maybe six hours to live and to get down there fast. Poor guy. It must have been horrendous. Can you imagine his drive from home?"

"Where do your parents live?"

"Parent. Mum's dead. Dad lives on his own in Portstewart. That's what – about an hour and a half from the hospital? Anyway, so there he was, standing over me. Oh yeah, and only my dad. No one with him. Not even my children—"

"You've got two kids, right?"

"Yeah. They're ten and eight. A girl and a boy. So there I was slipping away, and then, *bingo!* An effing miracle. I start fighting back. Well, with the help of some heavy-duty medication, that is. And I turned a corner."

"How long did you say you were in the coma for?"

"Comatose for about two months."

"And then you came round?"

"Yes, but gradually. Very slowly. About eight or nine weeks after the accident."

"And do you remember regaining consciousness?"

"No, not really. It wasn't like waking up from a deep sleep or coming out of a trance. It wasn't as if someone clicked their fingers and I woke up. It was more of a gradual process. Very controlled. As I say, I was heavily sedated. And, as it turns out, I *had* suffered brain damage—"

"Oh."

"Progress was then both slow and painful. I had to learn to walk again, learn to talk again. And then, as I mentioned, there were the complications with my legs. I mean, they could set one of them, but the other needed an operation and they couldn't operate whilst I was in the coma. As I mentioned, they still need to operate. But they won't risk giving me an anaesthetic until they're sure the blood vessels around my brain have healed."

"God, you're lucky to be here, aren't you?"

"Yes. They're delighted with my progress now though, but I've had to put in a huge amount of work: speech therapy, physiotherapy. I mean, learning to walk again isn't easy, believe me. There are others – people I've met in neurology – who can't hack it."

"So, what's the first thing you remember after regaining consciousness?"

"I don't know if it was the first thing, but I do remember lying in bed and asking for my wife and kids. I was so glad to be alive for them. I was just so glad that they wouldn't have to grieve for me. But then, little did I know."

"And how long ago is that now?"

"About four months."

"So, what have you been doing for the past four months?"

"Getting to the point where I could walk in here, sit down and talk to you."

"Really?"

"Yeah. This is my first day out and about unaccompanied. It's only my second day out of hospital."

"*Really?*"

"Really."

"An achievement, Mr String."

"Yes. Four months of learning to walk and talk again to get to a point where I can stagger in here, only to find out that you can't help me."

"Well, that's not strictly true. Your case *is* very unusual."

"But you still won't help me, will you, Mrs Heywood?"

Susan Heywood took a deep breath.

"I can't promise, but we'll see. I'll definitely have to refer this, but I will get back to you as soon as I've had the conversation. Look, I'll do my best."

"Please do. I've travelled a long way to get here. It's been a real struggle."

"I can see that." She paused. "No promises, but I'll see what we can do."

Harry smiled politely.

"Well, OK, Mr String. I think we've covered enough ground for today, but before you go I want to ask you a question about your wife."

"OK."

"Do you still love her?"

Harry paused. He looked up and shrugged.

"As I told you before, it feels like we're still married. I have no idea how we came to be divorced—"

"Except you are divorced."

"Yes."

"So. Do you still love her, Mr String?"

"Look, she is ... I mean ... She was my wife."

"Have you talked to her about this?"

"No."

"Didn't she visit you in hospital?"

"Yes. Just the once. I was unaware of it at the time, obviously. I was still comatose. Apparently she came when I was out of danger. She came with the kids. However, my father intervened. Wouldn't let her near me. I'm afraid they don't get on. Either that or – as well as that – he took advice from the staff. I have to avoid stress, you see. I don't know what he said, but she didn't come back."

"So you haven't seen or spoken to her since you regained consciousness?"

"No. I suppose she could have tried ignoring my dad, but maybe thought it was for the best."

"And the kids?"

"Dad brought them."

"Have you tried phoning your wife?"

"No. My dad has been acting as an intermediary. Funnily enough, they appear to be getting on much better now. He relays messages to her whenever he picks the kids up. And, as I say, I have been told to avoid doing anything stressful."

"But you came here."

"Yes, for some counselling, for some therapy. That should help. Phoning my ex-wife however, could prove stressful. And that definitely wouldn't be helpful. My neurosurgeon advised me to try and distinguish between that which is therapeutic and that which is detrimental to my recovery and to avoid the latter. That's what I've been doing, and so far it's worked."

"But now you're thinking of deviating from that advice?"

"Well, no. Not if I can help it."

"Fair enough."

"There are a lot of things I'm not supposed to do. Like, I'm not supposed to drink alcohol or fly. Well, not for a while. I'm also not allowed to drive. But we'll see. I need to be able to get about."

"Look, you really are going to have to talk to your ex-wife sooner or later. Won't you see her when you see your kids? You will be seeing your children sometime soon, I presume?"

"Oh, yes. Tomorrow. It'll be the first time since I left hospital. It's been agreed that I'll have them to stay over at mine a couple of nights a week and every other weekend. I'm to collect them from the family home. I don't have to see my ex-wife when I do that, but I could."

"Well, perhaps you should. If you think carefully about what you want to say and do your best to avoid conflict, I'm sure it might not be as stressful as you imagine. It could prove to be quite cathartic. And who knows? It might provide a way forward for you both."

"Maybe."

"And how's your relationship with your children?"

"Fine."

"*Fine*, Mr String?"

"Yeah, fine."

"Could you talk to them about the divorce?"

"Look, I don't think they're old enough. And I don't want to make life any harder for them then it already is."

Susan Heywood was suddenly distracted by the digital clock on her desk. The alarm was on silent mode, but the flashing numerals indicated that the hour was up.

"Well, I think that's enough for this session, Mr String."

"God! That was quick. Anyway, do you think we can do this again?"

"We'll see. It would help if you could bring your wife—"

"*Ex-wife.*"

"Ex-wife with you. And, as I say, it's not up to me. Did you leave your contact details with the receptionist?"

"Yes."

"Good. And a mobile number?"

"Yep."

"Good. I'll have a word with my colleagues. If I don't call you by the end of today, I'll call you tomorrow morning."

"Would *you* like to see me again, Mrs Heywood?" Harry asked, staring into Susan Heywood's eyes.

"Yes. But then it's not up to me, Mr String."

"*Harry.*"

"Harry."

Outside the rain had stopped. Harry String stood on the front step of the marriage guidance counselling offices drawing breath. An hour of discussion had exhausted him. He felt that he wasn't a good subject for analysis anyway. Too self-conscious and shy. His working-class upbringing encouraged him to believe that if times are tough, you knuckle down and make do. No whining.

Harry sighed at his vanity, took a deep breath and hobbled off towards Botanic and the train station. Slow progress. He wobbled for ten steps, rested for a moment then limped for ten more, wincing the whole way.

6

3.30pm. Tuesday, 25 November 2008.

It worried Clive Heywood that the flash of blue sweeping across the washing machine window might have been a five pound note. If so, then perhaps it was one of a few. It then struck him that he might have left his wallet in yesterday's trousers. He couldn't afford to have his money whirling around in soapsuds getting boiled to mush.

Heywood plonked down his tea, lurched across the kitchen, switched off the machine and bent down to open the small, round door.

It wouldn't budge.

Bugger!

A time lock.

He'd have to wait a couple of minutes or so.

Chauvinistic dogma roared to mind, fuelled by the adrenaline rush of lost cash.

"*Of course, the woman's place is in the fucking home*," he grumbled under his breath.

He didn't believe that kind of claptrap, but in a time of crisis it seemed a tantalising proposition to a self-pitying Cinderella.

He tried the door again and smiled when it popped open, then scowled when soapy water poured down onto his recently cleaned floor. He snatched the sodden pile of mixed colours and pulled it into the puddle below, raking his fingers through assorted arms, legs and fibres, fumbling for the fiver, or fivers, and/or his wallet. None were there. There was a light-blue pop sock, but no wallet and no cash.

Shaking his head, he bundled the damp clothes back into the machine and slammed the door. He grabbed the business and travel sections of *The Sunday Times* and draped them over the puddle to arrest its advance on the lounge carpet. Time for a nap; Clive retired to the bedroom.

Clive Heywood had enjoyed the house husbandry at first, but after four or five months the initial thrill had passed and cabin fever had taken hold in Knockbreda Close.

When Clive was offered early retirement from his teaching position at Camberhill College, he had seized the opportunity with his wife's blessing. He felt exhilarated, believed he had drawn a get out of jail free card and was going to play it. The proposal was accepted and signed off in the spring of the previous year.

At first the domestic chores proved a pleasant distraction from the tedium of being home alone, once the novelty of quitting the nine-to-five had diminished. The domesticity was only supposed to be a temporary arrangement whilst his wife got acquainted with her new position as a marriage guidance counsellor and he planned what he was going to do with the rest of his life, but he sensed a permanency setting into his routine.

He was fifty-three. A young fifty-three. He would like to try something in retail or human resources, or both, but five months on and he was still no nearer to finding a job. The boredom had become paralysing, crucial momentum had been lost.

Clive had grasped his household responsibilities with enthusiasm: organising his wife, helping her get ready for work, food shopping and taking care of the laundry. He had even enjoyed cleaning – had taken a pride in it. But above all he relished the extra time he now found for playing golf.

But there is only so much golf you can play in a week, and their house was of such a size, a three-up two-down semi, that it proved a little too easy to keep clean, especially without children. Given the free time he had on his hands, therefore, he quickly tired of the new way of life. Although he had valued the peace and calm of home and being away from the constant interruptions of the classroom and the demands made on his time by other people's problems, he soon realised that his early passion for this quieter lifestyle was something akin to a holiday romance. An exciting novelty, whose attraction had quickly worn thin. He now yearned for the security of school and the camaraderie of the staffroom.

Once he had been a team player, a key member of a large family, now he was a soloist. A self-isolated idler. Apart from time spent at the golf club, he spent long hours on his own. At school, contact and interaction had filled his days. Now he lived in solitary confinement, marooned. Lethargy flourished.

Since he'd had no success in finding long-term employment as he had hoped, he now found that he had less mental energy to fuel the search for it.

He was half asleep when his wife arrived home but fully awake once he heard the door slam.

"Clive?"

"I'm up here!"

"What's with the kitchen floor?" Susan Heywood asked with a sigh, leaning against the post at the foot of the stairs.

"Oh, just a small accident. Don't worry. Come up! I'm in the bedroom."

He listened for her footsteps. Heard her tut.

"What are you doing in here?"

"Snoozing."

"It's all right for some, Clive Heywood."

She sat on the edge of the bed. Smiled. Was within range. He leant across, took her wrist and gently pulled her over till she became snuggled up under his arm. She didn't resist.

"What happened?"

"Mmm?"

"The kitchen?"

"Oh, just a spot of money laundering."

"Wha—"

"Oh, nothing."

He leaned over and kissed her cheek.

"Have you gone mad, Clive?"

"Probably."

Inactivity had left Clive Heywood with an excess of energy. His wife, knackered after her day at work, spotted the warning sign when she felt something hard pressing against her upper thigh. She sat up and combed a hand through her hair.

"I'm going to make some tea, Clive. Fancy a cup?" she said, springing to her feet.

"Mmm, lovely," Clive chirped, in as bright a voice as a deflated ego fired up on testosterone can muster. He watched his wife leave the bedroom and smiled. God, how lucky was he, job or no job, that he had her in his life?

Susan was young. Thirty-three. He pretended not to care, but was flattered by the age difference and felt it ensured that she would always seem youthful and attractive to him. He looked over at the wedding photo. Ten years ago. He was forty-three, she twenty-three. The age gap seemed wider then. They had hoped to have children, maybe just the one, but that didn't seem so likely now. They had tried, but it had been a long time and still no sign. They valued their independence, however. That they were childless was a concern that had eroded over the years. It didn't seem to bother them so much now. They rarely thought about it and no longer discussed it, had become resigned.

The wedding had been an informal occasion. Once their respective families had got over the shock of the engagement – his because he had always struck them as a confirmed bachelor, and hers because of his age – Susan and Clive decided that they wanted a wedding that would suit *them*. Intimate. Just their parents and a few friends. And *their* choice of venue. Small. Their favourite restaurant in Belfast.

She looked stunning in the photo they'd framed. Beautiful. Dark. Ten years later and she looked almost unchanged. She had a natural beauty, shoulder-length raven hair, curvy figure. In the wedding photograph she was wearing a tailored suit in cream silk wool, simple make-up. Chic; a classic beauty. The only difference was that she now wore glasses, which, if anything, added to her allure.

The specs were a prize possession. Expensive. Chanel. And once lost, she knew, unlikely to be replaced.

Clive Heywood cringed whenever he looked at himself in the wedding photo: didn't like the change in his appearance since. Maybe it was the stress of teaching, but he seemed to be ageing at a faster rate than she. Whilst once his hair was thick and black, it was now grey, floppy and thin; his face more lined and puffier. But at least he had listened to her and got rid of the walrus moustache.

"How were the poor unfortunates today? Anyone get nasty?"

They sat in the kitchen with tea.

"Oh, they never do, Clive."

She knew not to rise to his bait.

"Anything interesting happen? Any happy ever afters? Any divorces to celebrate?"

"No. Nothing out of the ordinary."

She didn't like to discuss her work with him and so didn't – with anyone for that matter. She thought it would demean and undermine her efforts and compromise the confidences she held. And it was exhausting work that she would rather leave at the office.

"Plenty of tears and tantrums, I take it?"

"No, Clive. No tears or tantrums."

She resented Clive characterising her counselling work as though it comprised scenes from a soap opera. He seemed too keen to distil her cases into the stereotypes of his own imagining. A trivial view of her job that irked her. But she was well aware that he was bored at home and was winding her up out of frustration and could forgive him for that.

He would have to find meaningful work soon, however. The financial pressure of relying on his meagre pension and her modest salary alone was starting to tell. She would need to give him some ideas and nudge him in a direction. It was a sensitive subject and she knew she had to proceed with caution. Her job had taught her how to handle many difficult scenarios though, and that it is often easier to dispense advice than to follow it. She loved him and wanted to help. Didn't want their marriage to become another casualty. She saw too much of that at work.

But, as Clive finished probing her about her day, she remembered the blue-eyed man, Harry String. Until she had arrived home, she'd thought of little else. And the more she mulled over the complexities of his situation, the more she found herself wanting to help. There was an honesty about him; a vulnerability, and she felt he didn't deserve to be left to suffer alone. And he did seem lonely. Lonely to the point of depression. His *was* an unusual case. One of the most unusual she'd come across. A challenge, but probably a hopeless one.

Contemplating the pathos of his situation saddened her.

"You OK, Susan?"

She didn't answer. Clive walked over and wrapped his arms around her. She leant her head in against his shoulder.

"You OK?"

"Sorry, Clive. It's just ... it's just. Oh, I've got to give someone some bad news tomorrow, and I haven't got a bloody clue how to do it."

To his credit, Clive said nothing. Holding his wife tight, he noticed the headline on the front page of *The Sunday Times* Business Section spread across the floor: "CBI predicts jobs crisis in new year".

7

10.06am. Wednesday, 26 November 2008.

Harry caught the train into the city centre again the next day. It left Holywood shortly after ten o'clock; an hour past the commuter rush. That his carriage was two-thirds empty made him wonder whether the small coastal line was profitable.

Once the train had left the seaside station and was out of sight of the lough, the view grew more suburban: greyer and less green. Within a couple of miles the track passed by Belfast City Airport and then the backstreets of East Belfast.

Towards the Harbour Estate on the other side of the Sydenham carriageway, the dockland was being redeveloped. In an area once dominated by shipbuilding, modern apartments could now be seen sitting in close proximity to the old harbour offices, dry docks and storage tanks for gas and petrochemicals.

The journey into the city was brief; the train soon approaching the River Lagan. The Albert Bridge provided a broad view of the new waterside penthouses ring-fencing Belfast city centre. It reminded Harry how much Belfast had changed. The city, whose development had been thwarted by years of bombing, was now in bloom, the skyline transforming. A decade of peace had paid dividends in concrete and glass.

Harry disembarked at Central station to continue his journey on foot heading for May Street: the major artery running down towards Belfast City Hall on Donegall Square; a painful limp on frail legs. He cursed his disability.

As Harry hobbled down towards the office workers, tourists and shoppers swarming around the city centre, he observed that it wasn't just the buildings in Belfast that were changing. For years the city's streets had been dominated by the same gene pool, but now Harry could hear foreign accents and observed a broader palette of skin tones in contrast to the traditional Ulster pink.

At last! Some bloody diversity, he thought.

Along the way he called in on some old acquaintances, mostly retailers, clients for whom he had undertaken photo shoots; small commissions squeezed in between the food-book projects he favoured. It was reassuring to see some familiar faces, good to be able to thank them for their get-well messages and good to test his memory for names.

He picked up a camera lens which, judging by the receipt, he'd left in for repair over a year ago. Then made for the Europa Hotel for a coffee before catching the train home from Great Victoria Street station next door.

Nearing Great Victoria Street, Harry stopped for a breather. Panting and wiping his brow, he propped himself up on the edge of a large bin whilst flexing his legs to regain some feeling.

Bending down to massage some life back into his calves, he was surprised when the light suddenly dimmed. As he looked up he was startled by the appearance of an amber-haired girl looming overhead. She was staring down at him, arms locked across her chest, legs firmly planted; a pose which reminded him a little of Wonder Woman. And even though the sun was behind her and obscuring his view, he could sense that she was angry and imagined that if she were a dog she might bite.

"What the hell are you doing here?" she barked. "You're not following me again are you, by any chance?"

"I'm sorr—"

"Look, if you're going to start following me around, I'm going to have to call the police, get a court order or something."

"Excuse me, but do I know you?"

"Stop playing the weirdo, Harry."

"I'm sorry. But I'm afraid I don't rem—"

"Look. I don't know what you're playing at, but stay out of my way. OK? I've told you before ... Stay well out of my way."

As she turned to survey the small crowd drawn by the kerfuffle, the sun illuminated her face in a radiant glow. A pretty face, he noticed. Freckled, but with a tight-mouthed sternness that was a little too serious and begged a smile. Her eyes were ablaze with anger.

She punctuated the ensuing pause with a sharp nod then spun round and stomped off.

Harry watched her bustle through the crowd and observed her long enough to catch her glancing over her shoulder to make sure he wasn't following before she disappeared into the scrum shuffling towards City Hall. Elegant deportment, but a tad stiff, he thought. He looked down, studied the outline of his emaciated legs and shrugged.

Stunned for a moment, he dismissed the incident with a snort. Whatever was bugging the amber-haired girl and whatever their connection had been, he didn't see how he posed the slightest threat to her, or anyone else, in his present condition.

But, who the hell was she? He wondered.

He puffed out his cheeks, struggling to stand upright whilst ignoring the bemused glances of those who'd witnessed the spat.

A ghost. She was only a ghost.

He wished he knew who the ghost was, though, and what he'd done to deserve a haunting.

Harry spent a moment or two fast-forwarding through his library of faces. No, hers didn't register. Then he remembered the face in the dream the night before last, the face that had been staring at him from the opposite pillow. Could it have been her?

Maybe. Possibly.

A depressing thought then crossed his mind: how many more anonymous faces were going to pop up from his past to scare him half to death?

Having rested his legs and caught his breath, he felt ready to continue on to the Europa and was about to move off when he felt his iPhone throbbing in his breast pocket. It wasn't a number he recognised, but took the call all the same.

"Hello?"

"Hello, Mr String?"

A woman's voice.

"Yes?"

"It's Susan Heywood from the counselling service. Are you free to talk?"

"Yeah, sure. Fire ahead."

"Well, it's not good news, I'm afraid."

"Oh."

"I don't think you're going to like what I've got to say, Mr String."

"Really?"

"Well, I'm afraid we can't take you on as a client. I referred your case to my supervisor and she says that you don't meet any of our criteria for counselling. There's a long waiting list, you see. And it doesn't make sense to put you ahead of the married couples. I'm sure you can understand. We simply don't have the resources to help everyone. I'm sorry, but I did warn you."

"Oh, right. I see. No. Well, I guess that's understandable."

Susan Heywood detected disappointment in his voice.

"Look, it's not that I don't want to help you, Mr String. It's just that we don't have the facility to handle your case. I think that your current problems stem from your recent neurological history, and that's way beyond our expertise. But there will be – *is* – someone out there – a specialist – who can help you. I'm sure your GP can refer you to someone."

"I don't think you follow. Don't think you understand my problem. I did try and explain the crux of it to you, but you obviously don't get the point."

"Maybe. Maybe so. But I'm afraid my hands are tied. Look, Mr String, I do feel every sympathy for your situation, but unfortunately there's nothing I can do."

"Of course. Of course. I know. And thank you for trying."

He sounded resigned. Resigned and deflated.

"I'm sorry, Mr String. I tried my best."

She regretted the statement the moment she'd uttered the words. They sounded hollow and insincere. And her training had taught her that it is a poor counsellor who feels the need to seek reassurance from the client.

"Mr String, please go and see your GP. I'm sure he or she will help."

"Thank you, Mrs Heywood. And, yes, I know you tried. Thank you. Thank you very much. Yes, thank you. Goodbye."

He pressed the button to end the call.

One step forward, two steps back. After months of intensive therapy Harry String was used to setbacks. The physiotherapy might have him in tears from the extreme pain and the frustrating struggle to reawaken those senses compromised by an unresponsive nervous system – bullying his brain to move the muscles in legs he could barely feel as he supported himself on his arms in a hopeless stagger along the parallel bars – but it had hardened him.

Nothing could break his will now. And nothing could depress his mood further than the constant state of numbness to which he had become accustomed. He could bear it. It was a state in which he could weather the storm of his condition until he was fully recovered. And that *would* happen. His day *would* come. Of that he was certain, and to that ideal he clung when the blows got a little heavier and the disappointments more cruel.

And there were others less fortunate than he, after all. Others he had left behind in the neurology department who wouldn't be getting up and walking, who wouldn't be sitting up and talking, who wouldn't have the opportunity to stroll through Belfast unaccompanied. Ever. Never again.

Harry String strained his hips and leaned forward to start the short walk to the train station. The temperature was cooling; he could feel the chill in his legs and see it on his breath.

Then the phone was throbbing in his pocket again.

"Mr String? It's me, Susan Heywood. Sorry to bother you, but I was wondering if you would like to talk?"

"What?"

"I was wondering if you would like to meet me somewhere in Belfast?"

"An appointment?"

"No. As I say, I can't do that. Not at the office. But – and I know it's short notice – if you're free later, would you like to meet me for a quick coffee?"

"Today?"

"Yes, at lunchtime if it's convenient."

"Well—"

"It's just that before I heard from my supervisor this morning, I conducted a little research for you. I've a couple of ideas. You know, got some useful contact numbers and found some info online which I think might help."

"Are you sure?"

"Yes. It'll be relaxed and informal. There's a nice coffee bar up the road from our offices – Black's. Do you know it?"

"Yeah."

"It's on the Stranmillis Road—"

"Yeah, I know the one."

"I could meet you there at around half twelve if you're free? Just twenty minutes or so. I might be able to help you a little. At least point you in the right direction. You never know. As I say, I have some suggestions, some contacts."

"Sure. Why not? Yeah, I'll see you there. Black's at half twelve. Sounds good. Thanks."

Harry ended the call then dropped the phone back into his breast pocket. He looked up at the wispy clouds and shrugged.

8

12.30pm. Wednesday, 26 November 2008.

Black's coffee bar.

Harry String was disappointed that he was the first to arrive. Felt uncomfortable. Hated having to wait for anyone or anything. Insecurity would have him doubting whether the other party would turn up at all. Soon he would start glancing at his wristwatch over and over like he had a tic or was OCD or something.

He queued for a drink then took a table at the back of the room, not wanting to sit in the window and appear overeager.

Black's interior was typical late nineties – once fashionable but now dating fast. Despite the name the decor was predominantly brown; brown, beige and burgundy with a dash of orange and a hint of lime green. The subdued lighting suited Harry. He sat and daydreamed whilst attempting to blend into the wallpaper, and sipped his builder's tea, which was a healthy tan colour, brewed with care, not like the hundreds of watery cups he'd make for himself at home that usually resembled whitewash; a testament to extreme impatience.

Harry glanced at his watch. She was five minutes late now.

He tried to fill time by exercising his memory; running over the pieces of his jigsaw-puzzle life that he'd already recovered and put back in place, and then straining to salvage other fragments to add to the picture. Apart from his recent dream there were still no memories that featured the amber-haired girl.

He glanced at his watch. Seven minutes.

"Hello, Mr String."

"Hi."

"Sorry I'm late. Can I get you anything?"

"Er, no. I'm fine, thanks. I've got a cuppa. I was early. But let me get *you* something."

"No, no. No, thanks. That's OK," Susan Heywood replied, blushing, unsettled by his nervousness, and then bustling over to the counter to order.

Harry thought she looked tense too, as if she were also unsure as to whether she should be there. She returned to his table, taking pigeon steps whilst balancing a large cappuccino in one hand and a ream of papers and a briefcase in the other, then manoeuvred herself onto the banquette opposite him. She avoided eye contact.

"Right! Down to business, Mr String—"

"Er ... Harry."

String spoke slowly and deliberately to inject an element of control over the proceedings. But to little effect.

"Harry. Yes. Look, I'm sorry I can't see you at the office, but as I said, yours is an unusual story. You know ... Doesn't fit our criteria. The point is, I have done a little research on your behalf and have some ideas that might help you. I've got some addresses that could prove useful, websites and contact numbers. You see, I didn't want you to feel totally abandoned."

Harry String was beginning to switch off – wasn't interested in her research. Didn't want to be driven by her, or anybody else's, agenda. He didn't suffer fools gladly, not that he thought her foolish, but didn't want her pity and couldn't be doing with being patronised. He sensed that there was little in what she was about to say that could be of much interest.

As Susan Heywood babbled on String preoccupied himself with scrutinising the shape of her face and features which, he observed, were quite classic: good cheekbones and succulent, full lips with a hint of the Mediterranean.

In her office he hadn't let his eyes wander much beyond the metal nameplate on her desk, but, sitting with her here in the coffee shop, he noticed that she was really quite striking and possessed a natural beauty that couldn't be compromised by the lenses of her glasses and shapeless, grey two-piece. He was then drawn to her hands: they were constantly moving. Her fingers, long and well manicured, were for the most part splayed; palms waving wildly to emphasise a point. It revealed an energy and passion that surprised him.

Professional curiosity kicking in, he reached for his iPhone lying on the table between them. Tilting the device without picking it up, Harry directed the lens towards Susan Heywood's face. He sneaked a shot then peeked down at the screen to see what the camera thought of her. It agreed with him.

She didn't notice what he was up to at first.

"... And then there's a good support group for divorcees in East Belfast. It meets every Thursday. A friend of mine has been going for months. Loves it. It's held in a church hall in Belmont. I'll get the address for you, if you like. Belmont would be handy enough for you, wouldn't it? And then in Bangor there's ... Harry ... Harry ... Excuse me, Mr String ..."

When she first noticed that he was fiddling with his phone she tried to ignore it and talk on regardless, but was then thrown out of her stride when it became obvious he was taking photographs. She lost her train of thought and forgot the point she was trying to make altogether.

"*How fucking rude!*" she murmured under her breath, a dark mood descending. She didn't like bad manners. The humiliation burned in her cheeks, the anger glowered in her eyes.

"The name's Harry," he muttered, raising his mobile, taking another shot and then turning the device around so she could see the result.

"See. The camera likes you, Mrs Heywood."

"What the hell are you doing?"

"I'm sorry, I'm a photographer. It's what I do."

"Well, don't. I'm not here to have my frigging photograph taken. By you or anybody else."

"Sorr—"

"Look, *Harry*. Do you want help? I am starting to get the impression that you're not in the slightest bit interested," she said, pulling herself upright and looking fierce.

"No. Sorry. I am. Seriously."

"Then what about these self-help groups?" she said, thrusting a pile of leaflets at him.

"Sorry, but I don't think they would suit me."

"Harry, what do you mean: *I don't think they would suit me?*" she repeated with disdain.

She wanted to get up and leave. Would get up and leave. Was about to get up and leave. She was too busy to be playing games. Too busy for time-wasters. And, having exhausted her script, Susan was at a loss for something useful to say.

Harry reached for her hand.

"Look. I'm an idiot. Right?"

"An idiot?"

"Total idiot. I'm sorry. Sometimes I can't help my—"

"Can I give you a top-up?" A waitress in a brown polycotton shirt and black acrylic trousers interjected whilst brandishing a jug of coffee and wearing a smile that suggested she was offering them the elixir of life.

Susan snatched her hand away and covered her cup.

The waitress turned to Harry.

"No, thanks, I'm tea," he said in his most charming voice, looking up at the waitress and then over to Susan. "Are you sure, Mrs Heywood?"

Their eyes met. Harry chanced a smile.

Though she felt compelled to go, his attempted apology and change in demeanour tempted her to stay. And, anyway, she didn't want to let him get away with such poor behaviour without giving him a piece of her mind first. She slid her hand away, uncovered her cup and nodded at the waitress.

"Look. I'm not here to play games, Harry," she said in a stern voice, lowered for effect and still angry.

"Yeah. I know you're not. But you've got to understand. I am *not* joining a self-help group. It isn't my style."

He placed his phone back down on the table and slid it to one side.

"Are you a snob, Harry? Do you think you're too good or something?"

"Possibly. Or maybe I'm reluctant to throw my hat in with any one group of people. I don't want to join a divorcee's club, sign up with the tribe. I don't see myself as a divorced man, simply someone who happens to be divorced. There's a difference."

"Strikes me that you're in denial. And maybe you can't afford to be too fussy. Maybe 'style' is a bit of a luxury for you right now."

"What do you mean?"

"You've admitted that you've got a problem. Well, I've come here to help you in my lunch break, in *my* free time. Give you some constructive options. And you can't even be bothered to listen. How do you know if you don't try? How do you expect me to help you if you're not going to listen? Harry, what the hell *is it* that you want?"

"I want *you* to talk to *me*."

"What? Counselling? I've told you: I can't do that!"

"OK, but I need to talk to *someone*."

"Sounds to me like you're a wee bit lonely. A middle-aged man yearning for a little company—"

"Eh?"

"Look, there are plenty of men who'd like to come and see me on a regular basis just to get a little attention, a little kindness. Is that what you're after, Harry? If it is, then this ain't going to work. It's why I can't be your counsellor and why, as it turns out, that it's not advisable for me to come and meet you here like this."

"But—"

"Look, I came here because I thought I might be able to help point you in the right direction, but it seems to me that you are more in need of attention than counselling. That's it, isn't it, Harry? That's what's at the heart of the matter. You're lonely. That's the real problem, isn't it?"

"Yes and no."

"But you are lonely, aren't you? You don't really need counselling, do you? You probably think you do, but no. No, you don't. You need company. A shoulder to cry on. And I can't do that. Whatever chance there was of you receiving my professional help ... Well, you've blown that too. No wonder you're lonely. I'm hardly going to want to help you if you're going to sit there and prat about like a delinquent schoolboy. Sorry, but that's just the way it is. Look, Harry, under the circumstances I think I'd better go."

"Won't you stay and finish your—" But she was up, away and out the door.

Susan Heywood felt embarrassed. Though her intention had been to handle the situation in a professional manner, he had made her feel as though their meeting was an illicit assignation or something akin to a date. It was all too awkward and frustrating. She questioned her motives and then determined that it would be inadvisable to see him again.

Harry waited for a few minutes, then followed her out onto the street. He, too, felt disgruntled. Yes, he had been looking forward to the social interaction, but he had wanted more than that, a strategy to win back his wife and family being a priority. They hadn't even touched on that subject. Also, it was Susan Heywood who had contacted *him*, who had arranged to meet *him*. It baffled him that she could give up so easily and was unwilling to accept the challenge.

Back on the street and walking down to the station, Harry's iPhone rang.

"Ah, Harry! It's me, Mr Patterson. How are you doing? I believe your physio's going well. Apparently you're the star patient. I've heard glowing reports from physiotherapy."

It was the hospital. Mr Hugh Patterson, his neurologist.

The voice was altogether too jolly for Harry String's mood. He grunted a reply.

"Hang on. That doesn't sound like the Harry String I've grown to loathe and laugh at. What's up?"

"With a bedside manner like yours, Mr Patterson, you'd have been better off joining the prison service or the priesthood rather than the NHS."

"And you're right, Harry. I *was* once heading for holy orders. My mother's idea. Desperate to have a priest in the family. Went and got my A-levels, though. Good grades too. After that my parents saw pound signs."

"And now?"

"Spiritually bankrupt, but with a healthy bank balance."

"OK, Doc. Look, my battery's going to be dead in a minute. What can I do for you?"

"Just wanted to see how you are, Harry. I hear you've been escaping into Belfast."

"News travels fast."

"I have my spies."

"My father?"

"I couldn't possibly comment."

"So?"

"So ... be careful."

"So ... don't patronise me."

"Mmm, you do sound a bit touchy today. Everything OK?"

"Yeah. A little setback on the social front. Nothing for you to worry about, though."

"Well, just take it one step at a time. We all know how impetuous you can be."

"Look, Mr Patterson, would you mind telling me exactly why you're calling?"

"We need to get you in to take a look at your legs. A little bit routine, a little bit to check you out for surgery."

"Surgery? What? See if I'm ready?"

"Yes."

"Oh, thank the Lord!"

"Good, I thought that might cheer you up. No promises now. But your last scan was encouraging. Come by tomorrow after your physio. I'll see you at twelve. We'll give you a thorough check-up and I'll talk you through the possibilities."

"And then? When do you reckon?"

"As I say: no promises. However, if all looks well, it could be as early as May. But, and it's a big but, try and avoid overexerting yourself in the meantime. And avoid stress."

"That's easier said than done."

"I have every faith in you ... er ... Harry ... I've got to go. We'll speak soon."

Hugh Patterson rang off. Another plate to spin.

If Harry had been able, he would have danced a jig along the paving slabs of the Stranmillis Road. God knows what sort of treatment the hospital was lining up for him, what agonies he would have to endure on the operating table, but little could compare with the painful state of his legs right now.

That they might consider surgery in the new year indicated that Mr Patterson had confidence in his continuing recovery and that the lesions in his head were healing well.

Harry ambled through the station entrance at Botanic and tottered down the ramp to his platform wearing a satisfied smile. A morning at the clinic would take his mind off Susan Heywood's inability to help. Not that he was convinced she had given up on him completely. Why would she have gone out of her way to meet him for a coffee if she didn't have some sympathy for his plight? Feeling positive, he decided that given another chance he would be more diplomatic; try and repair the damage and win her round.

9

1.30pm. Wednesday, 26 November 2008.

Harry stopped off at his studio when he got back to Holywood. It lay along the route between the station and home. Popping in on a whim made a tricky hurdle easier to cross.

Harry had always thought of his workspace as more of an office than a studio. His idea of a studio was a loft at the top of a Victorian wharf building flooded with natural light. It would feature wooden floorboards and lots of exposed brick. Harry's "studio" was a large ground floor room with double windows facing onto a car park. It was tucked in behind the reception area of a commercial property built in the seventies, just off the high street.

Harry was a photographer, however, and photographers have studios, so a studio it was called whatever the reality.

The reality was a utilitarian environment where light flickered over magnolia walls from rows of fluorescent tubes, one in three of which was dud. These sat overhead amidst a grid of polystyrene tiles that jumped in their aluminium frame whenever the door opened or closed. Underfoot, a sea of blue carpet tiles sat in loose proximity to the concrete floor.

The room wasn't large enough to accommodate most photo shoots. For more expansive photography he would rent fit-for-purpose facilities in Belfast or, if he were photographing food, would shoot on location. He found that chefs, cooks and food writers often have spacious kitchens at home either designed to a high specification or full of character or both and usually with plenty of props to hand.

The studio in Holywood proved useful as a base for taking calls, storing stuff and for keeping on top of admin.

The rest of the building was colonised by a PR company: a warm-hearted group of chatty women who were kind enough to keep an eye on things for him whenever he couldn't be there and generous enough to include him in their office shenanigans whenever he was. They would also employ him to take the occasional promotional photograph. Handy bread-and-butter stuff.

Harry's unscheduled visit distracted his female colleagues from their daily grind. They stopped to greet him with enthusiastic hugs, cooing and ahhing to welcome home the office pet; the first time most of them had seen him since the accident.

In the workplace he was often the only man present and therefore usually spoilt rotten. Their greeting made him realise just how much he had missed them, and was relieved he could remember them all by name.

Half an hour of tea and banter in the foyer and the hubbub subsided. Everyone back to work. Harry took a deep breath and entered his room.

His studio was dominated by two desks, piles of ageing computer equipment and, along one wall, a large storage system made up of chipboard cubes screwed together into something that looked like a barricade. The unit contained file copies of every issue of every publication he'd ever contributed to. Twenty-five years of hard labour.

From time to time he had tried to reorganise the piles of printed matter into neat rows, but had never succeeded in a total eradication of the sprawl. The top of the unit was covered in a thick layer of magazines, newspapers and books too big to fit on a shelf or in a drawer. It was a challenge to find anything in a hurry especially if the item hadn't been seen for a while.

The studio, though comfortable enough, was too scruffy for his liking. The clutter reminded him of a schoolboy's bedroom or a suburban garage, with a musty smell to match, and made the room almost impossible to clean. He had been promising himself for years that he would have a clear-out, redecorate and upgrade his computer system, but there was little sign of that.

Once alone with the door shut, Harry made a start on the mountain of mail. It wasn't till he'd opened the last envelope that he remembered the photos he'd taken of Susan Heywood in the cafe. He uploaded the files onto his Mac. There were half a dozen and, considering they had been snatched in haste, weren't too bad for snaps. There was one Harry liked in particular. It was a shot where he had caught her spinning round in anger; her hair swishing past the camera, her eyes glowering over her glasses as her head tipped forward. Her eyes loomed large and green and fiery.

He tweaked the image in Photoshop, personalised the file name, saved it and binned the rest. Then he rushed through his emails, thanking the Lord that someone had thought to put an out-of-office notice on his mailbox. There was nothing worth responding to anyway, so he switched off his computer, locked the door and hobbled off in the direction of home.

En route he bumped into one or two familiar faces. There were always plenty of people to nod to or wave at on Holywood's high street. The friendliness was a big draw for Harry, who liked being part of a small community.

As he turned off the main drag onto the backstreet heading for home, he spotted his ex-wife coming down the hill towards him. It was a shock he wasn't prepared for.

She was approaching on the same side of the road, head down and in a hurry. He didn't think she'd spotted him, but wasn't going to avoid her, even though it had crossed his mind to dodge into a doorway or cut back onto the main road.

"Keira!" he beamed, trying to sound enthusiastic and calling out early before she got too close, not wanting to make her jump. He tried his friendliest smile.

"Keira?"

No answer and no eye contact.

"Jesus! Can't you even say hello?"

He stood firm. Reached out and touched her gently on the arm as she neared.

"Why would I? Really, why?" she muttered, shrugging him off and squeezing past.

Then she stopped, turned and looked up at him. There was a coldness in her eyes, her mouth taut and sullen. No flash of her bright white smile for him, then. Such a change from his first memories of her as a young and carefree twenty-something, always smiling and laughing. And brilliant hazel eyes, shiny, searching, intelligent, her face full of inquisitiveness beneath a bouncy blonde bob. A graceful fawn.

"I don't know," he replied, trying to sound kind and submissive. "Unfortunately, I can't remember why you wouldn't, Keira."

"How is your amnesia, by the way?"

"You know. Good days. Bad days."

"A selective memory, then."

"Not intentionally."

"Convenient, though."

"Actually, it's improving. I'm remembering more all the time, thank God."

"*Actually*, I'm not that interested. Anyway, what *do* you want, Harry?" she sighed, looking bored and world weary; a bespoke look Harry imagined she had tailored just for him.

He shrugged.

"Er, to talk? Yeah. But not for long."

"Why?"

"I don't know. I just want to talk to you, Keira. Ask a few questions. That's all."

"Well, I don't see why you would think I would want to talk to *you* after all you've put me through. But then, of course, you wouldn't remember any of that, would you?"

"Well, no, as it happens, I don't. But maybe if you gave me a moment to ask a few questions then maybe things might become a little clearer and I might be able to get some things into perspective."

"Oh, really."

"And I'd very much like to try and put things right."

"Oh, you would, would you?"

"Yes."

"Don't be so bloody stupid, Harry. It's far too late for that. Too much water—"

"But you'll talk to me?" he shrugged.

She turned and started to walk off.

"I don't know."

"Ten minutes?"

"I don't know—"

"Five minutes, then?"

He was almost shouting.

"Oh, for God's sake, Harry," she said, turning to face him.

"Three?"

"Oh, all right. Look, you're collecting the kids tonight. Pop your head round the door when you bring them back. I'll answer a few questions. But only a few. Five minutes, though. No more than five minutes. I can't promise anything. You're not exactly my favourite person these days."

Without waiting for a response she moved off towards the town centre. He'd felt an urge to present his case there and then, try and win her over, but knew it would be better to keep his mouth shut and let her go.

Seeing her exasperated him. He had missed her and yet knew it probably wasn't his place to be telling her such things now. In any case, he guessed she wouldn't listen.

Harry watched till she turned onto the high street and out of sight. After a brief pause to catch his breath he set off again, hoping that it was the wind gusting off the lough that was causing his eyes to water.

10

4pm. Wednesday, 26 November 2008.

"I'll have a consonant, please, Carol."
  "L."
  "And a vowel."
  "I."
  "And a consonant, please, Carol."
  "V."

Clive Heywood was spreadeagled on the sofa watching the game show *Countdown* on TV. And rather than concentrating on constructing a nine-letter word from co-host Carol Vorderman's random selection of vowels and consonants, was distracted by the physical attractions of Carol Vorderman.

"I've got a seven-letter word."
  "OK, what is it, please, Philip?"
  "It's VAGINAL."
The studio audience guffawed, whilst the hosts strained to keep straight faces.
  "Ah, yes. Very good, Philip. Vaginal. Susie?"
  "Yes, of course ... here it is." Lexicographer Susie Dent smiled, hands hovering over the appropriate entry in the *Oxford English Dictionary*, *"Vaginal. An adjective. The noun being, as I am sure we are all aware ...Vagina."*

Clive didn't hear the last sentence having closed his eyes and drifted off into a doze accompanied by the cymbal-like splish-splash of the audience applause that in the imagination of a dreamy half sleep had become waves crashing on a Caribbean shore.

Neither did he hear the key turning in the front door, nor the front door open and close. He was, however, awoken by Susan Heywood's briefcase as it sailed through the air and then crashlanded on the armchair beside his head, the backdraft ruffling his hair as it soared past. It was half past four and he felt like he'd been caught with his pants down.

"Carol Vorderman! What are you watching that crap for, Clive? Have you got nothing better to do?"

Clive sensed his timing in choosing that particular afternoon to slob out in front of the TV was somewhat unfortunate. He knew that the most effective line of defence was silent indifference.

"Bloody hell! Daytime television, Clive."

She was in a foul mood.

He knew it best to avoid becoming a sparring partner at all costs.

"A crap day at the office and then I have to come home to this!" she muttered under her breath, but loud enough to be heard.

Clive knew if he could keep his mouth shut for another minute or two, her storm would pass. Better to let her move round the house and throw a few things, bump into a table and kick some doors. If he were to speak to her prematurely, she would sit down and concentrate her anger on him. Better to keep her on her feet and moving so she could shake off what was bothering her by abusing whatever lay in her path. But, then, she sat down. And, against his better judgement, he opened his mouth.

"Bad day at work?"

"What the hell would you know about work, Clive? Very little, I'd say, judging by your current recreation."

"Oh."

"You do know that you're turning into a couch potato, don't you? An overweight one at that. A giant jacket potato. I bet you don't even know what day of the fucking week it is. And what do you care about my work, Clive? Let's face it, you've got little sympathy or time for my clients – social lepers, isn't that what you call them?"

"Oh, I don't kno—"

"Self-centred egomaniacs. Sound familiar? The morbidly obtuse."

"Oh, I was probably just a little grumpy then. Hey, relax! Let me fix you a drink."

"No, Clive. That's not going to help."

She got up, flicked off her shoes, which careered into the skirting board, and stomped off to climb the stairs, shed her work clothes and take a shower.

"*I'll have another vowel, please, Carol,*" Philip asked on the TV, a handful of points away from winning the last round and today's competition. His glasses slipped down his nose in the excitement of the moment.

Clive fell back into a doze only to be reawakened by his wife's mobile phone ringing from the briefcase by his head.

"Your mobile's ringing!" he shouted up the stairwell.

"Answer it!" came a muffled cry.

"Hello? Susan's phone."

A pause.

"Hang on, please. I'll get her."

Another pause.

"It's a Harry-somebody-or-other," Clive called to Susan, his hand covering the mouthpiece.

Susan Heywood reappeared in a bathrobe, scurrying down the stairs, flushed and furiously rubbing her wet hair with a towel. She grabbed the mobile out of her husband's grasp and then flapped her free hand to usher him away. Clive raised his eyebrows in resignation and sloped off back to the sofa. Susan wandered into the kitchen.

"Mr String? Why are you phoning me? And how did you get my number?" she whispered, snappily.

"Don't you know? You call my mobile then I have your number. Everybody knows that. Look, I'm going to talk to my wife tonight. To my ex-wife, that is. I wanted you to know."

"Well done. Congratulations," she said sarcastically. "But, look, I don't think for a minute that you've called just to tell me that. I'm not stupid."

"No. No. You're right. I also wanted to apologise. I guess I blew it this afternoon."

"Yes, you most certainly did. Big time."

"Well, I'm sorry. Is there anything I can d—"

"Yes, don't phone me. And never out of office hours."

"It's only half past four."

"Well, I'm not in the office. Look, what do you want?"

"To say sorry."

"OK. Well, you've done that now. What else?"

"I'd like to see you when I've talked to my wife?"

"No. I don't do tea and sympathy, Harry."

"I would be interested to know what you think. You know, a kind of debrief, I suppose."

"Look, I'm a marriage guidance counsellor, Harry, not Bomber Command. And I'm not here to hold your hand."

"I really think I need someone to help me on this one."

"Understood. But I can't. I've already explained that to you. Look, I don't know you. I'm not an old friend. I have no attachment or commitment to you. It's not like we met socially, like we were introduced at a cocktail party or something. I don't have a duty of care to you. And we're not becoming friends, Harry. There's noth—"

But he was gone. She tried to call back, but his mobile was switched to answerphone.

"*Shit!*"

She thought about texting.

"Who was that?" Clive called from the lounge.

"Hang on, Clive!" She yelled.

"Sounded like one of your wounded birds."

"Shut up, Clive!"

Susan Heywood took a deep breath, tried to think calmly, then typed into her mobile:

Harry, text me and let me know how you get on. But don't phone! SH.

Pressing the send button felt like pushing down the plunger to detonate an explosive charge. She wasn't sure if she should do it, then regretted doing it and then wondered why she had done it at all.

She put the phone into her dressing-gown pocket and went into the lounge to sit with Clive, feeling furtive.

"Who's Harry String, then?"

"Oh, a client."

"Thought so."

"He wanted to reschedule an appointment."

"Couldn't he phone the office?"

"Couldn't get through. Short notice."

"So, what's he doing with your mobile number? I'm not even allowed to phone you on that bloody thing!"

"He got it when I phoned him earlier. Oh, does it matter? Anyway, what have you been doing today, Clive?" she asked in a listless voice which barely concealed a slight pang of guilt.

"Oh, I ran down the high street stark bollock naked this morning, held up the local post office at lunchtime and strangled next door's cat with my bare hands before tea. Why? Do you really care?"

"God, Clive, you worry me sometimes," she said, getting up to retreat into the kitchen, wondering how soon it would be before she and Clive were sitting across the desk from one of her colleagues at the agency.

Clive sat impassive, stymied by his wife's mood. Her residual anger troubled him. She seemed more angry more often; it was becoming a regular feature of their domestic life. He knew that it was a symptom of a greater dissatisfaction and prayed that it had more to do with a lack of fulfilment at work rather than anything to do with him.

Having left her to rummage around in the kitchen for ten minutes and cool off, Clive followed her through.

"You OK?" he asked from the doorway. She had her back to him and was leaning over one of the worktops reading through the appointments section of the *Belfast Telegraph*. Ominously, she had a red biro in her hand, was ringing job ads and then scribbling details on a Post-it note. Clive walked up behind her, folded his arms around her waist and kissed the back of her neck.

"Looking for a job, sweetheart?" he asked quietly.

"Yes."

"Fed up with counselling? I'm not surprised."

"No, it's for you, Clive."

"Oh."

"Look, someone's got to do something to help you before your brain turns to goo."

"Of course, of course, you're right. And, of course, I will start looking soon. Very soon. But there's time enough."

"I think the time is now, Clive. You've got to do something before you lose all self-respect, or, even worse, find yourself on the committee at the bloody golf club. That'd be like landing a starring role in *Night of the Living Dead!*"

"There's talk of me being made club captain next year."

"No, Clive. I couldn't bear to see you reduced to wearing a navy blazer and grey slacks. Plus, a V-neck in canary yellow just isn't your colour," she laughed.

"I wouldn't worry. It ain't going to happen," Clive replied with a sigh whilst crossing his fingers behind his back.

Clive responded to her lightened mood by nibbling at her ear, a familiar chink in her armour, and smiled when, for the first time in a long time, she responded by arching her spine and pushing her backside into his crotch.

"I miss the old Clive," she whispered.

The old Clive? His blood began to boil, and he would have taken issue with her but he could tell she wanted to have sex, and it had been such a long time that he would rather bite his lip and take the abuse than miss the opportunity.

Emboldened, Clive moved his hands from her waist to cup her breasts and then slid his fingers inside her robe until they found her nipples. She leant her head back, extending her neck for him to kiss.

For once, Clive's timing was good. He took full advantage of his wife's change of mood on the lounge sofa, being mindful to turn off the TV before helping her slip out of her dressing gown, but was left wondering if Philip would solve the last conundrum and go on to win today's episode of *Countdown*.

11

5.20pm. Wednesday, 26 November 2008.

It was a clear night and the view across Belfast Lough came as an unexpected treat. The lights glimmering on the far bank reminded Harry String of the view across the bay of Saint-Tropez, it amused him to observe as he hobbled down the hill. He was on his way round to the old family house; a four minute walk away.

Harry was to collect his kids on the dot of five thirty. As he approached the front garden he paused, leaning on one of the stone pillars at the top of the path to take a good look. It seemed an age since he'd passed through the imposing front door. And even though he had lived at the tall Georgian terrace for at least ten years, he stood before it now without keys, a stranger. It was a homecoming of sorts, but felt like a homecoming in a parallel universe.

That the door was now Downing-Street black when it had been pillar-box red only added to Harry's feeling of detachment. There was a time when he would have been involved in the choice of colour and a veto over the final pick.

I'd have had plenty to say about gloss black, he thought.

There had been other changes: new plants in the window boxes, new window boxes, the hedge was cut lower, the door furniture changed from silver to brass to complement the paint job; details that accentuated the passing of time and his sidelining from the present.

Harry rang the bell. He pressed just once with a light tentative touch. Before, if he hadn't had his keys with him, he would have rung two or three times and ended with a cheeky flourish. For now, though, and for his wife's – his ex-wife's – benefit, he thought he'd hold off on extravagant campanology.

"Daddy!"

"Emily! You ready, poppet?"

"Yeah. I'll get my stuff. *Danny!*" Emily, the older child, yelled as she ran back into the house.

Harry glanced through the doorway into an empty hall. The cream paintwork now bore a grey patina that intensified as it rose towards the cornicing. Keira had finally got her way over the hall carpet: gone. The floorboards were stripped bare save for a coat of varnish. All change except for the familiar smell of fresh coffee brewing in the kitchen at the far end; a comforting aroma in normal circumstances.

And no sign of Keira. Harry was pretty sure that she wouldn't come near him unless she absolutely had to. He didn't want to enter the house either. Didn't want to annoy her, but felt a need to make contact of some kind. He crept into the hall like a Comanche stalking prey, cringing at every creak in the boards. A few feet would be acceptable, he thought, but no further.

The photographs lining the walls had been rearranged. The black-and-white wedding photo was gone, so too the framed print of the giant Highland stags. He'd bought it for her in their early days when he discovered that she had a thing about them.

"Is there any post for me, Emily?" Harry asked his daughter in a quiet voice, almost a whisper, as she darted up the stairs to fetch her overnight bag.

"Any post for Dad, Mum?" she shouted as she made her ascent.

"No. Tell him Grandad lifted it," a voice barked from the distant lounge. Harry took a deep breath.

"Hi, Keira. You OK?"

No answer.

Within a couple of minutes both kids were with him and ready in the hall.

"Right. Better go. I'm getting hungry."

"How long's tea?"

"*About six inches*," Harry whispered.

"What?"

"*It's sausages.*"

"Oh, Dad!"

Harry was keen to go. It was too weird standing in the house feeling like an alien when he felt he should be collapsing onto a sofa to wrestle with the kids or watch TV. The urge to leave became overwhelming.

Though he was impatient to talk to her, he knew it would be poor timing to attempt to have a conversation with Keira now. He'd hold her to her word though and suggest a brief chat when he walked the kids back later.

"What time will you be bringing them home, Harry?"

Keira's voice. Stern. Harry knew she was well capable of being warm and endearing, but this was her voice of admonishment. The voice of a school ma'am. Every comment premeditated with the precision of a chess move.

Her head appeared from behind the sitting-room door in pursuit of a response.

"Hi, there. You OK?" Harry asked in a friendly tone.

"What time?" she repeated, sticking to her subject.

"Much better, thank you," Harry replied, petulantly.

Keira emerged into full view with a knitted brow and fierce eyes.

"Eight, and don't be late. They've got school tomorrow," she said testily, moving down the hall and kissing each child on the head before ushering them out.

"We're only round the corner. Don't worry," he smiled. "It's good to see you."

She gave the subtlest of nods then closed the front door before they had time to turn around to walk down the path.

As they headed off, Harry noticed that the garden gate was missing. He'd been meaning to get it repaired for ages, but now it seemed to have been scrapped altogether. This really was another house in another life.

The kids could have stayed over at Harry's – there was a spare room with twin beds; a little cramped but comfortable enough. That they had school the next day and homework to finish made it a less practical proposition however. It was early days, anyway.

When they arrived back at the family home, Harry asked Emily to fetch her mother. Keira came to the door, ushered the children upstairs, grabbed a fleece and then led Harry into the front garden. They sat under the bay window on an old garden bench. Keira sitting straight-backed and stiff. The night was pitch black, the steam on their breath illuminated by the amber glow of the street lights beyond the hedge.

The solemnity of the moment encouraged a pause.

"OK. What do you want to talk about, Harry? What do you want?" Keira eventually asked, offering him a cigarette which he declined.

He noticed that her hands were trembling, but then again it was a cold evening for sitting out.

"I'd like to know what happened – I mean between you and me, that is. No one will tell me. Like they're frightened I might have a relapse or something. It's just that one minute I remember being married, the next I find I'm divorced."

"That's a tad dramatic."

"Well, it was bloody traumatic waking up in hospital and finding out and then not knowing why."

"Well, that's to do with your accident. It's got nothing to do with me."

"Still."

"Look, Harry, I don't want to go over old ground. We're divorced. What's the point? It's over now. And you did nothing to stop it happening at the time. In fact, it seemed to be what you wanted."

"Well, I'm sorry, but I don't remember. Can't remember. The point is, to me, it doesn't feel like it's over. For me, time has stood still since around about two years ago. I was a happily married man then. How did I end up being a divorcee living on my own?"

"That's the point. You weren't a happily married man two years ago, Harry. You were just *a married man* and making heavy going of it. You made life pretty miserable for me, too. I tried so hard to make our marriage work, but you did little or nothing to help. I got the impression you grew bored. Bored of me. You *were* bored of me. And that's a very unpleasant experience when you are intending to spend the rest of your life with someone. That's *traumatic*. Extremely traumatic. In actual fact, you were an absolute shit."

Harry, who was staring at the ground, didn't flinch.

"I was your wife," Keira continued. "I should have been your priority, but I always seemed to come off second best to anybody else who happened to be around at any particular time. You had loads of time for other people but very little for me and the kids. All those other people ... None of them cared for you. Not like I cared. But that didn't matter to you. Actually, I don't know why I'm bothering to tell you this. We've been over it so many times before."

As Harry processed every word and syllable, he wondered whether his ex-wife's account was accurate and had no way of knowing.

"The whole thing made me quite ill. From before the separation and then right through until the divorce," she continued. "The stress made me really quite sick."

"What started it?"

"What?"

"Us ... splitting up."

"How does it ever happen? A gradual growing apart, a lack of commitment, betrayals, infidelities."

"But we were so happy – even two years ago. I remember."

"Look, Harry, we were happy for about the first seven or eight years, but thereafter – the last two or three – it became a struggle. You were hardly skipping through life with a smile on your face. It takes two to make a marriage, and there were too many times when you just didn't seem to be there for us."

"Yeah, but times were very testing. I was always overstretched at work, and really had to struggle to make ends meet. We were always short of cash. I remember that much," Harry said, letting a little anguish creep into his voice.

"Who doesn't struggle, Harry?"

"It was bloody tough supporting all this!" Harry said sweeping his hand through a dramatic arc.

"Look, Harry. There's no point us continuing this conversation if it's going to become a platform for your self-pity. I've done all the arguing I'm ever going to do with you and I'm not doing any more. God knows why but I'll help you fill in some of the gaps, but you'll have to shut up and listen or we're going to stop right now! Overwork and poverty are feeble excuses for failure, in any case. It's the same for most of the adult population. And we had options. We didn't have to live here – we could have sold this place."

There was a long pause.

Aware that he was walking on thin ice, Harry decided that he'd better back off and be done with arguing.

"OK. Sorry. I'll listen. I'm listening."

"Right, cos I'm only good for about five minutes or so and I don't want to do this again. Ever. So you'd better concentrate."

"OK, OK."

"Right, here's the facts. Things were fine most of the time between us. A bit up and down but mostly fine. All that changed once you lost interest. After that things were never going to be the same—"

"Lost interest? How so? I don't understand."

"Well, neither did I. I thought you were having an affair."

"Oh, come on!"

"I couldn't be sure, but I sensed something was going on."

"That's ridiculous."

"I didn't think so at the time."

"So *everything* was my fault?"

"Maybe. Maybe not. But I never wanted a divorce. I never wanted any of this. You could have stopped it at any time but you didn't. You were the one who went to see a solicitor. Where did that leave me? What was I supposed to do?"

"I don't know. I really don't know. That's the thing! I just don't remember!"

Harry stood up, clapped both hands to his face and let out a long sigh.

"Look, Harry, if you're going to get agitated—"

"No, sorry ... sorry," Harry said, trying to smile, catching himself on and sitting down immediately. "It's just ... it's just ... Oh, I can't get my head round any of this. It's all so surreal. Lying in a hospital bed you get plenty of time to think through stuff. My very last memory before the accident is of being at home with you and the kids, and it's a happy memory, so it comes as a bit of a shock to wake up and find that I'm on my own. Divorced. It's a bit like, one day I'm the dad in *Little House on the Prairie* and the next I'm Robin Williams in *Mrs Doubtfire*. And then there are times now when I'm lying in bed, piecing the memories back together, and do you know what I recall the most?"

He paused so she could say "What?" but assumed that she wasn't going to bother.

"I remember the good times: the summer holidays, the kids' birthday parties and the Christmases."

"I'm sorry, I've filed all the good times away, Harry. They're all too long ago now anyway, I'm afraid. I'd rather live in the present and look forward."

"Yes, but we *did* have good times. You know we did. You've only got to look at the photos."

"They've been boxed up and packed away, too."

"Fair enough. But there *were* some happy times."

"Look, Harry. God knows why I'm telling you this, and it might surprise you, but ... I do love you. A part of me always will, but I don't love you as I did. Not now. I've moved on. And I'm sorry about your accident, but that's not my fault. And it's not my fault that you've lost a couple of years of your memory or whatever. And even though you've had a terrible accident, you're still culpable for what you did during those years your memory has selected to erase – amnesia or not."

Keira paused for emphasis, turning to stare into his eyes to ensure she had his full attention.

"Do you know what finally tipped me over the edge?"

"What?"

"When you did your vanishing act."

"When was that?"

"A couple of Januarys ago."

"I'm sorry, I don't remember."

"That's handy."

"Well—"

"We'd been arguing. Hadn't been talking for days. I was at the end of my tether. Then you disappeared. Took off without saying a word. Deserted us. No note, no phone call. No trace of you for a whole week. I still don't know where you were or who you were with. You just ran off and left us. Years of marriage and then it seemed that you just didn't care any more, had given up, resigned. It was just too cruel. I concluded there and then that there was no way back for us."

"Maybe I thought it would help break the deadlock."

"Harry, maybe you were just feeling sorry for yourself, I don't know, but it really seemed that you'd dumped us ... Thrown it all away. And why? You had it all!"

"So what happened when I came back?"

"Very little. We continued where we left off: arguing, then not talking."

"Didn't we try and make it work?"

"*Again*? Why? Why would I want to? There's only so much cruelty anyone's going to take."

"That's very sad."

"Of course it is. But you're the one who blew it. And now, just because you're feeling a bit lonely and realise that you really *have* lost me, it seems that you've decided that you don't like it. Well I'm glad, because it serves you bloody well right."

"Didn't you think, when I went away for a week, that maybe I was just trying to shake things up a bit? Maybe you were supposed to react differently?"

"Maybe it was the last straw."

"But maybe I was trying to get your attention. Maybe you were supposed to react more positively ... you know ... Give things another go. I mean ... Can't you be more positive?"

"I don't need to be. And I don't want to be. Not now. Circumstances change, and they *have* changed."

"Ah, I see. Hang on, don't tell me. You've met someone. You've got a new man."

Silence.

"You have?"

"Yes. And you knew, as a matter of fact. Well, you know. Well, used to know ... a while back. Before the accident, that is. It's obviously something else you've forgotten."

"Oh."

"Why 'Oh'?"

"Just 'Oh'. Who is it?"

"It's James."

"Not Little Jimmy Johnston?"

"Don't call him that! He's called James."

"You're dating Little Jimmy Johnston? That's brave. No! But you've got to be kidding!"

"You know something, Harry? You can be a complete arsehole at times. He's a good man. And I'll tell you what, he's a lot more reliable than you were or ever could be."

"Reliable? But, Jesus, Keira ... Jimmy Johnston, the line-dancing king of Killyleagh? Someone needs to tell him that wearing a Stetson with spectacles is *not* a good look."

"Fuck off, Harry."

"I suppose he's well capable of keeping you in the lavish style to which you've become accustomed, though. What's he in? Animal feeds?"

"Stop being such a wanker, Harry. And anyway, when I come to think about it, why the hell am I bothering to discuss this with you?"

"Why wouldn't you?"

"You don't know, do you? God, you are such a bloody hypocrite."

"I'm sorry. I don't kno—"

"You're sitting here whining about us not being together, about us being divorced, but do you know the real reason why we're divorced? I'll tell you. Well, we were only separated at first, but then you sued me for divorce. *Sued me!* So it's your own bloody fault. All of it. All of your own doing. And then, as soon as you got your decree nisi, you managed to find another woman to pester. I wasn't talking to you by then, of course, but I heard."

"Another woman?"

"Yes!"

"No."

"Yes!"

"When? Must have been before the accid—"

"Obviously."

"God! That's hard to believe. You know, I really don't—"

"I know. You don't remember anything about it. Well, apparently you were quite cut up about the whole thing."

"The divorce?"

"No. Your girlfriend."

"*Girlfriend?*" Harry shrugged.

Keira took a last draw on her cigarette, flicked it away, exhaled a geyser-like plume and smiled.

"Harry, you had a girlfriend."

"Who?"

"Don't know. Haven't a clue. No one I knew."

"You're kidding?"

"No."

"Wow!"

"She was called M-something. Mary, Melanie, Missie ... I don't know. The kids told me. Apparently you were totally besotted. Or so I heard."

"Really? That's amazing," he chuckled.

"What's so funny? No, hang on, don't tell me, I suppose it tickles your ego."

"Oh, come on. So what happened?"

"I heard you were dumped."

"Really! Why?"

"No idea. Why the hell would I be interested in your tawdry love life? Whatever happened, it served you bloody well right. And anyway, hardly a woman. Not much more than a schoolgirl though, or so I heard."

"Seriously?"

"In her twenties."

"*Shit!* What the hell? Weren't you upset?"

"No, I was not. I didn't give a damn by then. As I say, it was after the divorce had been finalised."

"OK. But you'd think *I'd* remember something about it."

"Don't know and don't care."

"I couldn't have been that bothered."

"Are you sure about that, Harry?"

"Why?"

"Because I heard on the grapevine that you couldn't stop talking about her."

"Did the kids meet her?"

"No."

"Thank God!"

"Yes, I'd agree with that."

"Blimey. What else do you know?"

"Not much. It obviously didn't work out. The kids said that you were getting a bit impatient with them around that time. Seemed upset. And then I heard you'd parted company."

"Er, when was that, then?"

"Well, that's something *I* can't remember, I'm afraid. What you got up to after the divorce was of little or no interest to me. Just as long as it didn't affect the kids."

"Fair enough. Anyway, that's all in the past. What about now? What about us?"

"There is no *us*."

"Are you sure there's no way back? Are you sure you don't want to give it another go?"

"With you?"

"Why not?"

"Why the hell would I?"

"I would."

"Don't be so naive, Harry. Time's moved on. Looking back gives me a headache. I don't want to go back there, and I don't want to go back there with you. You had your chance. You had many. I've moved on. I suggest you do the same."

"OK, but where do we go from here?"

"I've told you."

"No, I mean ... Can't we be friends?"

"Now? No. I don't want to be friends with you."

"Later then?"

"Do you know, Harry, I can't even be bothered to think about it."

"But you're my best friend."

"I don't think so, somehow. Not now."

Harry shrugged. Forlorn. His heart told him to keep trying, convince her, win her round, but his head knew he was staring defeat in the face. At least for now.

The conversation wilted.

"One thing, Keira."

"What?"

"Did you ever meet whatever-her-name-is?"

"No. Why? Why the hell would I?"

"I just wondered what she looks like. I don't know, but I think I might have bumped into her earlier today. If it was her, she's quite a fiery little character."

"Just how you like them, eh, Harry?"

"Amazing. I didn't recognise her, but that's the funny thing about memory. I never forgot about you and me, though. Do you really expect me to give up and go away?"

"Yes. And please do. I don't want you creeping around trying to win me back. Especially now I'm having an uncomplicated and very enjoyable time with somebody else."

"Oh, I'd hate to come between you and Little Jimmy Johnston."

"It's James. And don't be a pig. Anyway, what makes you think you're so special?"

"*You* did once. Don't you remember? What about all the great times we shared? You're my ... were ... my wife. Doesn't that mean anything to you?"

"Of course. Well it did till you buggered it all up. I'm afraid I moved on a long time ago. And so must you."

Keira stood up. Harry's cue.

Back at home Harry String lay gazing up at the bedroom ceiling, couldn't sleep, his head full of uncomfortable thoughts. Remorse, guilt, regret, doubt, loathing. His self-esteem had plumbed new depths.

He'd gone to bed early but became preoccupied with thoughts of M, the amber-haired girl. He pictured her face and tried to imagine being in her company; concentrated on retrieving the smallest fragment of something familiar – one episode, just one moment they had shared. Nothing came. It seemed implausible that they'd ever enjoyed any kind of intimacy or happiness in light of their recent encounter in Belfast.

Then memories of the early days with Keira came to him followed by an overwhelming sense of shame. Rather than count sheep he tried to recount the story in sequence.

Where did they first meet?
Racing at The Curragh.
When?
Spring, 1996.
She, a student nurse from Lisburn. He, a staff photographer on a Dublin paper.

Keira McKinley didn't think he was interested. Didn't notice he was trying to chat her up.

Feisty and funny, he liked her quick wit and superior intelligence.

Harry was thirty-two and ten years older than her. They arranged a date in Belfast. Hit it off. The real deal. Got engaged within seven or eight months, married within a year of that, and the kids soon followed.

They were happy for a good while, but the loss of three parents in quick succession was an emotional strain. It was hard for Keira: she was also an only child and now an orphan of sorts. It was also hard for Harry's dad to cope with the expectations and petty resentments that followed with being a sole survivor.

But Harry and Keira were a popular couple and seemed well-suited. Made for each other, it was said.

"*Made for each other. We were made for each other,*" Harry mumbled, as his eyelids grew heavy, fluttered and then closed.

12

9.20am. Thursday, 27 November 2008.

Harry was gazing into his tea, annoyed that it was a pale white when it should have been a light tan. Slopping in the milk, he'd forgotten it was Earl Grey and had ruined the brew. He took a sip, winced, but couldn't be bothered to boil the kettle again. At least this cup was hot even if it reminded him of the taste of Milk of Magnesia.

He was sitting in the dining area beside the galley kitchen of his two-up two-down. That end of the knock-through was dominated by a piece of garden furniture snapped up for buttons in a sale at B&Q and recast in the leading role of kitchen table. It had chrome legs with a smoked-glass top. The seats, wooden folding chairs bought in Habitat many years before, were a feeble support act.

Despairing of his tea, Harry switched his attention to the cardboard box lurking at the other end of the table. He had been reluctant to peek under the lid, wary of any of the stuff salvaged from the car crash; didn't fancy fingering through his belongings if they were scorched or blood-spattered. And whilst a look inside might spark memories from around the time of the accident, coming after a bad night's sleep and feeling a bit depressed (a mood worsened by his poor tea making), he decided that the rummaging could be left for another day.

But then, maybe? But then again, maybe not. But maybe? But no, definitely not.

He gave the box a petulant shove and went for a shower.

Harry took a long time in the bathroom. He was due at the hospital for his regular physiotherapy session and then for an appointment to have his legs examined by an orthopaedic surgeon, and wanted to make sure that when facing those twin humiliations he would at least do so smelling fragrant and appearing well groomed.

Following his accident, getting ready to go anywhere took Harry an age. The effort of putting on clothes, most of which seemed a size too big now, drained him of energy and left him short of breath. Before his incapacity he would never have considered the vast amount of bending and back movement involved in putting on a pair of jeans and a shirt. The struggle frustrated him and threatened to make him late.

Then he had trouble with his shoelaces. They were right at the outer limits of his reach. The strain of stretching his arms in order to get his hands in position to grasp the laces meant that he couldn't find any feeling or strength in his fingers to tie a knot once they'd reached their destination. He leant back across the bed, roaring with frustration, and, for the first time since he had left the ward, found he'd developed a headache. He swallowed a couple of paracetamol tablets, pillorying himself for allowing the routine to get him so stressed.

"*Just count your blessings. Count your blessings, you twat!*" he muttered, unclenching his fists. "*Just be glad to be alive,*" he rambled, whilst staring at the ceiling and taking deep breaths.

The last few days had been disappointing: the failed attempt at counselling and the meeting with Keira, but then he considered the condition of the patients he would encounter at the physio session. Some would be crying in pain with the exertion, others because the therapy appeared to be failing and that they were destined for what the hospital notes whispered would be *a negative outcome.*

By the time Harry was dressed and ready to leave, he was running late. He rushed down the stairs as best he could, tottered into the dining room, downed the dregs of his tea and, curiosity seizing the upper hand, found time to snatch a peep inside the box.

He had a quick fumble, but was disappointed by the insignificance of the contents unearthed: a tartan car rug, some battered CDs, an empty can of de-icer, an ancient phone charger, a deodoriser tree and his old waterproof jacket. However, thankfully, no blood.

Harry was about to abandon the search when he thought to check the pockets of the waterproof. He struck gold. Jackpot! His old mobile phone and wallet came to hand.

Looking up he caught a glimpse of the kitchen clock: ten fifteen. He grabbed the phone, the charger and wallet, stuffed them into his chest pocket – wondering if there was still some money in the wallet and hoping that the mobile had some battery power – before making for the train to Belfast.

As soon as he was sitting on the train, Harry started a closer inspection of the wallet and phone. Doubting that there would be any juice in the mobile, he was surprised when it fired up. Meanwhile, the wallet looked intact: credit cards, a crumpled tenner and a random collection of business cards. There was also a dog-eared snapshot of a couple in close-up, staring into the camera, shoulder to shoulder, heads pressed tight: Harry and the amber-haired girl. It reminded him of the kind of snap teenagers used to take in photo booths before the advent of mobile phones with cameras. Harry was stunned, couldn't take it in, and kept staring at the shot throughout the journey.

Though it didn't seem to have suffered any damage, the mobile phone, an ancient Nokia, still whiffed of diesel.

Fiddling with the phone, Harry went straight to the messages folder, brought up *messages in* and found one or two from his dad and also the kids, and then a plethora, about twenty, signed off with the initials MB. M-something. Mary, Melanie, Missie, the amber-haired girl?

He checked the phone's address book, but there was no listing for anyone like a Mary, Melanie or Missie. Just an MB.

Harry navigated back to, and then opened, all the messages received from MB in chronological order. The first had been sent the previous November:

Do you mean Nick's Wine Bar or Nick's Warehouse? If it's the latter, I can meet you there at 9.30.

A first date?

The next:

Yes. Monday's good. Meet you there at 7.

A second date?

Harry kept reading. An instinctive hoarder of anything, there were a lot of messages to read through. After the first ten or so, the chronology took Harry on into a second week. The messages grew jokier, then more intimate.

I wish you were here, we could chat, kiss ... go to bed. MBX

Harry found it difficult to equate the eagerness of the text messages with the hostility of the woman he'd encountered in the city centre. Were they really the same person? And, if so, what the hell could he have done to upset her?

He navigated to the *sent* folder and was about to read through the messages he'd texted to her when the phone bleeped and died, the battery drained. Frustrated, he tried to switch the phone on again, but to no avail.

As the train pulled into Great Victoria Street station, Harry pocketed the phone and wallet. On the concourse he bought a copy of *Auto Trader* to flick through whilst waiting for his appointment at the hospital; there was always plenty of waiting to be done. Anyway, he'd decided that, driving licence or not, he needed transport; he'd prefer a battered estate like the last one. Another Volvo. They were bulky, safe, reliable and good value for money. He'd need an automatic.

That he didn't have his licence back yet mattered little to him. *Bugger the consequences*, he thought.

Harry's physiotherapy at St George's took an hour. It was an intense and painful session, but – as some people can become obsessive about dieting once they see the numbers starting to drop on the scales – Harry was well-prepared to endure the pain if it meant taking another step towards a full recovery. And he had been growing more confident of achieving that with every milestone passed since waking from his coma: from learning to talk again, to walking unaided, to being discharged from hospital. But even though this progress marked him out as one of the luckier neurological patients, Harry was still urged to put in the hard graft during the physio sessions to ensure a complete recovery.

There were only two others in the physio suite when Harry arrived, both inpatients. One was recuperating from back surgery and progressing steadily. The other was a long-term paraplegic whose condition showed little sign of improvement.

The two were working on the parallel bars. Harry, who had graduated from the bars a month before leaving hospital, was to work on the general manipulation and strengthening of his upper and lower limbs. Meanwhile, he found somewhere to charge up his old mobile and then changed into his kit.

"So, Harry, how's life in the outside world?"

Harry was lying on his back on a yoga mat whilst the male physio contorted his arms and legs through what he imagined was something akin to a Spanish Inquisition.

The inanity of the question led Harry to believe that, if he closed his eyes he might imagine he was reclining at the barber's rather than being tied up in knots in the physio unit.

"Very good, Rory ... Ouch!" he replied through clenched teeth. "Yeah, a bit strange at times ... Ow! But it's ... Ooo! Good to have my own space and independence ... Agh!"

"Yeah, I can imagine. Any holidays planned?"

Yeah. I'm planning on jogging round Australia dressed as a nun, Harry thought to say, but didn't. He shook his head instead, which killed off the conversation and revived his headache all at the same time.

"Ever fancied taking up hairdressing, Rory?"

"What? Why?"

"Oh, nothing ... Ouch!"

Harry imagined that to anyone glancing in through the door it would appear that a very big bloke had got a much smaller bloke pinned to the floor and was trying to extract vital information through torture: like the combination to a safe or the little man's PIN numbers.

"See those two?" Rory grunted under his breath as he nodded towards the inpatients, "they haven't got your stamina, you know, Harry."

"*Uhuh?*"

Harry didn't like where the conversation was heading, didn't want to tempt the guy to bend his limbs further than they would comfortably bend. He also felt a stronger loyalty to his fellow patients than to Rory the physio.

"I'd be surprised if they ever reach your level, you know."

Harry closed his eyes and would have attempted sleep if it hadn't been for the lump of a man trying to wrench his arms from their sockets.

"Yep. Rory, you're doing a great job there, mate ... Aagh!"

After the physio session Harry got changed and moved on to his appointment with Mr Patterson, the neurologist. They were to meet in the office of a *Guy Bannister*, an orthopaedic surgeon.

He followed the blue vinyl strip running through the corridors until he reached a row of four plastic chairs hugging the wall opposite the surgeon's office whose name was displayed on the door with a jumble of impressive letters.

Sitting in the corridor reminded Harry of his schooldays and being sent to sit outside the headmaster's office to await punishment.

Harry preoccupied himself by flicking through his copy of *Auto Trader*.

"Good morning, Mr String! I don't know why you're looking through that. You can forget about driving for at least another four or five months yet!" Mr Patterson bellowed cheerily as he approached from down the corridor, his shoes squeaking on the polished grey lino.

Oh, God bless the bourgeoisie for their obsessive obedience to rules and regulations, Harry thought, tearing out the page he wanted and tossing the rest of the magazine into a waste bin beside him.

"Yes, but of course, Doc," Harry replied with a defiant twinkle in his eye.

Mr Patterson opened the door and beckoned Harry into the empty office and gestured for him to sit in front of the large and cluttered desk.

"Right, Harry. How are we today? Any headaches, vomiting, rashes, fever, nausea, diarrhoea, migraine, itchiness, bleeding, swelling or tiredness?"

"No."

Mr Patterson was circling as if he were a hungry hawk and Harry a field mouse.

"Sure?"

"Slight headache."

"Where?"

"Across here."

"Anything out of the ordinary?"

"No, I don't think so."

"Mmm. Let me know if it persists. I'm seeing you this time next week I believe, so I'll ask you about it again then. But come in straight away if you think it's getting any worse. Sleeping OK?"

"Ish."

"Smoking? Drinking?"

"Smoking, no. Drinking, yes. Just the odd glass of wine."

"The odd glass?"

"Very occasionally. One with a meal."

"Good. The odd glass is OK now. Two or three's bad."

Mr Patterson moved behind Harry and proceeded to handle Harry's head like it was a crystal ball and he a clairvoyant. He checked over his handiwork and, judging by the self-satisfied smile, liked what he saw.

Another white coat entered the room.

"Ah, Guy. This is Harry String. He's one of our star patients. He was a real mess not so long ago, but we've patched him up pretty good, don't you think?"

"Morning, Harry. We're just going to take a look at your legs to see what we can do with them," Guy Bannister said in a plummy Home Counties accent.

"Replacing them with something that works would be good. Wheels maybe."

"Mmm."

They made Harry drop his trousers; a common practice of late. There then followed much umming and ahhing and tapping and touching.

"X-ray? Time for an X-ray, Harry."

Harry was whisked away in a wheelchair.

"OK. We're going to take a careful look at these and get back to you, Mr String," Bannister mumbled, once they were back in his office, his face illuminated by the warm glow of the lightbox on the wall as he pawed over two sets of X-rays: the old and the new.

"I'd say, though, that unless there's any deterioration in your neurological condition we'll be operating sometime in April or May," Bannister continued. "Leave it with us for a week and we'll have a clearer idea of what we can achieve for you and a provisional date for the procedure. But let's be positive, shall we?"

"Can we be?" Harry asked, turning to Mr Patterson.

"I'd say so. There are no guarantees, of course, Harry, but your most recent scan suggested that the lesions are healing well. Everything's looking much improved. And, as long as you stay calm and avoid stress for the next while, there's little reason why things shouldn't go to plan."

"Sounds good," Harry replied calmly, even though he felt like screaming: "STOP TELLING ME TO STAY CALM!"

"Yes, you're doing well. But, Harry, just the odd glass of wine and no driving, right?" Mr Patterson added with a wink.

Harry nodded and gave a polite smile to signal acquiescence.

Back out on the street Harry wandered down towards the station, his mood lifted by the latest news. Rummaging through his pockets for the torn-out page from *Auto Trader*, he reached for his iPhone and called the contact number for a Volvo Estate he'd spotted.

"Hi, I'm interested in the car you're advertising. Yeah, the Volvo. It's an automatic, right? MOT'd? Taxed? Sixty thousand on the clock, yeah? Eight hundred and fifty quid, right? Yeah, I'd like to see it. Where are you? Right. Right. Great. Clean and tidy, but not showroom condition. Yeah, yeah. Sounds good. If I like it, can I lift it? Yeah, yeah. Cash. And she's ready to go, right? Any chance I can come now? Yeah ... Oh, good. What's your postcode? Right. Right. Got that. In about half an hour to forty-five minutes then, OK? Right. Thanks. Right, see you then. Aha. Yep. Bye then."

As he was putting his phone away a message beeped in:
How did it go with your wife? Susan.

Harry called straight back as he limped down towards the Europa Hotel. Susan's mobile rang five or six times before she took the call.

"I can't talk, Harry, I've got clients waiting."

"OK, meet me and I'll tell you about it."

"I don't kno—"

"*If that's a good idea*? Well, it probably isn't, is it? But what the hell? What time are you finishing today?"

"About six."

"Right, I'll see you in the bar at the QFT at half six. I'll buy you a coffee."

"The Queens Film Theatre?"

"Yeah. Know it?"

"Of course, but why there?"

"Why not? Will I see you there?"

"Maybe."

"Maybe's no good. Yes or no?"

"One coffee, then. A quick coffee. Just to discuss how—"

"Yes, yes. I kno—"

He heard a knock on her door as she rang off.

Harry wandered on past the train station, heading into the city centre to withdraw cash from the nearest ATM before making for the Europa to get a cab.

Four or five hours to kill and a car to buy.

13

12.30pm. Thursday, 27 November 2008.

Clive Heywood was cleaning his clubs in the kitchen at 112 Knockbreda Close. He had just returned home from the golf course in triumph, pumped up with pride – a competition winner at last – and a tad light-headed. The combination of victory, fresh air and a couple of pints of Guinness had had their effect.

But then Clive's mood changed. Standing at the sink, wiping down the heads of his irons with a J-cloth, he suddenly became overwhelmed with a sense of anticlimax. A sensitive man, it dawned on him that there was more to life than golf and, more relevant, that there should be much more to *his* life than golf.

It had taken weeks of practise on the driving range and no end of golf lessons to play himself into contention and win his first competition at the club, but in the aftermath Clive now knew that it hadn't been worth the effort and that he had dedicated too much of his early retirement to chipping away at his golf handicap. (It was now down to a respectable 14 from a very average 22.)

The sense of achievement, and he had achieved little else of late, was marred by the realisation that he had become addicted to an activity which, whilst being sociable and fairly active, was never going to win him a Booker, Turner, Pulitzer or Nobel Prize. It was a selfish obsession, unrewarding and almost pornographic in its intensity.

Today's win in the Taylor Cup was scant reward for a man who'd had such high hopes when embarking on a career in education. He was conscious that he should be doing more to find gainful employment rather than gorging on a diet of golf and TV game shows.

Maybe it had never been his destiny to win a Booker, Turner, Pulitzer or Nobel Prize, but he'd given up trying.

That he was now preoccupied with buffing his golf clubs just underlined his lack of drive and the extent of his obsession, but the world of work had given Clive Heywood a bloody nose and he was reluctant to go back for more punishment.

On reflection, he considered teaching a brutal profession; felt betrayed by the establishment; was bewildered by an *Alice Through The Looking Glass* society in which those who work the hardest are often the least well-rewarded whilst those who seek to extract the maximum profit are often rewarded disproportionately to the value of their product or service. It was enough to drive a traditional conservative like Clive Heywood to consider embracing socialism. And he did.

Clive cursed when he remembered the banter in the staff room when he announced that he'd signed up for early retirement.

"Good on you, Clive!"

"What are you going to do, Clive?"

"I'm going to give the private sector a bash. I'm going to work in the real world. A bureaucracy-free working environment with appropriate remuneration. Can you imagine?"

Many of the older teachers had expressed the same or similar aspirations when their opportunity came to jump ship.

Clive had likened the working culture in education to life in communist East Berlin: suffocating and restrictive, and thought early retirement a chance to flee over the wall to a brave new world of free enterprise.

However, having made his escape, Clive found he was drained of energy; burned out – too exhausted to plan the immediate future and explore the myriad options available to him. It became easier to defer the tough decisions and then, lacking enthusiasm, too easy to put his feet up for a while. And then for a while longer, and then for a while longer after that.

And then, within only six months, the lethargy had crept over Clive Heywood with the vigour of a vine: entangling his limbs, ensnarling his thought processes and pinning him down. The idea of becoming a businessman or entrepreneur was withering fast and becoming a vague and distant dream. Once there had been excitement and expectation for the new direction, now there was fear and inertia. Much easier to concentrate on honing his pitching and putting and refining his golf swing.

Then there was Susan.

Clive Heywood treasured his wife and appreciated his good fortune in having her as his partner. It was becoming obvious, though, that he needed to get his act together to regain her respect.

Clive had seemed an impressive character when Susan had met him. Tall, dark and handsome, and successful at work, he exuded charisma, energy and power. Eyes would turn when he entered a room. Qualities that had drawn a young and naive Susan Thompson to the older man. And although he wasn't old – he was in his forties then – he had maturity and confidence. A raconteur, he was fun and funny, interesting and experienced. She was mesmerised.

Susan was a chameleon. She was quick to learn from her husband, admired his ambition, observed his social skills and mimicked them. She grew more assertive. He was her role model and she recreated herself in his mould, but with one or two modifications of her own. And with his blessing she completed her higher education, gained qualifications and trained. Pregnancy and childbirth were put on hold as her career blossomed.

Then the blossoming brought guilt. For whilst *her* career was developing, she became aware that Clive was growing disenchanted with his. At first there was just the occasional whinge, but as the years passed this grew into a constant moaning.

First came the frustration with the ever-increasing paperwork, then the demoralising transfer of power from the teacher to the pupil as all means of control were removed: no more cuffs round the ears, no more bollockings. Without the ability to impose discipline on his pupils, Clive felt emasculated. Where there had once been scope for discretion, now there were regimens and lines that could not be crossed. Every aspect of his work was subject to clearly defined rules and regulation. The system eliminated common sense, employed little imagination and encouraged none. How could he fire up his classes with passion and zeal if he felt none himself?

Susan watched and supported, but he was changing, suffering. It pained her to see it, but there was little she could do in a practical sense. Clive grew more cynical, more introvert, less upright, more hunched, less confident, greyer.

Meanwhile, Susan's career progressed well. She had found a job she liked and excelled at. She was good with people, and counselling, though modestly paid, was a job she was well suited to and well qualified for. And whilst she loved her husband, noted the change in him with a growing disquiet. She had become the confident one, was a positive thinker, an achiever imbued with power and magnetism. The shift was unsettling for them both.

Susan offered Clive moral support, but he soon came to rely on her for reassurance and constantly sought approval.

So when the question of his early retirement arose, she immediately spotted the possibility of a renaissance for him. It excited her to think that her handsome, talented husband might flourish and find a second wind once he had left the unrewarding world of education for the vibrant world of commerce. She therefore urged him to share her vision, sold him the idea. She didn't have to force or coerce, just sell the vision. And it was an attractive future that she portrayed. He would be freer, more relaxed, more confident and at last his talents would be appreciated and well rewarded. Their joint earnings would open doors; create broader horizons for them as a couple.

When the option of early retirement became available to him, therefore, her enthusiasm became the tipping point and Clive seized the opportunity.

For a while early retirement brought a refreshing change. The honeymoon period brought optimism. For the first two or three months away from the school Clive seemed calmer and happier, his confidence restored. Susan was pleased with the transformation and looked at her husband with renewed affection. Eventually, for he was in no rush, Clive applied for a couple of jobs. A marketing post with a leading packaging company and then an executive role with a headhunting agency. He was granted interviews, but wasn't appointed.

And as the first cracks in his new-found confidence appeared, he decided to take his time before choosing the next step. In the meantime he developed his hobby, golf, in an attempt to prove that he still possessed youth and ability through sporting prowess.

Deep in thought at the kitchen sink, Clive failed to notice his clubs overbalance and then slide along the edge of the drainer. He jumped when the bag fell onto the tiled floor with a loud clang. He grasped the golf bag and reset it, leaning the clubs against the cabinet at a more upright angle before turning back to busy himself with rinsing out the sink. But the bag toppled over again, this time clattering onto the floor and creating an even louder din.

Clive seized the golf bag in both hands, opened the back door and hurled it down the lawn in frustration; clubs, balls and tees splaying across the grass in all directions like jackstraws.

"*Fuck this for a game of soldiers!*" Clive yelled as he slammed the door, his eyes staring maniacally.

14

1.30pm. Thursday, 27 November 2008.

"It's past Templepatrick and on towards the lough. We can work it out as we go."

Harry's instructions to the cab driver were reliant on blind faith rather than science as they drove off in search of the Volvo he'd sourced in *Auto Trader*. They were twenty minutes out of Belfast, without satnav and heading towards the International Airport.

The vendor had given Harry directions from the roundabout at Templepatrick. The address turned out to be a farm somewhere in the hills overlooking Lough Neagh. Harry had to strain to decipher the man's broad accent over the phone.

After a protracted search they approached what both driver and passenger agreed was probably the right property. The farm, a damp fifty-acre smallholding, stretched away from the B road across the bogland above and was veined with drystone walls patched up here and there with chicken wire, blocks and wooden pallets. The surrounding fields were peppered with pond-sized puddles. Below the road the farmland stretched down to the shore and was dotted with sycamores.

As they turned to drive up the lane to the farmhouse, they passed a large rusty horsebox parked in an adjacent field. It bore the message: *Jesus loves you!* hand-painted on its side in worn three-foot characters. The cab driver raised an eyebrow. Harry took a snap with his iPhone. Nothing was said.

The potholes pockmarking the lane were brimming with mud; the yard at the front of the house was a quagmire. Once the taxi had pulled up and Harry had prised himself out and paid up, the driver offered to wait on in case Harry didn't like the car and needed a lift back. At this point he thought he probably would. Harry tiptoed his way through the mire; trying to follow the shallowest path and stepping with care to avoid losing a shoe in the muck.

The farmhouse was two-storey and looked like it had been built in the twenties or thirties. It was grey and pebble-dashed, with a couple of extensions added over the years. It needed repainting. There was a boarded-up window on the first floor that Harry imagined had been a temporary fix turned permanent fixture. A wooden porch with glass-panelled sides enclosed the front entrance, the glass patterned with sixties-style swirls and circles in blues and yellows. Harry rang the doorbell then picked at the paintwork whilst waiting.

There were few signs of life. No lights and no noise except for the mooing of a bedraggled herd in the field beside.

Harry glanced back towards the lough stretching away towards the Sperrin Mountains in the distance. It looked like an ocean from his perspective in the hills; the view diminishing in the hazy light.

Before long a middle-aged man came scuttling up behind him, shuffling round the corner of the house wearing what looked like a granny-knitted beanie and an exhausted scowl. A shrug of steam wafted about his shoulders. He was unshaven and seemed unconscious of the sausage-meat skin and sprouts of white hair protruding through the mesh of his string vest. Pyjama bottoms lurked below baggy jeans, visible where they were stuffed into mud-splattered wellies. A Jack Russell on a choke chain followed at his side, which, as soon as she spotted Harry, pulled hard and barked.

"Don't mind the dog, son," the man said with a smile that boasted few teeth. "Doesn't like men, so she doesn't. *Goo ... er!*" he roared at the dog, prodding her into a shed with his boot.

No wonder, Harry thought.

"Car's over here," the man said, turning away from Harry and leading him towards the largest of the corrugated outbuildings. The air was heavy with the stink of cattle. He scraped back the barn door to reveal the car standing on a concrete floor and surrounded by bales of straw.

The condition of the car took Harry by surprise. A 1980's Volvo 200 Series Estate in metallic silver complete with sunroof and tow bar. Clean and tidy.

"Taxed and MOT'd?" Harry asked, a little elated.

"Yep, as advertised. And for just under a year."

"How much do you want for her?"

"What it says in the ad. Eight fifty. I've had a lot of interest today, so I have."

"Mmm, I'm sure. Would you take eight hundred?"

"No. I've been offered the full price."

"But I've got the cash here and now."

"Mmm ... She's worth more, you know. Much more."

"Still, my offer's eight hundred in cash."

"Would you split the difference, son?"

"Eight twenty-five?"

"OK, eight twenty-five."

"Eight twenty-five it is, then." Harry said with a grin and extending a hand.

"Done. But aren't you going to look under the bonnet? You can take her for a test drive too if you like."

"As long as she starts up, is taxed and MOT'd and you've got the logbook, I'm sure she'll be fine."

The man gave Harry's hand a firm shake, then passed him a red plastic folder.

"All the paperwork's in there. Full service history, receipts. Everything," he said, looking disapproving of Harry's impetuosity.

Harry flicked through the logbook, checked the MOT certificate and then handed over the money. The man made a meticulous count then pocketed the cash before passing Harry the keys. He seemed reluctant to let go of them, as though he were parting with a family heirloom.

"Are you sure you'll be able to drive her?" The man asked bluntly, before nodding at Harry's legs.

"If she's an automatic, there won't be a problem."

Harry offered what he hoped was a confident smile, opened the door and levered himself into the driver's seat then adjusted the mirrors. It was the look of the car that had won him over. It was in tidy order and, for a second-hand vehicle, didn't smell too bad either. And she fired up first time.

The Volvo was almost identical to his last. Same colour, same engine specification and a similar age. Big and reliable. It also had a radio cassette player that was a bit of a giveaway when it came to estimating the car's vintage. Harry grinned with satisfaction. The man in the string vest stepped back to one side of the barn door, his arms wrapped tightly around his chest whilst he shivered from the cold, the skin on his forearms and shoulders turning lobster pink, his smile gone.

Harry didn't delay. Shifted the car into drive and then pressed down on the accelerator to move her off. The first few yards were jerky and he could see panic on the old man's face when he glanced in the driver's mirror. But Harry didn't stop, just tooted the horn – a limp squeak – waved and then continued to rock and bump down the pitted lane as puddle water splashed dirt over the Volvo's gleaming panels. The taxicab followed in his wake.

Once out on the open road, Harry turned north and headed for the M2. There was about a quarter of a tank of fuel and time to fly up to Portstewart to drop in on his dad before his rendezvous with Susan Heywood at the QFT.

Freedom! Harry thumped the steering wheel in triumph, shook his head and roared in jubilation. The feeling reminded him of the exhilaration he felt on the journey back from Belfast the day he passed his driving test.

When Harry popped home to Holywood he just had long enough to change out of his mud-stained jeans and clean his shoes before heading off to the QFT. He also seized the chance to put his old mobile on charge and check through the *messages sent* folder. The first of the old messages was blunt and to the point:

Martha - See you in Nick's at 9. HSX

Bingo! He had a name: Martha. But still no recollection.

He read the rest of the texts in sequence, jotting them down on a pad as he went and noting the times and dates, then spliced together her messages to *him* and his replies to *her* to complete the picture.

He read through them carefully in chronological order.

I think about you all the time, Harry, and it scares me.

But he still couldn't imagine a connection between the Martha of the text messages and the amber-haired girl in Belfast.

It was dark by the time he left home for the city.

15

6.35pm. Thursday, 27 November 2008.

Harry String had a soft spot for the Queen's Film Theatre. The QFT was the only cinema he'd found in Belfast that regularly screened foreign language movies and old classics. That he could rarely, if ever, persuade anyone to accompany him was a source of frustration. Why he had chosen it as a rendezvous now he wasn't sure, except that he felt at ease there and presumed it would create a positive impression.

When Susan Heywood bustled into the foyer she seemed as flustered as she had been the previous day in Black's: out of breath and nervous. She was carrying another armful of folders and files. Harry String was sitting at the back of the bar and cafe area and gestured for her to join him.

"Hi! Mr String, I can't stay long. Shall we—"

"Can I get you a beer?"

"Oh. That's tempting bu—"

"Right."

Harry stood up and made a beeline for the bar before she could say no. He imagined Susan Heywood was probably too uptight to drink anything stronger than water in normal circumstances, still water at that. When he returned with the necessary they retired to a leather couch by the entrance to screen one. He passed her one of the bottles. She took it and tutted, but didn't refuse and fired him a smile in thanks.

"So?" Susan asked, emboldened by a gulp of lager.

"So?"

"You know ... How did it go?"

"What?"

"With your ex."

"Oh, crap, to be honest. Terrible. If you'd been there, you'd have thought she hated me. I guess it's revenge of a kind. She knows I like to be liked and can't bear to be unpopular, and she knows I don't like confrontation."

"Mmm, I'm sorry. But then, I guess, I'm not surprised."

"Well, it was your idea that I go and talk to her."

"Yes, I know. But it was never going to be easy. And you had to talk. I thought that at least it might bring you some closure. Anyway, her behaviour is nothing out of the ordinary. I see that reaction all the time," Susan said, arching a brow and offering him a businesslike expression.

"I don't know. I guess I'm just too much of an optimist. I kind of thought there was a chance things might have gone better. Much, much better. You know, a slim one, but a chance. You have to remember that my poor brain still thinks we're married. And I never give up anything without a fight."

"Well, I suppose you've proved that by being here. I mean above ground, up and walking."

Harry shrugged.

"So, you don't think there's even the smallest chance she might come round?"

"No. Sadly not."

"Is there anything I can do? Do you think she'd come along with you for counselling? Maybe if you both came—"

"No. It's over. Definitely over. And you know as well as I do that my expectations have been unrealistic. It seems that it was over months ago and I'm just going to have to accept that. There wasn't a lot of feeling there when I saw her, to be honest. No spark. She was cold. She could barely look at me. She's moved on."

"Oh."

"No, I can see that it's a pointless pursuit. Sad, but true. I guess I must have been a real shit. Not that I recall any of the details. All the same, I was kind of hoping there might still have been a flicker of something, you know. That given a little oxygen the fire could be rekindled, but, really, it looks like the flame has definitely gone out, I'm afraid. *And* she laughed at me. Like I was a joke. Like me suggesting we give it another go was total lunacy."

"Unfortunate."

"It was quite disorientating. I feel like I've arrived here from another planet or have been cryogenically frozen for two years or something. And I suppose in a way I have. I feel a bit of an idiot right now, as a matter of fact. And on top of that there's the guilt and the shame of the family breaking up."

"How did it go with your kids?"

"Really well. Great fun, actually. Nice to have them to myself for a while."

"Good."

"But I feel bad, though. I mean, if the break up was my fault, well—"

"You shouldn't be so hard on yourself. And you shouldn't be so ready to take *all* the blame. It can't all be down to you, Harry."

"How do you know?"

"Because this is what I do. Look, it's rarely one person's fault."

"Whatever. Anyway, that's another door closed, I'm afraid. I have to face facts. Live in the present."

"Well, it's good that you see it that way. There you are ... closure!"

Harry drained what was left of his beer in one long swig then thumped the bottle onto the table.

"Actually, Susan, I've just discovered that there was somebody else."

"What do you mean?"

"Apparently, after the separation and/or during the divorce, I don't know which, I met somebody else."

"Oh. Another woman?"

"Yes."

"As in a girlfriend?"

"Apparently so. I was amazed."

"And do you have feelings for her?"

"None. How could I? I don't know anything about her."

"Nothing?"

"No, nothing."

"*Nothing at all?*"

"Absolutely nothing."

"Must come as a bit of a surprise then, huh?"

"Yeah. Total. I've no idea who she is and have no recollection of her."

"So?"

"So spooky, no?"

"For you, I guess."

"And I find that I'm kind of curious now."

"Are you going to contact her, then?" Susan asked, frowning.

"I'm reluctant."

"Why?"

"I'd kind of like to know what happened first. How it ended. I don't know what I said or did, but I must have done something to upset her or she'd still be around now, I guess. I'm worried in case I did something awful, and, if that's the case, I'd like to know in advance. She probably won't want to talk to me anyway."

"You don't seem to have much luck with the opposite sex, do you, Harry?"

"No comment."

"Did any of your friends meet her? Can't they fill you in?"

"Well, I've only got a small circle of friends. Good friends, that is. And none of the people I've seen since the accident, and that's only one or two, have mentioned anything at all. Except Keira, of course. I don't think anyone could have met her. I must have kept her to myself. I imagine I would either have been too worried about what my kids would think or that my friends might scare her off. I don't know."

"Why would your friends scare her off?"

"The age thing. There was quite an age gap, it seems."

"How old was ... I mean, *is* she?"

"I don't know. Twenty-something. You know, mid to late twenties. Here, see for yourself. What do you think?"

Harry produced the battered snapshot.

"Twenty-eight, twenty-nine. I'd say about four or five years younger than me. Where did you get this?"

"Found it in my old wallet this morning."

"She's got a chipped tooth," Susan observed.

"Maybe in that photo but not now."

"Oh, and how do you know that?"

"I bumped into her yesterday in Belfast."

"*What?* I'm getting confused. How did you know it was her? Did she talk to you? Was she glad to see you?"

"It wasn't like that. She just came up to me in the street and started having a go. I didn't know who she was or anything. She wasn't at all friendly. Actually, she was very *un*friendly. Practically accused me of stalking her."

"Were you?"

"No. No way! How could I? I didn't know she existed till she approached me. She was like a total stranger."

"Oh. Weird, huh?"

"Totally. I know it sounds odd, but it was only when I thought about it afterwards that I kind of recognised her from a dream I'd had the other night. And then when I found this photo earlier today it was easy enough to put two and two together."

"OK."

"But her reaction in the street is why I'm worried about what I may or may not have said or done, or whatever. I mean, she was shouting at me for God's sake."

Harry got up to go to the loo and left the photo lying on the couch.

Susan Heywood studied the two faces. She smiled at the photograph's naive charm, the innocent enthusiasm of a courting couple.

When Harry returned, he was carrying two more bottles of Heineken.

"Er, who are they for?"

"Us."

"Jesus, Harry. I can't. This is supposed to be a quick cup of coffee not a piss up."

She straightened her back and sat upright as if to regain authority. Ignoring her protestations, Harry planted one of the beers down on the glass table top in front of her. She looked stern, but was surprised that she no longer found his assertiveness as offensive as she had previously. Anyway, it had been a long day and the alcohol was taking effect, and she was starting to enjoy being somewhere else other than at home or the office.

"So, what's your advice?" Harry asked, picking up the photo and slipping it back into his wallet.

"I have none. There is none. I don't know what advice I am qualified to give you, Harry. We've already established that you're divorced *and* now you're telling me that you've been in another relationship since the marriage ended. I'm a marriage guidance counsellor not a miracle worker."

"Oh, OK—"

"And now you're single again, anyway. A bachelor. You confirmed that for yourself when you saw Keira. You've no strings attached. What more can I say? As I've already told you, your biggest problems are clearly physical and relate to your accident. You need to stop living in the past. You seem a little out of sync with the rest of us on that score. My advice is simple: *enjoy being single.* Yeah. Enjoy being single. That should do it. There are huge advantages to the single life, you know. For a start, you don't have any responsibilities and you don't have to answer to anyone. There's no one to disappoint or hurt and *you're* not going to get hurt either. Perfect. Enjoy it. Enjoy being single for a while."

"Is that how you see relationships? Like they're emotional minefields?"

"Maybe."

"Brutal!"

"That's marriage guidance for you."

"And is that how you'd describe your relationship with your hus—"

"Hey! Leave my personal life out of this. My personal life is totally off limits, Harry."

"Oh, I see. We're not allowed to talk about you, is that it?"

"Yes."

"So who do *you* talk to?"

"I don't need to."

"Are you sure?"

"Look. We're here to discuss your problems, not mine."

"So you do have some?"

"I'm not saying that. I didn't say—"

"I thought you just did."

"Look, Harry—"

"Yes. I hear you. *I should enjoy being single.* And you're right. I should. The problem is, I'm lonely."

"That's natural. How long had you and Keira been living together?"

"About ten years or so, I guess."

"Well, it's bound to feel a bit odd being on your own, then. But you'll get used to it."

"That's easy to say."

"It's common."

"Great."

The conversation stalled as they both took a sip of their fresh drinks.

"Well, I guess my work is about finished with you, Harry. There doesn't seem much for me to do. As I said before, what help can I give you as a marriage guidance counsellor now you're divorced?"

"Very little. Maybe none. In fact, *none*. But we could become friends."

"Is that really a good idea?"

"Maybe. Why not?"

"What if I don't want to be your friend? Maybe I don't need *you* as a friend, Harry," she grinned.

Harry shrugged and smiled back.

Susan Heywood took another, longer sip of lager. Her initial discomfort at being in the bar was waning fast. She now sensed a growing reluctance to leave and go home. An unwillingness that was growing stronger as her resistance to drinking beer withered.

Sober, she might have asked herself what the hell she was doing in the company of the puzzling, blue-eyed man with mangled legs, concluded her business and left, recognising that there was no professional context that gave good reason for her to be in his company. But the more she drank the less she cared, and the less she cared the more she relished the hedonism of being in a different environment with a different person; someone intent on giving her his full attention.

"Do you drink a lot of beer?" he enquired, leaning back against the wall.

"Rarely."

"What do you normally drink?"

"An occasional glass of wine, I suppose."

"Red or white?"

"Usually white. Why?"

Harry got to his feet without answering, picked up her files and put his unfinished Heineken down on the table opposite.

"Maybe we should find you one," he said with a confidant smile and offering her his arm for support.

"What?"

"I think we should find you a nice bottle of white."

"Where?"

"Don't worry. Just a bit up the road. You're quite safe."

She froze for a moment. Then surprised herself by standing up too and allowing herself to be coerced into whatever was to come.

"Er, can I ask you something? It's a little bit personal," she said, straightening her jacket.

"Shoot."

"Where do you get your money from, Harry?"

"What?"

"Well, you're obviously not broke and you haven't been at work for God knows how long."

"You're right. But that's a *very* personal matter." Harry paused, then smiled. "However, if you must know, I'm a photographer. I'm good at my job. Sometimes it's quite lucrative. Not always, but sometimes. Especially if I get a book to photograph and if the book does well, you know, becomes a bestseller here there and everywhere. Also, I'm not a total idiot with money."

"Ah."

"Now, does that answer your question?" he asked, turning to leave.

She hesitated again then shook her hair loose and set off behind him.

The heavens opened over the streets of the university quarter releasing rain in torrents. When Harry hailed a cab outside the QFT Susan Heywood ran ahead to get out of the downpour, splashing through the puddles in her heels and leaving Harry to limp behind as best he could. He'd leave his car. Pick it up in the morning. They squeezed into the back of the taxi.

"Coco, please. It's the restaurant at the top of Linenhall Street. Do you know it OK?"

"Yep." The driver nodded as he whisked them away.

Clive Heywood was standing in the kitchen washing lettuce.

Yes. Time to turn over a new leaf, he thought whilst rinsing a handful of cos under the cold tap.

He'd proposed so many new initiatives in recent months, faced so many mornings fuelled with optimism, but so far none of the fresh starts had got him very far or ever quite got underway.

Tonight, however, Clive was filled with a new determination. He was fed up with the boredom of his domestic prison and had decided that from now on he was going to be positive, energetic and, to this end, eat healthily, drink less and exercise more. He wanted to be fitter and leaner; all of which, he believed, would help his mental sharpness and stamina. He wanted an end to the lethargy, wanted to get busy.

And, he'd tell Susan when she got home. No grand speech, no great claims. He would simply inform her that he was going to get active and be proactive about finding a job. Might even try education again. But first he was going to feed her, and feed her well. She was due home by seven and he would surprise her with a meal fit for a queen. He'd also run her a bath, have her favourite jazz playing in the background and would dress smartly for dinner. He would surprise her with his culinary flair and spontaneity, and she was sure to love him for it and reward him with renewed passion.

Clive wasn't a great cook, but he would try his best. He'd cook a menu he was familiar with and sure he could master. The first course was to be a simple plate of Parma ham and melon with black pepper, to be followed by baked trout with almonds, new potatoes, asparagus tips and a little walnut salad. Then for dessert: roast peaches with honey and pine nuts and a dollop of vanilla ice cream – Häagen-Dazs, their favourite. He'd also buy a couple of good bottles of dry white. Two of the more expensive on offer in the local off-licence.

He was excited and pleased and knew his efforts would be appreciated. And even if Susan was merely showing her appreciation out of politeness, he knew that it would be a positive start to the new regime and she would take note.

Giving the lettuce a vigorous shake, he wondered if they had any scented candles.

Susan was eating her main course at the restaurant and had stopped wondering what the hell she was doing in the company of the blue-eyed man. Sensible thinking had been put on hold. The wine helped. She was tired of thinking and done with worry. This was novel and she had been bored by the mundane for such a long time.

She was staring at Harry String's features and analysing his lines and wrinkles. He was talking animatedly and laughing. And though she found him amusing, she wasn't listening much now, just looking. And when he stopped to laugh at his own witticisms, she stretched her smile a little in acknowledgement and to encourage him to continue his monologue so she could continue to study his face.

His eyes were beautiful. They were such a deep, iridescent blue that she wondered if he was wearing tinted lenses. They were quite mesmerising, and she felt that she could stare into them all day. His head was close-shaven. He was lucky that his skull had a good shape. More disturbing was the lattice of scars that ran across the back of his scalp. A shaved head suited him, though, and looked more like a fashion statement than the hallmark of surgery. His skin was quite swarthy, which was surprising considering his recent incarceration.

Despite the wear and tear, his face was youthful for a forty-four-year-old. The lines, she imagined, had been etched by continuous mirth; a good sign that gave him a kind, reassuring appearance and made him look younger than his years.

"But then, you never know, do you?" Harry babbled on.

Silence.

"Do you?" he urged.

"I'm sorry?"

"You never know what you should say to people begging on the street. It's a dilemma. Actually, have you been listening to a word I've been saying?" he asked, smiling.

"Oh, yes. Yes. And no. No, you're right though. I grin and try to look friendly and hope they think I'm a nice person."

"I'd arranged to meet up with a friend in Belfast once. I was leaning against a wall on a street corner waiting for whoever it was to arrive, trying to keep out of the flow of pedestrians. I was a bit knackered, a bit hung-over, a bit stubbly. I'd just finished a takeaway double espresso and was still holding the foam cup when suddenly an old lady came by and, out of the blue, dropped a pound coin into it and said: 'Buy yourself a cup of tea, love. And don't you be spending that on drink.' I was gobsmacked!"

Harry was laughing again. She smiled too.

He loved her smile. Loved her teeth. They were perfect, shiny and white, but not too white. Not like an A-list celebrity's teeth you could see by in the dark.

And he loved her great mass of hair. It gave her a wild and untamed appearance. Latin. Was taken with her generous, thick lips. It was easy to imagine kissing them. He imagined they would taste sweet.

"Do you get to travel much with your work, Harry?"

"Er, I have done, yes. But not lately, for obvious reasons. It's something I'm looking forward to doing more of later."

"Later?"

"Yes. You know, when I'm fully recovered. Actually, it's always been an ambition to buy something in France—"

"Really?"

"Yeah, a fermette or something. You know, a little bolt-hole. But I guess that's a way off yet."

My God, he said fermette. What the hell's a fermette?

Susan's mobile beeped.

"Sorry, Harry, it's a text. Hang on."

It was Clive: *Where are you? CX.*

Home soon. Problem at work. X, she replied, then switched her phone to silent.

"Harry?"

"Mmm."

"You're not eating."

"I'm not that hungry."

"Oh?"

"I think it's the adrenaline. I haven't been on a dinner date for quite a while," he said grinning.

"I really, really hope that's not what you think this is."

"What?"

"A date."

Harry raised his eyebrows.

"It's not, Harry. I think we're just friends. Don't you?"

Harry shrugged.

"God! You're such a fucking predator."

"Just a man."

"Well, try pretending that you're not one when you're with me, please."

He smiled to reassure her.

She smiled back.

"OK. Tell you what, though. I've really got to go. *Really got to go.* Let's pay up and get out of here. I'll order a cab and drop you off on the way home," Susan added.

"No problem," Harry replied, wanting to appear cheerful even though the thought of going back to an empty house felt as uplifting as a kick in the bollocks.

Harry insisted on paying the bill and they were away within minutes.

Outside it was still dark and showery. The taxi she'd ordered was waiting. They dashed across the pavement to avoid the drizzle and shuffled into the back. The cab drove off into the rain, which in the gloom, and punctuated by the Christmas tree lights outside the city hall, seemed to suit the time of year.

Neither of them spoke in the car. Holywood was a quick ten-minute journey at night in light traffic; a mile a minute along the dual carriageway.

"Just up to the junction on the ... er ... Here will do. Thank you!" Harry instructed the cab driver.

He leaned back and turned towards Susan.

"Thanks for a great evening, Mrs Heywood."

"No, thank you. But—"

"But, look. You don't have to say anything. I'll text you."

Harry bent forward and offered her his cheek. She leaned in as if to kiss it, but, at the last minute, he turned his face towards hers to ensure that their lips met instead.

He smiled. Was right about her lips. Held the contact for as long as he could.

She slapped his face.

"Bastard!" she hissed.

He knew he'd overstepped the mark, so was sure that he was out of the car, had shut the door and was out of earshot before she could react further. The cab driver rolled his eyes as Harry slipped him a twenty.

Clive Heywood's special meal had been ready since six thirty as he'd expected Susan home around seven o'clock. It was now almost eight thirty. The bath had gone cold, the tea lights had burned out and Clive had dispensed with his tie.

Clive was sitting with his Parma-ham starter and wondering if his efforts had been premature; that maybe it had been a mistake to try and surprise his wife, especially if she wasn't going to turn up. But then, she was normally more predictable. He could usually guarantee she would be home by seven on a weekday. It was so unlike her to be any later. However, he wouldn't make a fuss, wouldn't make her feel self-conscious. He was keen to deliver his surprise, but then, like the ham on the plate before him, his confidence was starting to wilt.

Then he began to worry about her well-being.

Clive pitched his fork into a slice of the meat and was on the verge of lifting it to his lips when he heard the clunk of a car door outside and then the fidgeting of a key in the front door.

"Hi-yer!"

Susan.

The door slammed.

Clive's heart sank a little lower when he heard her clomping up the stairs.

"You not going to say hello?" he shouted, frustrated that she wasn't coming straight in to see him, whilst trying not to sound overanxious.

"Down in a sec!" came a muffled cry.

But, goddamn! She was supposed to stroll into the lounge, see the table laid out, then run over and kiss him, delighted by his surprise. There was a time, he thought, when she couldn't wait to see him, would rush into the house and jump into his arms. Clive stuffed the forkful of ham into his mouth. It was good, but too much pepper.

Then he heard footsteps coming down the stairs.

"Clive!" she gasped, catching sight of her husband's handiwork: the napkins, the wine glasses, the subdued lighting and the cutlery, polished and laid out with precision. Her heart melted. His face was wracked with the disappointment that a feeble smile couldn't disguise.

"I hope you're hungry," Clive said calmly.

"Starving!" she lied, fluffing her hair up with trembling fingers, struggling not to cry and immediately downing a glass of wine to mask the scent of the previous three.

16

11.45pm. Thursday, 27 November 2008.

I'm in bed thinking of you. I wish you were here too. I could hug you, kiss you. We could have sex.

Harry String was lying in bed scrolling through MB's messages. A diary of a romance acted out in texts; one in which he had performed a leading role. How strange, he thought, that he now felt like a peeping Tom.

The climate of the relationship was easy to chart: from the one-text-a-day drip through the first week, to the flood of texts a month later. However, the flow of messages suggested that the relationship had only lasted about six months including the breaks when one or the other were on holiday. There was talk of a holiday together in Tuscany.

Five months on and the texts dried to a trickle. No more flirtatious banter. Something was wrong. Whilst his texts grew wordier, hers grew more abrupt. Then they stopped altogether. There were no clues as to why.

Harry felt detached from the couple in the texts. The old messages depicted another Harry, not him. Those that he'd sent seemed too earnest. Also, it was hard to connect the witty text messages sent by MB with the angry woman he'd met in Belfast. And odd, he thought, that she hadn't been in touch later on to enquire about his health. Surely she must have heard about his accident and cared enough to have made a polite enquiry at the very least.

Harry turned off his old Nokia and put it aside; tried to sleep, but was kept awake by a sharp pain behind his right temple and a TV blaring from a bedroom in the house next door. He buried his head under a pillow but couldn't cut out the din. When he listened more carefully, he thought he recognised the voices. There were two. Definitely two. A man and a woman. A film or a play. The woman's sounded reminiscent of Keira's and he thought the male voice sounded a bit like his own. They were arguing.

The more he tried to shut out the din the louder it seemed to get. It was only when he put his fingers in his ears that Harry realised that the noise was in his head. He tried to make out words, then sentences, but the row had descended into a slanging match. The mood seemed familiar.

Harry sat up, then got up, shaking his head and then slapping his forehead. And as the din subsided, he decided to flee downstairs to the kitchen for a cup of tea and a handful of strong tablets.

Waiting for the kettle to boil he thought about Susan Heywood. *Did he really want her as a friend?*

It was obvious to him now that that was what he'd wanted from when they'd first met. But he was also aware that he'd have to back off a bit and treat her with a lot more respect if that was ever going to happen.

The next morning Harry was up early to fetch his Volvo. He'd left it in a meter bay round by the QFT. A cab had been booked for six o'clock to avoid the rush hour traffic and a clamping. He was therefore back home and fixing himself breakfast by seven.

Harry's neurologist had cautioned him not to go back to work until the new year to avoid stress, but Harry was finding inactivity more stressful than work. Not that photography was that mentally or physically demanding anyway and, as Harry himself admitted, was a lot less stressful than coal mining, bricklaying or factory work. Anyhow, he was bored.

There were no therapy sessions at the hospital on Fridays, so having watched an hour of daytime television – which Harry found more brain numbing than his hangover – he wandered across Holywood to his studio in search of greater stimulation.

Within half an hour of checking his emails and sending some replies he'd drummed up a little work. A local lifestyle magazine wanted some profile shots taken of an *Ulster Television* newsreader at their home overlooking the sea. The editor wanted to feature it in the magazine's interiors section.

A job!

The house was near Strangford, about a forty-five minute drive from Holywood. Harry called the newsreader and arranged to go over the following day, Saturday morning.

Harry checked the satellite forecast: the weather was set to be dry and sunny, and then looked around the studio for suitable lighting equipment. As usual it was a challenge to find what he wanted amongst the piles of junk.

The office accommodation was comfortable enough, and there was plenty of space for one, in fact, there was plenty of space for two or three, but he hated the clutter. He hated that his computer systems were so archaic. Very low tech. Old tech: huge, slow and heavy. He hated the shelving, the carpet tiles, the desk, the blinds, the lighting, the dirt. His was an industry that thrived on artifice, on youthfulness and state-of-the-art newness, and yet his working environment smacked of dusty, dyed-in-the-wool, second-hand shop grottiness. He berated himself for allowing the dirt, fluff and cobwebs to take over; hated that he hoarded books and magazines; hated that he didn't have the courage to throw anything away. Ever.

If the viability of his photography business was to be judged by his working environment, then most would say it was pretty down-at-heel. His was the kind of office that a moth-eaten private eye might inhabit, not the studio of a cutting-edge photographer.

Cutting-edge photographer? Who was he trying to kid anyway? He had been a successful photographer when he was based in London, but since he'd returned to Northern Ireland?

He had bags of talent, was damn professional, and everybody knew it, but it takes more than talent to build a profitable business in a provincial city. Youthfulness would have helped, business acumen, too. And some enthusiasm. Plus a materialistic streak that would have given him a taste for the latest technology and the inclination to inhabit a modern photographic studio closer to the city centre. But he wasn't materialistic.

Harry saved his passion for the field. On location, camera in hand, the adrenaline flowed and he moved with confidence. He had a gift for capturing the essence of a subject, bringing life to the mundane.

Since Harry's specialism was originally photojournalism, the move back to Belfast in the nineties had made sense. But following the ceasefires and the transition towards peace, there were fewer bombs, fewer bullets and fewer human interest stories to cover. The responsibilities that come with having a young family then deterred him from seeking out fresh trouble spots elsewhere. So food became his subject, and the steady diet of food photography proved a good compromise that suited both his lifestyle and his bank balance.

Harry was contemplating doing a little tidying, if not some filing, when his mobile heralded a text message.

It was from Susan.

Thnx for the meal. Probably shouldn't do that again. SH.

Harry chuckled to himself. Curious, he thought, that a trained counsellor could be so transparent.

In Strangford tomorrow. Why not come too! Be round at mine by 10. No 26 Vic Rd.

Harry reread the message to make sure it made sense, pressed the send key, leaned back and smiled.

He didn't expect a reply and didn't get one.

Day two of the regime and Clive Heywood's appetite for the task ahead was still healthy, despite the poor start. He was awake and up to make his wife's breakfast at seven-thirty and had already jogged round to the newsagents to get a copy of *The Guardian* to check the job ads. He didn't want to go back into teaching, but thought it worth taking a look at what was on offer. And, anyway, he wanted to be proactive and make continual progress to fend off any lethargic lapses or the lure of the golf course.

"Made you some coffee. Want a cup?" he called up to his wife.

There was an energy being exuded by her husband that Susan Heywood found disconcerting first thing in the morning; he was usually more subdued, but today he was bouncing around the kitchen like Tigger.

"Clive, what's got into you? You're driving me nuts," she yawned as she came down the stairs. "And why are you wearing a tracksuit?"

Clive Heywood wondered what it was about his wife that led her to respond so negatively to niceness. Why did she find his good deeds so offensive?

"I thought you might like it if I had your breakfast ready for you."

"Thank you," she said with caution while flicking through the previous day's post.

"No, it's just that I'm trying to make a bit more of an effort. Be more positive."

"Mmm. Good."

"I'm going to start looking for a job again. You know, give it my best shot."

"Good. Good. That's great, Clive."

Clive frowned. She didn't sound convinced, and he suspected that she wasn't listening.

"That's good, Clive. Well done."

And it irked him that she couldn't even be bothered to make eye contact. He sighed, remembering the time when she couldn't take her eyes off him and hung on to his every word.

"I'm thinking of taking up pole dancing, actually."
"Mmm. Good, Clive."
Is she asleep or just brain-dead? Clive wondered.
"No. I'm being serious ... That *is* good, Clive."
"What is?"
"The job thing."
"Oh. Right."
"I know you can do it. There's something out there for everybody, sweetheart."
"Don't you mean 'somebody'?"
"What?"
"There's somebody out there for everybody. That's the saying: there's somebody for everybody."
"You've lost me."
"Yeah, well, I certainly thought I had last night. I mean, it's not like you to get home so late."
"No. You're right," Susan replied dismissively, whilst reading through a credit-card statement.

He gulped before continuing in a jollier vein: "Would you like to go to Donegal for the weekend? The west coast? We could set off tonight. Pack a bag and I'll pick you up after work. We could go straight from there. Head up to Sheephaven Bay. Drop into the Harbour Bar."

"That's such a nice idea, Clive. But you know, I'm really knackered. Wouldn't you rather stay at home and cosy up? Play some golf? I've got to go to Bangor tomorrow, anyway."

"Oh," Clive grunted, his disappointment audible.
"Sorry, sweetheart."
"I thought it would be nice, that's all."
"We'll do it some other time, eh? In a week or two."

Some other time had become a phantom fifth season: coming soon, but never arriving. It had been mentioned much of late.

Clive Heywood felt deflated, but couldn't find the words and didn't have the heart to articulate his feelings. Going to Donegal, he had hoped, would show Susan he had listened.

Show that he had new energy and a willingness to be spontaneous, to get active and shed his couch potato skin. It was just so much easier to vegetate when they were at home and Clive had had enough of being a vegetable. But he would keep going with the new regime. Would be positive. Stay focused. Keep busy.

He walked round behind his wife and put his hands gently on her shoulders.

"Maybe we can stay home and ..." he whispered into her ear and paused.

"*Make babies*. Yeah, right. With me being the only one in work. How's that going to stack up, Clive?" Susan said in as sympathetic a manner as she could muster.

She's going to say, "Maybe next year" any moment now, Clive thought to himself. *Three ... two ... one ...*

"Maybe next year, Clive. Hey? Things will be different. You're bound to have found something profitable to do by then. And then maybe I could afford to take the time off."

She stroked her hand across his chin and smiled.

"Er-huh ..."

Clive slunk out of the room to go and get showered, repeating the mantra he had picked up from a daytime yoga show: "*Think positive. Stay positive. Be positive.*"

However, he felt less positive when coming out of the shower he heard the *pling!* of an incoming text on his wife's mobile and noticed that she blushed as she read it. When she looked up he gave her a curt smile and made a mental note to be alert.

Harry was walking as he was talking into his mobile on the high street in Holywood: "Ah, Mr Doherty. How are you?"

"Long time no hear, Harry. Where the fuck have you been, you plonker?"

"Didn't you hear?"

"Of course I heard. Didn't you get my flowers?"

"Oh yeah, right. And the grapes and the *Woman's Own*."

"Are you better, then?"
"Much."
"What can I do for you, H?"
"Fancy lunch?"
"No. But a quick coffee would be good. Got a lot on."
"You've always got a lot on, Robert."
"Yeah, nothing that shouldn't have been finished yesterday."
"Well, a quick coffee then, Robert?"
"Just a quick one."
"Where?"
"Holywood's OK."
"Good, I'm on my way down to the coffee bar near the post office right now. Can you make it in ten or fifteen?"
"Yep. See you there, Harry."

Coffee sounded good, and even though it was Harry's first day back at work and that he'd only been in for a couple of hours, he was already starting to feel a little jaded and work-shy. He needed little excuse to get out of the office.

With its creamy-domed top and sprinkling of cocoa powder, Harry's coffee looked like a cappuccino should but tasted like dishwater. He was sipping it anyway. The mental effort of calling the waitress over to complain when the service was so slow and surly in the first place was enough to deter any attempt to remedy the situation. That and his determination to stay calm at all times, though as always, the determination itself was causing him stress.

Harry was looking forward to catching up with Robert Doherty. They weren't bosom buddies, but might have been closer friends had it not been for Doherty's working hours. Doherty seemed to work twenty-four-hour days; not untypical in publishing, an occupation long on hours and short on remuneration. Theirs was a friendship forged through years of collaborating on photo shoots and maintaining a sense of humour when everyone else around them was losing theirs.

Doherty was a freelance graphic designer who supplied Harry with regular work photographing pack shots for a retailing magazine he laid out every month. Not Harry's favourite, but useful run-of-the-mill jobs that helped pay the mortgage. They'd met in the late nineties working on a food book at a time when celebrity cookbooks were rising in popularity.

Harry had winced his way through his first cappuccino by the time Doherty ambled in. Harry was leaning back against the side wall of the coffee bar, slouched on a banquette by the window. It was elevenish and the bar about a third full.

"Harry! Where have you been, you plonker? Here, have one of these," Robert Doherty said handing over a business card from the top of a thick pack.

"What's this?"

"My new card."

"How many brands have you designed for yourself by now?"

"Hey! I'm a graphic designer. It's what I do."

They clasped hands and hugged. Doherty hadn't changed. He was in his mid-thirties, a difficult age when some men go through something akin to a second pubescence. Nothing to do with balls dropping and voices breaking, just the awkward transition when many sense they are too old to wear lurid T-shirts and torn jeans and too young to wear a suit and tie. Robert camouflaged the onset of his middle age with a goatee and hair dye. He'd have had his tongue pierced and a Maori tattoo if he'd had the time.

"Do you remember when you last saw me, Robert?"

"Yeah, when I dropped by the hospital a few months back. You were still well out of it then."

"And before that?"

"No idea. Why?"

"Just wondering. Er, can't you think?"

"I'm not sure. Hang on ... Was it at Murph's last year? The barbecue in Belmont? Yeah, that's it ... Murph's barbecue."

"If you say so."

"Thinking about it, the very last time I saw you on your feet you were staggering out of Murph's barbecue with a girlfriend of mine. Well ... you know ... She's a friend."

"What? I was with a woman?"

"Yeah, and a good-looking one."

"Really?"

"Yes. I know ... It surprised me too."

"Name?"

"Actually, come to think of it, I've been dying to get your side of that story."

"Name?"

"That memorable, eh, Harry? Oh, come on. Spill the beans. What happened?"

"Jesus, didn't anybody tell you about my condition?"

"What?"

"You know, can't remember anything of the last two years."

"Drink problem?"

"Fucking amnesia."

"Amnesia?"

"Yes!"

"Of course I heard about it, you plonker."

"Seriously, though. Who was the girl you saw me with?"

"Martha. Martha Browne. Ring any bells?"

"God! Amazing! How do you know her, Robert? I was beginning to think she only existed in my imagination."

"She might as well do. She's usually quite reserved. Likes to keep herself to herself."

"OK. But who is she?"

"Just someone I know from around town."

"How?"

"We've some mutual friends. Some mutual interests."

"Right. So I met her through you, then?"

"Yes. Precisely. In Belmont."

"Right."

"But you don't remember that, Harry?"

"Nope."

"And you know nothing about her?"

"Nope."

"Nothing?"

"Well, apart from the fact that she seems mad at me for some reason. Let's say, she's not exactly a fan. It appears we were a couple ... went out for a while. Seems it didn't last long."

"OK. And what makes you think that's the case, then?"

"My mobile. It's all on here. Her text messages and so on," Harry said, waving the Nokia in the air.

"Mmm, that's peculiar."

"Why?"

"That's not the impression she gave me."

"Really?"

"Look, the last time I saw her I happened to mention your name and she wasn't very complimentary."

"Oh."

"She certainly didn't say anything about you two ever being an item."

"What did she say, then?"

"Not a lot. Just that you'd been hassling her. Asked me to have a word. You know. Warn you off."

"That's awful."

"Really?"

"Yes!"

"Why? What do you care what she thinks, Harry?"

"It's just that if I did something terrible to upset her, I'd like to know about it."

"Why?"

"I'm trying to become reconciled with my past. If I upset her, I'd like to know how and why. I want to know what I am ... or was ... capable of."

"Don't be daft. Why bother?"

"Because moving back to Holywood has been a bit of a shock to the system. I want to move on—"

"Well, *move on*."

"Right. And I am. But I can't very well start getting involved in a new relationship till I find out what went wrong with the last one. What if I hit her or something? I don't want to have relationships if I'm going to start slapping people about."

"Oh, come on. You? Hit people? I can't see that, Harry."

"Well, there's a possibility my behaviour might have got a bit erratic because of my neurological condition."

"But, still, I definitely didn't hear anything like that."

"Yeah, but I want to be sure. I don't want any more fuck-ups."

"I'd just forget about it if I were you."

"That's a hell of a faux pas, Robert."

"Oh, you know what I mean."

"So, she didn't say anything else to you about *us*?"

"As I say. She didn't give me the impression that there had been an *us*."

"Is that it, then?"

"Look, all I recall is her saying something about you being a weirdo. 'A bit of a weirdo' was how she summed you up. I'd leave well alone if I were you."

"Well, that'll be easy. Anyway, calling me a weirdo? That's not very flattering."

"No, but accurate."

"Oh, ha-fucking-ha."

"Actually, Harry, I did hear that you got a little wound up at the beginning of the year. What was it? Your marriage? The separation? The divorce?"

"I don't know. Can't remember. Seriously! I wasn't even aware I was divorced until recently."

"All the same, people were worried about you, you know. Said you were getting a bit flaky. Weren't quite yourself."

"Yeah?"

"Everyone thought you'd lost the plot. Then you had the crash, right? But you're better now, eh?"

"Well, so far so good. But I'd like to know more about Martha Browne, Robert. I mean, what does she do?"

"Works in retail. Manages Pravda. You know, the womenswear store off Royal Avenue? I mean, she does their buying. It does well. They've made her a partner. I'm not surprised. She's a sharp cookie. Pretty indispensable."

"And what's she like? I mean ... Is she a nice person?"

"She's great looking."

"Yes. But is she a nice person, you dipstick?"

"Course! She's lovely. She's a friend of mine."

Back in his studio Harry did a logistical run-through for the next day's shoot then tried to get to grips with the piles of paperwork on his desk.

It felt like trying to shift a sand dune with a cocktail stick.

17

9.55am. Saturday, 29 November 2008.

Harry String was sitting at his dining table with only his breakfast for company. In one hand, a mug of tea; in the other, a handful of pink pills that glowed in the sunshine strobing through the blinds. The sunlight encouraged Harry to feel optimistic for the location shoot later.

The headache that had been nagging him for the last three days still persisted. His right eye throbbed constantly. If he couldn't shake it off soon, he'd give Mr Patterson a call.

It was a few minutes before ten o'clock and if she were coming to Strangford, Susan Heywood would have to arrive soon. Harry was to be at the newsreader's house by half eleven, about an hour by car. The probability that she wouldn't show loomed large in his imagination. He would leave at ten fifteen no matter what, but couldn't help checking the clock on the back wall of the kitchen every thirty seconds or so.

In the meantime he distracted himself by tidying away the box of effects still cluttering up the table. Following the previous rummage he presumed that there was little of interest, but on scattering the contents across the tabletop found a small book he'd previously overlooked. It was brown with leather covers. Quite plain. It resembled a desk diary. He was surprised on closer inspection when he noticed the tiny gold lettering on the spine: *Holy Bible, King James Version.*

Harry opened the covers and found a handwritten inscription on the flyleaf: *To Harry String from Martha Browne XOX* and then below: *Read 2 Chronicles 15:13.*

He flicked through the pages, having a pretty good idea of where to find the reference. Chronicles. Second book. Old Testament. Midway through.

Though lapsed, Harry had had a traditional upbringing and what his father referred to as a "classical education".

And they entered into a covenant to seek the Lord God of their fathers with all their heart and with all their soul; That whosoever would not seek the Lord God of Israel should be put to death, whether small or great, whether man or woman.

A bit morbid, he thought. And Harry was no wiser. He couldn't conceive what possible relevance the verses might have to him and couldn't think of any reason why Martha would have given him a Bible.

Another look at the clock confirmed that it was time to go. Putting the book down, he grabbed his Puffa jacket and car keys and made for the door.

As he went out into the hall the doorbell rang.

When he opened the door he found Susan Heywood standing on the step with her back to him. She spun round.

"Hi, Harry. I'm just on my way to Bangor. I just thought I'd better call round and expl—"

"Come in, Susan. Cup of tea?" Harry said in a calm voice to counteract her nervous garbling and to disguise his surprise that she had turned up at all after his behaviour in the cab.

He turned and walked back into the house without waiting for a response to the question. And so, rather than make her excuses and leave as she had rehearsed in the car on the way over, Susan followed Harry into the lounge, sat at the table and did what she really wanted to do: talk.

And why not? She could forgive his brash behaviour the other night – could put it down to drink. So maybe they were friends now. Seemed like friends. And don't friends talk? She loved talking; had found that she liked talking to Harry. She was interested in him, and he seemed interested in her. Simple.

At this point Susan's experience as a marriage guidance counsellor should have warned her with flashing lights and a foghorn that: if you are having a problem communicating with your partner, it is not advisable to seek support from a member of the opposite sex whom your partner has neither met nor knows anything of, especially if there is even the slightest possibility you might be, or may become, attracted to them.

But no warning came.

Mid-conversation Harry interrupted and whispered: *"It's time we were going."*

And how could she say no? It was so lovely and sunny. Cold, but sunny. And he had made the assumption with such confidence and without sounding either too pushy, as in: "You must come to Strangford, I know you'll enjoy it," or too diffident, as in: "You wouldn't possibly want to come, would you?" – that it seemed far simpler for her to comply than not.

Harry could tell from what she was wearing that she'd had no intention of accompanying him when she left home. Anyone with any sense, he thought, if they knew they were going on a location shoot in November, would wear trousers, boots, something woolly and an overcoat. Susan had opted for a tartan mini over black tights, under a cropped denim jacket.

Harry got up and moved towards the door. Susan followed as though mesmerised. It seemed easier to go with him than continue on her way to Bangor as planned or go home.

"I thought you weren't able to drive, Harry?"

"Well, you thought wrong."

As they drove off, heading for Comber and the western side of Strangford Lough, Susan felt energised by the spontaneity of the adventure. And relaxed. Neither of them talked much, such was their ease. Harry shoved on the first cassette that came to hand from the clump he'd dumped in his manbag. A 50's compilation. First track: "I Put a Spell on You", Screamin' Jay Hawkins.

Amusingly appropriate, he thought.

The house was located a couple of miles out of Strangford, sitting on a hill with panoramic views out to sea, the beauty enhanced by a cloudlesss sky. It was a former presbytery, Victorian, hidden from the road by a winding drive and set in mature grounds. A peach.

"You know, whenever I have to do these kind of shoots, most of the properties I get sent to are new builds. There's such a dearth of good period homes in Northern Ireland. I'd much rather be doing a shoot at a place like this any day."

"What do you want me to do?"

"You can be my assistant for the morning."

"Oh, you'd love that wouldn't you? Bossing me around, telling me what to do."

"Yep, you've got it. Just pass me stuff from this," he said, handing her a large, black canvas tote bag brimming with kit. It was heavy and unwieldy.

"We'll probably be in and out of here in about three or four hours," Harry said, unloading a selection of battered lights and a large, clumpy tripod. He found a fleece to keep Susan warm.

The owner, the newsreader, was at the front door to greet them. He showed them around, pointing out the rooms that he thought would make suitable backdrops.

Harry spent half an hour setting up his equipment. He didn't speak much except to ask Susan's opinion from time to time. And once he started taking photos, he showed her the shots on the screen at the back of his camera and gauged her reactions as he progressed.

It was interesting to watch him work. She hadn't seen his face look so expressionless – so robotic. His demeanour seemed to transform when he was concentrating: tight-lipped and pensive. The images he showed her appeared to be of a high standard. She was no expert, but was impressed with what she saw.

A last portrait of the newsreader standing in the porch and they were done and heading for the car ferry to make the short crossing to Portaferry. They were going to drive back to Holywood along the east side of the lough. They were standing on the boat's viewing deck leaning against the guardrail and looking out over the mouth of the estuary towards the Irish Sea.

"Do you really not remember anything at all about your divorce. I mean the divorce itself. You know, going to court and all the legal ins and outs?" Susan asked casually.

Harry kept silent to a point at which Susan thought that maybe he hadn't heard her.

"No, not the actual event," he eventually replied. "Nothing at all really. I certainly don't remember the legal process. You know, meetings with my solicitor ... the barrister ..."

"OK. You don't remember the specifics. But you've got to have some idea about what happened between you and Keira. It couldn't have happened out of the blue?"

Harry was gazing down at the water as it sped past; the tidal race frenetic where the lough bottlenecked between Strangford and Portaferry.

"I had some flashbacks last night, as it happens."

"Flashbacks?"

"I get them all the time now."

"That's encouraging."

"Well, yes and no."

"Oh?"

"It's a good sign that my memory is coming back, but unfortunately most of the memories aren't that pleasant. To be honest, they don't really seem to be worth having."

"I'm sorry about that. So what have you remembered about the break-up?"

"That I played my part," Harry said, hunching his shoulders and resting his chin on the gunwale. "I find it hard to understand any of it with any sense of balance. I mean, I feel guilty for doing, or not doing, whatever I did or didn't do, but trying to form a balanced view is tough. I guess that's true of most history though, isn't it? Fault is subjective. I think that at times like this you need God to pop down for half an hour to give you an overview and provide some definitive answers. A heavenly stat sheet would suffice – something that lists the profit and loss of responsibility. I mean, I'm sure if God were summarising my marriage, he'd point a big angry finger at me. How can you swear an oath of loyalty to someone in front of all your friends and family and then go off and divorce them? No, I'm not proud of that."

"OK, so on a scale of one to ten, how responsible do you think you were for the divorce? With say, ten being 'it's all your fault'."

"Well, I guess this is precisely why we need God to step in. You know, blow his golden whistle and be the ultimate referee. Mind you, he's such a stickler for the rules he'd probably say I was a ten. Yeah, he'd show me a straight red."

"Oh, be serious."

"OK. Pass. I don't know. I guess a six ... Maybe a seven or an eight. Having said that, I do tend to feel guilty for pretty much anything and everything that happens to me or anyone else for that matter whether I'm actually responsible or not. And I'll also blame myself for not having the foresight to have stopped whatever it was from happening in the first place."

"There's a kind of distorted arrogance there – like you've got a God complex or something. Like you think you control yours and everybody else's fate."

"Maybe."

"What about Keira? What does she score on the scale of one to ten?"

That's not for me to say. I still feel a strong sense of loyalty and don't like to criticise."

"OK. Let me put it this way. Should she take *any* blame for the failure of your marriage? Yes or no?"

"I guess there are some things she said or did that maybe

she would say or do differently now and a few that she wouldn't do at all. But the thing is she tried and—"

"Yes or no?"

"Look, she is a good person. A really good person. Don't get me wrong, she could be really difficult at times – and when things didn't go her way, well ... Let's just say she didn't always react as positively as she might have done—"

"Aren't we all a bit like that?"

"Yes. Exactly. And she has a good heart. She may have made some mistakes, but she was committed to the marriage. The thing is, it was always going to be a tall order to keep the initial pace going. But then I imagine it's the same for most couples."

Susan touched Harry on the shoulder to encourage eye contact.

"You seem to have figured out quite a lot since you came into my office last week."

"I've had plenty of time to think. And the more I think, the easier it is to fit the pieces together."

"So tell me, I'll repeat the question: do you blame Keira?"

"No, not at all. Maybe we were just too young. And men can be very immature."

"Oh God, Harry, tell me about it. Believe me, I know."

"You must hear this stuff every day at the agency."

"Of course I do."

"Doesn't it leave you feeling a little bit jaded? Doesn't marriage sometimes seem like an unrealistic state of affairs to you? A waste of time and emotional energy?"

"Yes, sometimes. Well ... Quite often, really."

"And then there's my kids. I mean, there you go ... They are the main priority and I haven't even mentioned them. How selfish am I?"

"You said they were doing alright."

"Yes, luckily enough they seem fine. But they're the ones who are important in all of this. When I think of the wonderful childhood my parents gave me ... You would hope you could give your children the same secure upbringing."

"Just because you're divorced, it doesn't mean that you can't still be an excellent parent."

"Well, I try. Actually, I've got to a point now where I wonder what the hell marriage is for."

Harry paused for a second, looked up from the lough and stared into Susan's eyes.

"What do you think, Susan?"

"Oh, since I've been doing this I've come to understand divorce a bit better. I mean, if it's broke, why fix it? How long should you give a broken marriage before you give up? Sometimes life's too short. My job isn't always about saving marriages, it's also to help couples cope with divorce; to manage the process of splitting up in as humane and dignified a way as possible."

"Manage?"

"Well, help them come to terms with what's going on and to think of treating their partner with a little more understanding and respect. Maybe manage isn't exactly the right word, but I'm sure you get my drift."

"Absolutely. Maybe marriage needs redefining. Maybe the only thing you should get on your wedding day is a blessing, or whatever, a ring and a certificate. Maybe the razzmatazz ... the service and the reception should be given as a reward thirty years down the road if you're still together."

"Well, Harry. You seem to have got your wish."

"What's that?"

"Marriage guidance by default. Congratulations. I'll send you my bill."

Harry took Susan Heywood for a late lunch in Portaferry. They both ate fish and drank a little wine in a harbourside restaurant.

"What about your husband?"

"What?"

Susan's smile waned. She wasn't about to let a drop of reality tarnish the mood.

"Does he know where you are?"

"This has nothing to do with him," she said dismissively whilst refraining from using his name. It would have felt like a betrayal to utter his name or discuss anything about him in the present circumstances.

"You're kidding."

"No. This has nothing to do with him, Harry, and won't. I can befriend whomever I like and it's none of his business. That's as long as this *is* a friendship. And it is."

"So, we're just friends?"

"What else?"

"I don't know. I don't feel a need to classify things like you, Susan."

"That's too risky."

"What do you mean?"

"Look, I know how these things start. I meet plenty of people in the course of my work who have had affairs. Their stories, if not the same, tend to be similar; follow a pattern. Men and women who meet casually, have innocent friendships, enjoy a bit of company. Then before you know it, things get out of hand. A few drinks, a little flirting, a little kissing, a little petting and then *bang!* casual sex. And then it's too late. Both swear it has to finish. They stop seeing each other for a while; put an end to whatever it is they are doing. But, surprise surprise, they can't leave it at that. Curiosity or lust or the novelty of it all draws them back for more. So a friendship and a bit of company becomes a fling, and then once the genie is out of the bottle there's no getting it back in. One careless slip, sometimes quite deliberate, and the affair is exposed and the husband and wife end up sitting in front of me, blaming each other and trying to heal the rift."

"So, is that what you have planned for us?"

"As I say. We're friends."

"Fits the pattern, then."

Susan ignored him.

Harry stared out of the restaurant window. It offered a view across the moorings at the mouth of the lough. The ferry sped past with another cargo of cars and motorists, heading back to Strangford on the strong tide.

"And your husband," Harry continued. "What would he say if he knew you'd spent the day with me?"

"Let's not go there."

"I take it he wouldn't be very happy, then?"

"He *isn't* very happy."

"And what are you doing to help him?"

"Trying to keep my sanity. Oh God! It just isn't as simple as that."

"You need to talk."

"We do. He's struggling at the moment, that's all. He needs direction. He's not motivated right now. You know, he's just a little world-weary."

"And you?"

"It's challenging when you've been married for a long time. Married couples can be like tectonic plates: the two can shift in different directions almost undetectably. Then one or the other, or both, realise the sea between their continents has grown wider. They find there's more clear blue water separating them than ever before. A huge gulf, an ocean ... and then ... How do you get back to where you were? It's hard to recover the connection."

"So, why don't you take some of your own advice?"

"Uh?"

"What do you advise others to do? Isn't there a formula?"

"Well, funnily enough, and keep this to yourself, there is no magic formula. As I suggested, we don't have *that* much success in keeping people together. Whilst we can't always patch marriages up, we can often make the transition from separation to divorce more tolerable."

"You haven't answered my question, though."

"The advice? Talk. Talk through it. And make time for one another. And listen. Make sure you listen and hear what the other person is saying. Most problems in marriages arise from a breakdown in communication. A kind of panic mode descends over the situation that's not easy to budge."

"So?"

"So *what*, Harry?"

"So, are you listening to your husband?"

"Not that it's any of your business but, with us, if we do have a problem, it's not about bad communication, it's more that we've developed different interests, enjoy different things, have evolved separate lifestyles."

"And do you still love him?"

"Again, none of your business. But, yes, of course."

"So, what are you going to do?"

"Don't know. Cry?"

"Too pathetic."

"Shout?"

"Too aggressive."

"Scream?"

"Too childish."

"OK, so what do you recommend, Mr Clever Clogs?"

"Hitch a ride on a tomato lorry headed for Spain."

"What?"

"Hitch a lift to Spain and don't look back. I'll come too."

"Run away?"

"Yes. Run away."

"That doesn't solve anything."

"It does if you just keep going. But you need to be escaping to somewhere where it's warm and sunny. It's more fun running around in a hot climate, where the beer's cheap and people don't wear many clothes."

"Apart from being incredibly stupid, I think you're a bit of a hypocrite, Harry String."

"Thank you. You're not the first to say that."

"Well, I know you've had a rough time—"

"And thank you for acknowledging that too."

"You've had a rough time, but you're still here. You've survived. And, I mean, coming to me for marriage guidance counselling ... That isn't exactly running away now, is it? I'd say that's an attempt to tackle the problem head-on. In sporting terms that's a pretty full-blooded tackle."

"So we agree then, Susan."

"Huh?"

"You need to confront it. *Him*."

"Clive? Look, I was talking about *you*. Maybe you're braver than me. And, as I say: it's one thing giving advice to others; it's another taking it. Anyway, I thought we'd agreed that we're not going to talk about me. About my personal stuff."

It was dark by the time they pulled up outside Harry's place in Holywood. If it weren't that Harry String had gear to unload, Susan would have climbed straight into her car and driven home. But it was obvious that he needed help, and having wandered in and out of his house with armfuls of equipment, it was easy to accept the offer of a quick drink.

They sat on the small sofa below the window that faced onto the street and sipped white wine.

"What am I doing here, Harry?"

He didn't answer.

"Well?"

Harry kept quiet.

"How do you do that, Harry?"

"Uh?"

"How do you know when not to do or say anything? You've got good timing."

"Maybe I'm just thick. Anyway, why are you analysing me? I thought I wasn't client material."

"You intrigue me."

"Well I suppose that's better than being thought of as cute."

"Don't flatter yourself. You're intriguing like Quasimodo or the phantom of the opera. Kind of tragic and intriguing."

"And ruggedly handsome."

"With the emphasis on rugged."

"Mmm ... Beauty and the beast. That would be a flattering portrait. Thank you very much," Harry said laughing, which left a pregnant pause filled with tension.

"So, Harry. What—"

Harry suddenly leaned over and kissed her full on the lips. Startled, she responded and was receptive.

If Susan had known that there was the slightest chance this might happen, she wouldn't have entered the house, or so she thought as she closed her eyes. And she found, to her horror, that she liked his kisses; thought him an excellent kisser and had lost all sense of reason and restraint. Self-control, she knew, was losing out to reckless abandon.

She hadn't been kissed by anyone but her husband for such a long, long time and was surprised by her unwillingness to resist. The taste was luscious and it seemed such a natural thing to be doing. And when he started to massage her right breast with his free hand, she found she wanted more, she wanted to feel the warmth of his fingers on her nipples.

This was more than friends should be doing, she knew, but was entranced. And when he started to slide his hand under the hem of her skirt and onto her thigh, she was tempted to relax and open her legs but knew to stop and stop immediately.

She tore herself away, stood up and then froze.

Susan locked Harry with a fierce stare; both were transfixed, breathless. Susan ran out of the house slamming the door behind her. Harry sat with his head in his hands; couldn't understand what the hell had motivated him to be so reckless. And how could he justify *that*? So toxic!

Having screwed up his own marriage, why would he want to drag Susan into a situation that could destroy hers too? She'd already made it quite clear that she loved her husband. She'd mentioned that they were having problems, but it was not for him to be taking advantage and preying on her vulnerability. He enjoyed Susan's company and knew that if he had any respect for her at all, he wouldn't be trying to seduce her. He blew out his cheeks then rocked slowly backwards and forwards shaking his head.

18

5.30pm. Saturday, 29 November 2008.

"Look, I really don't know."
 "What?"
 "I don't know if I want to go there again."
 "Why?"
 "Well, what good does it do?"
 "OK, Dad. Water under the bridge and all that, but I'd just like a clearer picture, that's all."
 "Look, you're a smashing lad, son, but you know your problem, don't you? You think too much. You're always thinking, worrying, trying to work stuff out. You need to cut yourself a bit of slack, Harry."
 "I just want ... Och, you don't understand," Harry moaned as he ran a finger through the dust that had collected along the slats of the blinds; his attention starting to wander out the window and across the street.

With the dusk had come drizzle.
 He'd called his dad, Billy, within a minute or two of Susan leaving and had been ambling round the lounge with the handheld clamped under his chin and lost in conversation whilst tidying up the flotsam and jetsam of the day.
 "Look, Harry, we've been over and over this, time and time again—"
 "Yes, Dad. And I'm aware that it's not easy for you either. But, please ... Just help me out here."
 "All right, all right. OK, just give me a moment."

Harry heard his father take a deep breath before continuing: "So, you can't remember anything up until when? About a year before the accident? OK. Well that must have been shortly before you and Keira separated."

"Yeah. I have little or no memory of that. I remember we were having a few ups and downs, but that's all."

"Well, you didn't tell me much before or after your divorce, and, to be frank, I didn't want to get involved. But the first I heard about it was when you told me you'd sent Keira a solicitor's letter requesting a separation. You didn't appear to be at all comfortable about it. Though, I have to say, it didn't come as any great shock to me, son. Then, about three or four months later, we were at Geraldine and Richard's silver wedding do in Galway when you got a call from some mate of Keira's advising you not to go back home because Keira was suffering from stress. So when you got back from Galway you moved straight into where you are now. I remember coming round to see you. It was being done up at the time and was a bit throughother. No running water, no loo and no bath. I think you just had a mattress, a telly and a couple of chairs to start with. But you got it sorted and double quick. You needed to so that the kids could stay over."

"How were they then?"

"They *seemed* OK. A little confused, but OK. I guess it's not their fault they've got a couple of *eejits* for parents."

"Agreed."

"However, time moved on. You were a bit shell-shocked. I think your work suffered, not that you ever talked much about that. You were paying the running costs of two houses and I think money got tight – well, I'm sure you've seen the evidence of that. I mean, you must have been through your bank statements. So I had to sub you. And then about another six months on you got your decree nisi. Game over. Except I think the stress of the divorce had a bad effect on you. On your health, I mean."

"Yes, and aneurysms can be caused by stress—"

"And that's why you've got to calm down, son."

"I know, Dad. I know."

"Maybe you should focus on the kids and their needs and just get over the rest."

"Er ... *Get over it!* Is that what you're saying?"

"Exactly. *Get over it!*"

A sustained silence followed.

"Look. Time's moving on, Harry. I don't know about you, but right now I need to get my tea on," Harry's father said abruptly.

"Fair dos, Dad."

"Make sure you get plenty of sleep tonight, son. And try not to think so much."

As Harry put the phone down, he glanced out through the blinds. The drizzle had turned to rain. Then a shadow flashed across the window followed by a ring of the doorbell. Harry limped down the hall and opened the front door. Susan Heywood was standing on the doorstep soaking wet and shivering.

"Are you stalking me, Mrs Heywood?"

She ignored him, squeezed past and went into the lounge.

Harry followed close behind, and as soon as she had crossed the threshold into the room, she spun round and clasped his face in both hands and kissed him hard on the lips, her wet hair falling over his cheek.

Harry responded, wrapping his arms around her drenched jacket and pulling her in tight till he could feel the dampness soaking through to his skin. And although her clothes were icy cold, he could feel the warmth of her breasts pressing against his chest through her blouse. She tugged his shirt loose and ran her hands up his back whilst kissing him, her mouth open and urgent, then pulled away.

"Upstairs?" she whispered.

Harry looked into her eyes, nodded and then took her hand and guided her up to his bedroom where they fell across the bed fumbling with waistbands, buttons, zips and sleeves until they were naked.

When they had sex it was fast and urgent, as though a last act in desperate circumstances. Harry conscious that it was the first time in a long while and trying not to be awkward or clumsy. Later they were slower and more sensitive.

"Still friends?" he murmured as they lay in each other's arms.

"I can't stay, Harry," she said rolling away.

He didn't respond; was trying to gauge her mood but couldn't. Wanted to urge her to stay but knew better and therefore wouldn't. For her to leave and not spend the night seemed to reduce the significance of what they had just done, but he was in no position to argue.

"Look, I'm sorry, I have to go," Susan said quietly as she sat on the edge of the bed buttoning her blouse.

Harry smiled at her.

"Your legs," she said, running a finger along the scars on his right thigh, "do they hurt much?"

"A fair bit, yes."

"But they'll get better?"

"With luck, it's just a matter of time and some surgery."

She smiled, gently touching Harry's shoulder.

"Must go," she whispered before darting out of the room.

He heard the front door close, lay back and shut his eyes.

Harry slept well at first: a deep sleep that he hadn't experienced since leaving the hospital. But at about five in the morning he woke with a start. His head was throbbing and he felt hot, sticky and in a sweat, like he had a fever. The bedroom was dark, and, as he turned over to try and get back to sleep, he was alarmed by an apparition of the amber-haired girl. She, Martha, was lying next to him and smiling. And as he searched her eyes for meaning, a memory came back to him. It was of the two of them together in the bedroom. This bedroom. And he knew it was a memory because as the imaginary film ran in his mind's eye, he knew what was to come. In the clip he could see them the first time they'd slept together. Yes, he could remember now. Could remember what she had been wearing: a voluminous skirt tied at the waist with a sash. He'd had trouble undoing the knot. And ankle socks and brogues – ankle socks with brogues was her look then. And, being summer, a white organza blouse. Then he remembered her anxiety – that she was shy. But he was reassuring and gentle. And he remembered the tenderness, the closeness. And, yes, he remembered her smiling, her head resting on the pillow beside him.

Harry was about to fall asleep when he recalled another vignette. Martha in the kitchen of the small house. She was talking, but he couldn't make out the words. Then he could hear snippets; straining as if trying to hear a conversation on a badly tuned radio:

"*I can't do this, Harry.*"

"*I don't under—*"

"*I'm not supposed to, that's all. I want to, but I can't. In fact, I shouldn't be here with you now.*"

"*OK. But there's not much I can do about that.*"

Once Harry began to recall small snippets, longer episodes started to follow. But even though he was greedy for more and fought the onset of drowsiness, his eyes kept closing, and he couldn't help but succumb to sleep.

Harry woke with a jolt at around ten o'clock the next morning. Panicking that he might have forgotten the episodes that had come back to him the night before, he sprinted through the new material to lock it into his memory.

Then he worried about Susan Heywood. Felt hollow. But how dreadful must she be feeling? What kind of bastard was *he* for sleeping with her?

Harry distracted himself with thoughts of Martha Browne. He lay still to relax and focus, attempting to conjure up more incidents; trying to recollect the time when they had split up.

Then Harry recalled a dinner party they'd been invited to at a friend's house. It was early spring, and he'd just got back from a holiday with the kids. Martha had asked him if he would consider moving to London with her. It had seemed a serious proposal. As they left the dinner party, she asked him back to her place. They'd been drinking. Got a cab. It wasn't far.

He then had a clear image of the abandon with which they'd shed their clothes and fallen into bed. The passion. The sex. She'd told him she loved him. Was she drunk?

Then there was to be a picnic in the week that followed.

Ah, yes, the picnic. His idea. "*Love to,*" she had said. Then she blew him out. Sent him a text message an hour before he was due to pick her up: *Bad day at work. Not feeling well.* But he wouldn't take no for an answer. Panicking, he went round to collect her anyway. Bad idea. Too pushy. They fell out. Yeah. That was it. They had a row. That's when she told him. Yeah, he could remember now. Said that she wanted to split. He hadn't seen it coming.

Following the loneliness of the divorce came the exhilaration of a new relationship only then to get dumped. He could remember it clearly now. Was devastated. Attempted to win her round and wouldn't give up easily, but all to no avail.

Whenever he tried to talk to her she didn't engage. No explanation, nothing. Wouldn't answer his calls, wouldn't phone him back, wouldn't return texts, wouldn't see him. Maybe that was when she had told Robert that Harry was turning into *a bit of a weirdo*.

Maybe he was, but Harry realised that by then Martha would do or say anything to scare him off, and then say or do anything to keep it that way.

Maybe that's why she was so aggressive when I ran into her in Belfast? Harry thought.

But what did she have to fear?

Harry lay around for most of Sunday reading the papers and taking it easy. He hoped to hear from Susan, was worried for her, but knew it was unlikely she'd call. She had seemed to have enough problems before they'd slept together, and now, without doubt, he'd made her situation worse. He wanted to send her a text message but knew he mustn't. Must leave her well alone.

In order to resist the urge to contact her he scribbled her mobile number down on a piece of paper and dropped it into his studio and then deleted her details from his phone. He didn't want to give in to temptation and disturb her later when he'd had a drink or two.

But then she texted him in the evening anyway:

Bad day. Time dragging. Will call you next week when head straight SH.

When he received her text Harry was sat in a bar overlooking Belfast City Hall having a quick drink with Robert Doherty.

"People are going to start talking about us, Doc."

"Well, they're already talking about *you*, you bollocks."

"Well, you know what they say: it's better to be—"

"Look, I don't know if you're going to like this."

"Like what?"

"I've seen Martha Browne."

"No!"

"But yes."

"And?"

"I mentioned you."

"Shit!"

"Said that she's worried you've started following her around again."

"That's crazy!"

"Well, she didn't sound best pleased, to be honest. Says you were following her through Belfast last week. Says you're scaring her."

"Oh, for Christ's sake, it was a chance meeting! Not even a meeting. More *chance* than *meeting*. Just a complete coincidence. I had no idea who she was. Didn't recognise her. She could have been anyone. Doesn't she know about the accident?"

"Yeah, of course. Everybody's heard about your crash, mate. You're practically a celebrity."

"Right."

"Look, I'd stay well away from her. Told me she's warned her staff to keep an eye out in case you go into the shop, and then to call the police if you do."

"Is she nuts? You know, until I ran into her in town I probably hadn't seen her for seven or eight months. What's she got to worry about?"

"Look, as I say, if I were you—"

"Yeah, I know, you'd stay well out of her way. Well, that should be easy enough, unless she has a sudden brain haemorrhage or moves to Holywood. Anyway, what do you make of this?" Harry said passing Robert the Bible Martha had given him.

"Maybe not your typical present," Robert Doherty said, arching his brow whilst flicking through the pages.

"Don't understand," Harry replied, downing his coffee.

"Me neither. But tell you what, leave it with me," Doherty said, pocketing the book as he stood to leave "I'll check it out."

"Give it back to her if you like. Means nothing to me."

"Sure. Oh, and by the way, have one of these ..." Robert said, handing Harry his latest business card.

19

9am. Thursday, 27 November 2008.

Gillian McGuinness and Paula Smyth made a formidable team. They had been the backbone of the human resources department at Supermark since it opened in Bangor in the late nineties. Over the years they had hired and fired a sizeable proportion of the town's population.

A UK-wide multiple retailer, Supermark was well on its way to becoming Northern Ireland's largest supermarket chain at the time it built its flagship store on the Bangor ring road. With the square footage of four football pitches, it was the first shopping centre of its size in the north; a positive indicator that the Good Friday Agreement was bearing fruit, attracting inward investment and creating employment. However, it did little to support the turnover of the local shopkeepers struggling to maintain a commercial presence on the high street.

The majority of opportunities at Supermark were blue-collar. Common were the job titles incorporating the words "assistant" or "operative", as in: deli-counter assistant, cleansing operative, cafeteria assistant and trolley-return operative, and so on.

McGuinness and Smyth had learned much about human nature. They could spot a useful assistant or operative as soon as the candidate walked into the HR office for interview, and even before the routine questioning had begun.

The Supermark human resources department was situated in a Portakabin placed to one side of the vast aircraft-hangar style depository used for receiving goods at the rear of the store. Deliveries were constant. Customers were unaware that behind the bright, bleached inner skin of the Supermark supermarket lay a vast, gloomy cavern lined with the vital organs of bakery, cold storage and office accommodation.

It was to the HR Portakabin that potential recruits were escorted for interview. Most were sixth-formers and school-leavers looking for casual work or a Saturday job.

McGuinness and Smyth's role was made easier by the fact that job opportunities were scarce in the North Down area. There were always many more applicants for jobs than there were jobs being advertised. The HR pair could afford to be picky when appointing new personnel. The menial nature of the work on offer ensured that there was a constant stream of applicants to be interviewed. Low wages, however, contributed to a high turnover of staff.

The pair had worked together for so long and were so conversant with their responsibilities that they now worked by instinct. Conversation was brief. Though they were subordinate only to Mr Desmond, the store manager, Mr Desmond was an excellent delegator. The HR couple found that it suited their smooth management of the workforce to assume the executive power that his largesse made available to them.

That they spent the day together and were never apart gave them an authority that was rarely challenged. They ran the shop floor at Supermark with an iron fist. And since they appointed all new personnel and had a comprehensive knowledge of the personal details of each employee, it was easy enough to maintain the impression that the staff worked for, and were answerable to, them and them alone. On this basis they had established a formidable powerbase.

Their routine was written in stone. At nine o'clock sharp they toured the aisles, strutting stiff-backed, clipboards clasped to their bosoms like breastplates. And whilst the Supermark uniform was supplied in navy and yellow nylon, the two HR manageresses wore green cotton: light green blouse under a forest-green blazer combined with a forest-green skirt,

American tan tights and black, sensible walking shoes. They marched like camp guards, but with the frozen smiles of ballroom dancers. Pointing and wagging stern fingers at the supermarket sales staff, their bearing and body language had been ingrained through years of repetition.

Synchronised and crisp, they swept through the store like crack troops goose-stepping in a presidential march past: chests up, buttocks proud and hips rolling like the haunches of a seaside pony. They wore little make-up and both had their mousy hair scraped back into tight buns wrapped in a little black hairnet and fastened with a lacy bobble. Though they were both thirty-somethings they had the demeanour of the middle-aged: serious and short-tempered. Both were spinsters. They appeared like twins. There was much gossip concerning the nature of their relationship.

During the ten years they had governed from the HR Portakabin, Gillian McGuinness and Paula Smyth had finessed their technique and the process for spotting new talent. There was now a drill.

First the applicant would be given a warm reception at the customer service desk beside the tills in the supermarket proper. They would then be ushered through to the cavernous backstage storage area where their eyes would strain to adjust to the gloom. They would notice the cold.

Disoriented, they might sniff and wonder if the slight stench was from diesel fumes or something more sinister.

They would be led to, and then instructed to sit on, one of a row of cheap, plastic garden chairs outside the HR Portakabin. The applicant would be left to wait for five minutes and then, precisely five minutes later, would be hailed as their surname was shouted through the door – a sharp shout with a hint of boot camp menace.

The light inside the Portakabin would be bright. The candidate would be invited to sit on a simple wooden chair in the middle of the room below a glaring 150-watt bulb.

McGuinness and Smyth would be standing close by and would remain so throughout the process. They would circle the applicant, thrusting their heads forward to ask questions one after the other, hands on hips.

Some light-hearted questions about hobbies and lifestyle at first, and then, with a swift change of mood, others more direct such as: "Do you have a criminal record?", "Have you ever been sectioned under the Mental Health Act?" and "Are you, or have you ever been, listed on the sex offender register?".

The applicant would then be asked to fill in a questionnaire from which the HR officers would establish a psychological profile once the interview was completed. The questionnaire would comprise multiple-choice questions such as:

You are driving a car along a narrow country lane when a cat runs across the road ahead of you. Do you: a) Swerve to avoid it? b) Brake hard and hope you can stop? c) Keep driving without diverting from your course? d) Close your eyes and hope for the best?

That McGuinness and Smyth had experience as military policewomen would surprise no one. For reasons of personal security, however, this was never advertised or discussed. And, though the questioning of applicants could at times be relaxed and amicable, they got prompt answers. They also never failed to impress upon candidates the importance of smart dress and discipline at the Bangor branch of Supermark.

Over the past four or five years the pair had noticed an increase in the number of senior citizens and the middle-aged applying for work at the store. A welcome development. They found that their older employees were responsive to instruction, reliable and, though occasionally a little grumpy, generally had better communication skills. They didn't trust schoolchildren or students as much, but found that they were a necessary burden to keep the shelves stacked, the conveyor belts rolling and the tills ringing.

27th November: Hand in notice!

Clive Heywood smiled as he wrote this, the first entry in his new 2009 desk diary.

"Some fucking year this is going to be," he mumbled under his breath.

The plan was simple though: he would give himself twelve months. One year working at Supermark, and, if all went well – if he could climb the greasy pole to a managerial position – he would stay. If it didn't work out and he was still stacking shelves after that time, he would hand in his notice and leave.

Clive was pleased with his plan. It was simple yet inspiring. And, if all went well, he might shock everyone (including himself) and end up a branch manager. He knew that he had to try something, anything, before old age and/or dementia kicked in. Anyway, he was yet to find any other kind of work and since retail was one of the few growth areas in the Northern Ireland economy, decided to give it a go. If he were only going to be there a year, he would treat the experience as an experiment, a creative exercise, if not a game. And even though he would miss his afternoons with Carol Vorderman, anything was better than lounging on his backside at home watching daytime television.

Having written the diary entry it didn't feel so much like a life sentence, more a brief sojourn.

Clive Heywood found the job interview similar to how he imagined a prisoner of war might experience an interrogation: he sensed that it wouldn't pay to be overly defensive or too smart-arsed.

"Mr Heywood, I see you were a department head at Camberhill College. Won't you find collecting trolleys in our car park a bit of a comedown?"

"On the contrary, I see the position as a challenge. And, actually, I have experience in this area. I used to marshal the car parking at school open days."

God! he thought. *Way too smart-arsed!*

"And how will you find working alongside younger people? We have many teenagers working for us."

"Excellent. Not a problem."

"Are you good with young people?"

"Well, with *my* teaching experience ... very!" he lied enthusiastically.

The HR couple didn't warm to Clive Heywood. It was obvious from his CV that he had been successful in his field, had worked in management, and that worried them. Probably too ambitious and too intelligent. But they decided to take a risk. They offered him a job, and almost out of spite, as they imagined he would hate the work and be thoroughly miserable. To them he was little more than trolley fodder.

The interview was short. They didn't bother with the questions about his mental state and criminal record. They wanted him out of the Portakabin, into his blue nylon overalls and exposed to the elements in the drab Supermark car park as soon as they could get him there.

"Your working hours will vary according to the shift rota, Clive. We can offer you a minimum of forty hours a week at a basic rate of £5.75 per hour. If you like, you can start on Monday."

Clive Heywood allowed himself a chuckle as he left the HR Portakabin armed with his temporary name badge and bundle of uniform. The game had begun.

Confidence in his ability to shine led him to believe that he would be out of the car park and onto the tills more or less straight away. And he looked forward to the contact with the public that being a cashier would bring, though dreaded the possibility of having to serve ex-pupils and their parents. He would grin and bear those vengeful encounters as best he could. (Though he imagined that most of their kind shopped at Marks and Spencer anyway.) But for now there was no avoiding spending his first day as a Supermark employee out of doors sporting a navy parka, overalls and fluorescent-yellow bib, whilst herding the stray shopping trolleys scattered around the site back to the aluminium corral at the front of the store.

Inspecting himself in the mirror wearing his Supermark uniform for the first time before setting off to work on the Monday morning was an unsettling experience. He struggled to recognise the man in the navy boiler suit and hi-vis jacket staring back at him. Descending the stairs to surprise Susan with his news and new look he could imagine how it might feel to "come out" as a cross-dresser. As he arrived at the bottom of the stairs and wandered into the kitchen, he almost lost his nerve when he noticed her face drop.

"So, what do you think?"
"Bloody hell! Is it fancy-dress day at the golf club, Clive?"
"What, you don't like it?"
"I don't know if navy and yellow are quite your colours."
"Oh, I don't know. I think they take years off me."
"Yeah. You look like a child heading off to a Saturday job."
Clive frowned and explained his strategy.
"Look, I've got to do *something*, for fuck's sake!'
"Actually, good for you! No, seriously, I'm proud of you, Clive," Susan said, wrapping her arms round her husband to give him an encouraging hug.
"Look, it's a good job, right? We feed people, you know."
"And sell them toiletries and dog food."
"And we've over thirty varieties of biscuit to choose from."
"There you go. You're practically an aid worker. Bob Geldolf and Bono will be very proud of you."
"No one need starve in Bangor now. Not if I can help it."
"Quite."
"So, do you think I'm mad?"
"No. A job's a job. And it's a good one."
"And the retail industry *is* pretty hot right now."
"Well, good for you! And I don't want to hear you patronising your fellow workers, Clive."

"Would I?"

"Most definitely."

"We're just one big happy family at Supermark. Me, the schoolkids and the OAPs make a formidable team. We're like the *Dad's Army* of UK retailing."

"No. Seriously. Well done, Clive. I'm impressed."

"Really?"

"Really."

"What about you, Susan?"

"Me?"

"I've hardly seen you."

"Eh?"

"I mean. What time did you get in on Saturday? Or was it Sunday morning? One? Two?"

"Can't remember," she blushed.

"It seemed very late or very early."

"You know Tracey when she gets talking."

"Still. I was worried. And yesterday, I didn't see you from breakfast till dinner."

"You were on the golf course for most of the day, Clive. We could have done something otherwise."

"Well, you wouldn't deny a condemned man one last round of golf, would you?"

"Do you know, Clive, I wouldn't deny you anything, especially if you paid me a little more attention."

"Well, from now on I can shower you with all the biscuits, toiletries and dog food any girl could wish for."

"You're just too kind."

"And, anyway, I did ask you to come to Donegal with me for the weekend."

"True."

"Actually, I think you must be having an affair," Clive said with a reassuring wink.

Susan shrugged. She was happy to humour the subterfuge whilst hoping Clive wouldn't notice her reddening cheeks. She felt self-conscious, so got lost in the early-morning routine to hide her embarrassment and retreated to the shower.

Clive poured himself a fresh coffee, put on some toast and leant against the worktop waiting for the toaster to *ping*. He lifted Susan's mobile out of the way in case he spilled coffee over it. Put it down. Picked it up and stared at it for a moment. Put it down, thought twice and picked it up again. The hairs on the back of his neck stood up as he scrolled through the messages folder.

Inbox: nothing of interest. Sent items: nothing of interest. But then, scrolling down, he found a message tagged Harry String.

Clive opened Susan's text: *Bad day. Time dragging. Will call you next week when head straight SH.*

Clive scrolled up and made a mental note of the message details.

Harry String phoned Mr Patterson first thing on the Monday morning.

"We'll take a look when you come in, then, Harry. You're in this morning, aren't you? Don't worry. It might be nothing. We all get headaches. But I hope you've been taking it easy. Look. You know you're not – but in a way you *are* – out on parole from here. We're expecting good behaviour from you. If you're working too hard, partying or overdoing it in any way, you could be back in here for a long stretch before you know it."

Harry drove into the hospital grounds, but was careful to park the Volvo well away from Mr Patterson's department.

He did his hour of therapy with Rory but didn't feel as motivated as usual.

"You know, Harry, it'll surprise you, but these last sessions are going to be the hardest for you. It's like dieting: the first few weeks are easier to cope with because those are the weeks when the scales reveal the greatest weight loss. The later weeks much less so. And you're going to notice smaller and smaller improvements now. OK, so we've got you up and walking, but if you want to walk without a limp later in life, you've got to try and correct your gait before it becomes ingrained into your musculature with implications for excessive wear and tear on your hips and spine."

"Yeah, you're right, Rory. It's just, some days, you don't feel like you've got what it takes to go through the pain."

"What, because you're down or something? Well, fine. Take it out on the exercises. Take it out on me. Burn some adrenaline. That's the best way to shake off the blues. Come on, Harry! Channel that negativity into your rehab."

Harry discarded his tracksuit top, walked over to the weights and started pumping. The pain in physio was often intense, but combined with a headache was almost unbearable and had him close to tears.

"Come on. It's not that bad, Harry. Come on. Get stuck in!"

Afterwards, Harry kept his appointment with Mr Patterson.

"Whereabouts are you getting these headaches, Harry? Can you show me?"

Harry shaped a hand round his head to indicate the source and pattern of the pain.

"OK, some routine questions: have you been taking your medication regularly?"

"Yes."

"In the correct dosages?"

"Yes."

"Are you drinking?"

"No more than the last time you asked."

"Smoking?"

"Still no."

"Working?"

"Not really."

"Worrying?"

"A little."

"What about?

"Bit of baggage."

"Lost baggage refound?"

"Yes, kind of. I'm remembering more. All sorts of stuff."

"That's good. A healthy sign. Look, I'll be straight with you. The headaches ... Could be something or nothing."

"What would 'something' be?"

"An aneurysm."

"Shit."

"No, not good."

"So?"

"We scan you."

"When?"

"Now."

"Results?"

"This morning."

"Right."

Harry hated taking his clothes off in hospital. It seemed like the first nail in the coffin, lying down being the second. The last hospital bed had nearly been the final nail in his coffin and his last resting place.

Walking around in a hospital gown also felt like having one foot in the grave. Not only did Harry have to strip off, but also had to hang around in a badly tailored garment that exposed his bottom to anyone in the vicinity and that was no more substantial than a giant J-cloth with sleeves. He didn't like that it singled him out as a patient in the same way that shorts on holiday single out the wearer as a tourist. There were many times he preferred to be an extra rather than playing in the starring role. This was one.

Plus the waiting was interminable.

And people complain about service in restaurants? he thought. He didn't complain, though. In restaurants the staff handle your food, in a hospital they handle you.

The whole process of having a brain scan tested the patience: from waiting for the equipment to be free, to going through the procedure itself. Any time spent lying in an oversized cigar tube did not appeal to a claustrophobe like Harry String. It was also frustrating that, since his meeting with Mr Patterson, the headache seemed to have eased; and although he was instructed to lie motionless, he couldn't resist frowning to check whether his headache was still there. And when he did, it wasn't.

Harry preoccupied himself by daydreaming about Martha Browne whilst confined in the tube. Tried to remember her smile. He could picture them in bed now, could remember the sex and her hands, her body and could hear her voice, soft and gentle and clear. Could hear her whispering over and over: "*I love you, Harry. I really, really love you ...*" And it angered him. It angered him that she could profess to love him so much and then give him up so easily and then didn't even bother to explain why.

The results of Harry's scan were encouraging. The lesions were healing well and there were no further traces of swelling. But, an hour later, his headache returned. The pain had now spread down behind his left eye.

Harry drove over to South Belfast, parked up and walked along the Stranmillis Road looking for somewhere to have a drink to relieve his discomfort. Having copied Susan's number back into his iPhone's address book he wanted to text her, but still felt he should leave her in peace and wait for her to contact him.

He walked into the first brasserie he came to, sat at the bar and, no sooner than he'd downed a drink, got out his phone.

20

9am. Monday, 1 December 2008.

Susan Heywood's room at the marriage guidance counselling offices looked its grimmest in December; grey and starved of natural light. There was little relief from the gloom out of doors either. That morning, thick cloud had smothered the sunrise, enveloping Belfast in a dull cloak. Another dark, soulless day was now in prospect.

However, Susan still had to wear a pleasant smile for those desperate couples that traversed her Brillo-pad carpet in the hope of finding redemption. That and offer large doses of enthusiasm – a mix of boundless energy and extreme positivity.

Meanwhile, the lank, vertical strips of fabric that constituted the blinds did little to discourage the murk outside from dripping down the inside of the window as condensation. A rash of mould spores blossomed in a corner of the sill.

Today: more tears, more sad stories. The box of Kleenex emptying fast. From nine till twelve there were three groups of just-about-still-marrieds. An hour for each appointment.

Mr and Mrs Thompson: too young to be getting divorced. Too young to be wed.

Their problem?

Boredom.

The solution?

Take a lover and run away. Get out. Escape! Dump him. Dump her. She hates you. You hate her. So don't do it! Don't spend the rest of your short lives gasping for breath whilst slowly suffocating. For fuck's sake, get out. Get out before you reach some sort of sad, miserable compromise sealed at your golden wedding anniversary or funeral with brave talk about how you struggled through: "*Oh, it wasn't always easy, you know. We've had our ups and downs.*" But what about passion? Where was the love?

And now you're too old to even go to the loo on your own. And you never got to visit all those places you promised you'd see together. Too late to love those others you held a torch for and yearned for in secret and who have drifted away on the passing days; lost like a beach ball sucked out to sea on the ebbing tide. Too late. Too fucking late.

And it all ends in tears. Must end in tears. Every relationship. Even those that last a lifetime. Death. The funeral. The burial. The mourning. And what's left? Just so much ash in an urn on the mantlepiece. Or a plot. A stone. A name and a year.

Go on then – leave! Leave and rejoin the world a free citizen. Don't come and sit on my horrid plastic chairs and beg for mercy. I am no miracle worker. I cannot heal you. I cannot show you the way. I can only talk crap for an hour and then show you the door.

"Look at this diagram," Susan said, regaining focus whilst standing over beside her flip chart; thick, black marker in hand being waved like a magic wand. "See this?" she said, making extravagant vertical then horizontal slashes on the top page that had started to resemble a huge sheet of noughts and crosses. "This is where you are," she continued, sticking a blob in the middle of the lattice. "You are at a crossroads. And this is where you've come from, and this is where you're going. And these are the three stages of a relationship. Well ... of *your* relationship. And from here you can either go this way together, or take a path that diverts you to here and here."

The Thompsons where enthralled by the bold marks shooting out of Susan's felt-tip. It was at least a diversion from the bickering and the tears, but the doodle as hard to interpret as road directions given in Swahili.

But what could Susan say? What can you say to people who have become entrenched, who can't or don't want to hear their partner's cries for help or respond to the desperation in their eyes? Their need for love, for excitement, for reinvention.

The Thompsons seemed grateful, and, for the moment, hypnotised by the Magic Marker – stunned into believing in the fragile optimism which Susan was spinning that like a shot of adrenaline would carry them bounding out to the car and home with renewed enthusiasm, only to commence a slow slip back into the swamp of domestic bile from which they had emerged to attend Susan's clinic in the first place.

And then they were gone, their hour over. Susan rested her forehead on her desk, contemplating the enormity of another week of desperate and unhappy couples.

Tangerine walls, tobacco ceiling. Had to change. In the last day or two the old calendar had fallen and was now wedged behind the radiator and enveloped in dust, warped by the heat and developing a permanent wave.

One married couple down, two to go.

Next up, the McMullens. Fifties. She obviously adored him, whilst he obviously didn't give a shit about any of this or her. Her love was evident in her attentiveness and ability to find amusement in anything and everything he said, whilst his disenchantment was characterised by his hangdog expression, drooping shoulders and reluctance to make eye contact.

Susan could tell that Mr McMullen would rather have *her*, Susan. But not just Susan – any woman. Any woman his leering gaze fell upon. Any woman except his wife.

Mrs McMullen appeared to be sensitive and sensible. She was early-fifties. But, provoked by his neglect, had neglected herself too. A heavy smoker, the row of fine lines fanning out across her top lip were a giveaway. And comfort ate. Low self-esteem. She was now wrinkled and ageing fast. But she was demure and full of love for this oaf of a man. In essence, a beauty.

And the beast? A grinning monkey on whom few others made any impact and who sought his own reflection in every shop window and in every eye.

Susan was sure that Mr McMullen, the couple's mouthpiece, was also the main cause of the couple's marital strife. The wife was almost mute, *but could he talk*? And, of course, he disliked Susan. He disliked that a woman might gain even the slightest element of control over him, that Susan controlled the agenda, asked the questions and that she gave his wife equal status.

But what could Susan say to this idiot who made no effort to take on board the advice she was trying to impart? She couldn't fathom why he bothered to come at all. He didn't listen to her. Didn't listen to his wife.

And the poor wife, what could Susan do for her? Tell her to divorce him ASAP? Get proof of his infidelities, leave him and then sue him for every penny?

She didn't need a diagram for these two. They knew exactly where they were: off the map. Their earth was flat and their ship had well and truly plunged over the edge.

Susan needed to delve deep into the box of Kleenex herself after the McMullens had left. She wanted to take Mrs McMullen aside. Get her on her own. Talk some sense into her: "Escape! Your fate *is* in *your* hands ..." But she knew it wasn't. Wouldn't be. For Mrs McMullen there could only be a slow, lingering life until she or he – one of them – passed away.

How about him passing away at the sharp end of a kitchen knife? A quick thrust between the ribs, a twist and then a scream of joy? She'd get twenty years. Out in ten. Less if her barrister could prove extenuating circumstances.

Mercifully, the minute hand passed the hour mark and the LED started to flash in alarm.

"NEXT!"

Susan Heywood's third and last session of the morning was a one-to-one with Tom.

Tom came every week but, of late, on his own. She liked Tom. He was articulate and reasonably handsome. His wife had stopped coming to their session; had appeared to have given up hope. But Tom soldiered on. And Susan knew that he was really there to seek forgiveness for his mistakes. Forgiveness for the fling he had tearfully admitted to and that stood to wreck the marriage. The consultation more a confessional.

But even though he seemed remorseful, Susan knew it was probably too late to repair the damage. The emergence of the personality flaw that had driven his crass error of judgement now ate away at his wife's faith in him, defeating her like a slow and unstoppable cancer, undermining her strength and stamina for the fight.

Tom cried a lot. Susan wished he would stop. She'd have more respect for him if he didn't cry so damn much. Tears, she had come to observe, were often a sign of self-pity in the counselling context. And however much she liked this charming, young man, she resented that he felt more sorry for himself than he ever could for his wife.

Susan was strict with him, therefore. She visualised herself as a dominatrix: unforgiving and brutally honest. A role that encouraged him to cry further. However, she felt there was still the tiniest glimmer of hope for Tom and his wife. But only if he could start to think more about his wife's need for reassurance and love than for his need for forgiveness. Tom wanted a clean slate, and that was the key to his problem. For what Tom wanted meant more to Tom than what he knew his wife needed.

But, compared to most, Tom was good company for an hour. He had a sense of humour; there was also laughter with the tears. Susan could imagine how easy it must have been for him to give in to the temptation of adultery since his unrelenting need for approval came mixed with an ability to charm.

For once, Tom had to leave early: had a nativity play to attend at the primary school. The thought of this couple having children was doubly depressing.

Lunchtime!

Susan now had almost an hour to spare. She rested her brow on the edge of the orange desk and breathed a long sigh of relief as Tom pulled the door closed behind him.

Seconds later the door reopened. Susan deep in thought. Someone, she imagined a colleague, wandered in and sat down opposite her.

Susan raised her head.

"Jesus! What the—"

"Hello, I've come for some advice. My wife and I haven't been getting on too well recently. I'm starting to think she takes me for granted. And—"

"Bloody hell, Clive!"

Clive, much to Susan's displeasure, was wearing his new Supermark outfit. She hated seeing him in his uniform. Clive had been such a dapper dresser; had always gone for quality fabrics and tailoring.

"What are you doing here? I thought you were starting work this morning?"

"They called just after you left. They've changed the rota. I don't have to be in till four. Starting on a double. I'm shelf stacking till dawn. Almost sounds romantic, doesn't it?"

"Congratulations, Clive. I *am* impressed."

"Well, without wishing to sound rude, I don't really care what you think. Or is that too negative? Maybe you could draw me a pie chart or something to explain my terrible insecurities," he said, waving a hand at the flip chart.

Susan looked away, unamused and silent.

"OK, Clive. What do you really want?" she snapped, growing agitated.

"It's your lunchtime. We need to talk."

"Really?"

"Yes. Or maybe have some marriage guidance? Maybe both."

"That's not funny."

"Actually, I'm not being funny."

"Well, we don't need that, Clive. Whatever's bothering you ... whatever it is ... We can sort it out for ourselves. And certainly not here, not in my bloody office!"

"It's the perfect place."

"No. I'm not doing this. And marriage guidance, Clive ... It doesn't work. You know as well as I do: the majority of couples who walk in here together end up leaving separately."

"So, what do you suggest? Keep on drifting apart?"

"Are we?"

"Too bloody right!"

"You're starting to sound angry."

"I am angry."

"Is that necessary?"

"Damn right. And do you know why?"

"Because you care. Because you want things to be the way they used to be. You want to be the alpha male and me the dutiful wife. But I'm not—"

"Oh for God's sake, SHUT UP!"

Clive got up and started pacing the room.

"Well, we are in a bit of a strange mood today, aren't we?" Susan said, using a tone of voice she immediately regretted.

Clive didn't reply, but when he turned towards her she was startled to see tears in his eyes.

"Clive!"

She'd never seen him cry before.

"God, Susan, you must think I am so fucking stupid."

Susan passed him the box of Kleenex. It was empty. She felt driven to stand, and went around the desk to put an arm round him. He shrugged her arm off and turned away, tottering over to the radiator and falling against it in a slump whilst flattening the calendar welded across the top.

"Why *do* you have a fucking calendar of Coventry in here anyway?"

"I guess it's the finishing touch to this ghastly interior. Look, if this room was at all bearable, I'd never get rid of the poor bastards."

"Impressive psychology."

"Oh, Clive," Susan said, reaching for his arm, helping him up and then nestling him into her shoulder.

They stood still, hugging for a moment in silence.

"*You do know how much I love you. Don't you?*" he whispered into her ear with an intensity that induced a fresh wave of tears.

"Yes, yes, Clive. Don't you worry. It's going to be OK. Everything is going to be OK. We can talk through this. There's nothing that can't be fixed."

They froze for a moment. Clive, head bowed and clasped to her bosom. The only sound, that of his heavy breathing; his sobs and sighs dissipating as he regained his composure.

After a moment or two of calm, Clive broke away and slouched over one of the navy chairs in front of her desk. She noticed that a streak of his snot had dribbled across the sleeve of her cardigan.

"Sit down!" he suddenly shouted, snapping into a colder mood and making her jump.

His ferocity frightened her and was enough to make her comply immediately.

Clive paused. There was silence. Seconds seemed to be passing in hours.

"What is it, Clive? What's the matter?"

"Do you know something?"

He spoke with a wild stare in his eyes.

"What?"

"You think you know someone. Know them better than anyone else. You feel so close—"

"Clive—"

"No! Shut up, Susan!"

"OK, sorr—"

"Please, just shut the fuck up! There you are, Susan. That's it in a nutshell, isn't it? You make it your business to listen to all sorts of pathetic drivel from people you barely know every day of the week. For hours. For fucking hours. But you won't listen to me for two bloody minutes. So SSSSH!" Clive said, raising a shaky finger to his lips. "Ssssh!"

She wondered if he'd been drinking.

"What is it, Clive? What have I done?" she whispered.

"As I was saying," Clive continued. "You think you know someone. You think you can trust someone. They'll tell you they love you. They'll make out they care, but then one day BANG! It's over. It's amazing. The dynamic of a relationship is like an elastic band. At first, so, so tight. And then it stretches and stretches, the tension building and building and building, and then BANG! It snaps, and you've lost everything. The trust and the tension are gone. Broken. Gone forever. And you've got nothing salvageable. Nothing at all."

"And is that how you see us? Do you feel you've lost me?"

He nodded in silence.

"Do you know something, Clive? There's a simple trick to keeping a woman. Any woman. It's a matter of confidence. Even if you're not confident, Clive, you've got to pretend to be. It's that bloody simple. It's not rocket science. Your problem's always been that you overcomplicate everything, and then when things don't work out the way you planned you feel crushed and demoralised. You're the most intelligent man I know, Clive. You've got the brain of a rocket scientist. So, why does it seem easier for everyone else to get on and get by? Why are *you* the one who's screwed up and stacking shelves in Supermark? Not that there's anything wrong with … Oh, anyway … Don't you ever wonder why that is, Clive? It's because you try too hard. Stop trying so bloody hard. Stand up, stand tall, puff your chest out and bloody get on with it."

Clive was sitting with his head in his hands. Susan couldn't be sure if he was listening, couldn't see his face. She could almost hear him thinking though; could imagine the thoughts and ideas clicking and clanking through his head. Then he looked up.

"But what about you, Susan? What can we do about you?"

"I'll always be there for you, Clive."

"No, you won't. And ... You're not my fucking mother. I don't want someone who's *always there for me*. I want someone who *really* wants *me* to be there with *them*. Do you long for me to come home, Susan? Do you yearn for my company? I don't bloody think so."

"I love you, Clive."

"Yeah, like I love Dean Martin and the cat next door, but I don't want to shag them."

"Look, Clive, let's not do this here. This is my office. It's lunchtime. Why don't you take me out for a coffee and a sandwich or something? We can talk this through when I get home, or tomorrow when you've finished your shift."

"It's funny, you know, I can sense the angst in this room. It has a certain chill. It's cold. Like a coldstore. And it radiates sadness, reeks of betrayal or something. It seems quite appropriate to be sitting here with you now and talking like this. Congratulations, Susan, you've created the perfect environment for emotional discharge on a most excruciating scale. I can tell you've seen a lot of tears in here. It's one of those places ... haunted. Cold. Like Glen Coe. A chamber of horrors. Cursed with the ambience of atrocities past. Truly, truly morose. I pity you having to come in to this every day."

"That's awful. A horrible thing to say."

"Yes, it is."

"This helps to pay our bills though, Clive."

Clive looked at his watch. Ten past twelve.

"Well? Will we have a coffee?" Susan asked, tentatively.

She was nervous, wanted out of the room. Out at any cost. And she would have got up and left him sitting there, sitting and staring at her desk, but she didn't trust him not to do something reckless.

But he didn't respond. Simply sat. Sat and stared.

Then, out of the corner of his eye, Clive glimpsed Susan's mobile phone light up. Susan noticed it too, but a split second later, and just as the first chord of her message alert started to *pling!* he looked up into her eyes and read the look of panic in her expression as she stared back at him. And within the nanosecond that he registered this, he felt compelled to dart his hand across the desk, seize the mobile and snatch it back into his lap.

"Clive! Give it to me!" she yelled, standing, hands on hips to give weight to the command. But this time he was going to ignore her and she knew it.

Clive pressed "open" when the little message envelope icon appeared at the top of the screen.

Fancy lunch? Bar Zero, Stranmillis, 12.30? CU there, Harry X

Clive gave Susan a glimpse of the screen, switched the phone off and thrust it into a side pocket of his fleece.

Silence.

He walked over to Susan's flip chart, ripped off the top sheet with its noughts and crosses grid and little black blob people, tossed the scrunched-up paper onto the floor, grabbed the black marker and wrote the name HARRY STRING across the fresh page in large capitals, underlined the name with a sweeping flourish then punched the board with an inky-black full stop.

"There. There's a name to conjure with: Harry Bloody String. You must think I'm as thick as champ, Susan. Do you think I don't know?"

Clive hurled the Magic Marker across the room, yanked the office phone out of its socket, snatched Susan's laptop tucked them both under his arm and stormed out, taking care to remove the key and lock the door from the outside before heading down the corridor, through reception and out of the building.

"Holy fuck!" Susan swore under her breath, sitting down and lowering her head till her forehead came to rest on the top of her desk once again.

21

12.10pm. Monday, 1 December 2008.

Harry String was sitting at the bar stabbing olives with a cocktail stick. A social animal, he felt denuded without company: awkward, exposed, inept. Finding somewhere, anywhere to rest his eyes in Bar Zero was proving a problem. He felt shifty. To the regulars he looked like a misfit to be avoided at all costs.

Bar Zero was a near neighbour of Black's, just a few doors up along the Stranmillis Road. The interior of its dining room was postmodern, minimal and self consciously fashionable. Its lunch service was as popular as its young chef was talented. The ambience was defined by the proprietor's love of Myles Davis and Chet Baker.

A second drink was ordered to keep his headache at bay and ease his discomfort. Better make it a beer, he thought; a longer drink more likely to last without having to reorder. No, better stick to wine. Beer makes your breath smell. Not ideal. And Harry could drink a bottle of wine and still feel sober.

That he shouldn't be drinking more than one or two glasses a day bothered him. It wouldn't stop him, but it bothered him. The last thing he wanted was to drink himself back into hospital and fulfil Mr Patterson's gloomiest prognosis. To discourage the temptation to binge he'd come by car – a nod towards sobriety.

What he couldn't resist, however, was thinking about a further seduction of Susan Heywood. Like the drinking he knew he shouldn't, hated himself for even contemplating it, but couldn't stop the momentum that made another fling seem an achievable goal, if not inevitable, and felt powerless to withstand the appetite that drove the craving.

Another olive. And another. And another swig of wine. The lines starting to soften.

But he still cared. Still cared enough to abandon the notion, still cared enough to have a conscience about the manipulation of Susan Heywood and feel troubled for her husband. And why would he want to inflict misery on someone he'd never met? Though the anonymity would make the act easier to execute.

It was obvious that there was something amiss in their marriage. Was it his fault if Clive couldn't satisfy his wife? Maybe Clive was the wrong guy and theirs a bad match? Anyway, he was lonely. Needed company. Dennis Nilsen had murdered for company, Harry would seduce Susan to the same end. And no one need ever know.

Another olive. And with another gulp of wine more wild and irresponsible thoughts took flight, the lines blurring.

A glance around the room.

A quarter past twelve.

Why had he arrived so bloody early? Why was he always first? If Susan were coming, she wouldn't be there for at least another fifteen minutes.

Thinking on through he observed that his manipulation of Susan Heywood fitted a pattern. He'd done it before: isolate the target of affection, lure them away from their natural habitat. Disorientate them. Tranquilise them with wine. Be enigmatic. Entertain them. Be a listening ear. Then make a move.

Harry sensed he was about to pounce; was confident that his victim would be willing. She would have to want him too though, that was fundamental to a satisfying outcome, and Harry realised that he had been grooming her to be a willing accomplice. Seduction: a subtle and ignoble art. Suddenly he was overwhelmed with self-loathing.

Harry wondered if he'd employed such skills to seduce Martha Browne. Such an unlikely partner for him. Maybe the challenge was the attraction. But then again, maybe she had seduced *him*. He had no idea.

Another sip and another. Eyes calming. Another olive and another. He was growing accustomed to his surroundings now, but growing sick of bloody olives.

"Some nuts, please," he asked, smiling at the barman who nodded with a professional detachment that seemed to say: "*You can ask me for anything you like, sir, but please don't expect me to chat to you. I don't do small talk.*"

"Dry roasted or salted?"

"Salted."

"Would you like to see a menu, sir?"

"No, it's OK, thanks. I'm waiting for someone."

Well, almost a conversation.

Harry had another look around the bar. Fuzzy vision. He had trouble focusing on the fresh tide of chattering heads arriving for lunch. He blinked. Then his eyes started to dart about the room again, making him feel agitated and twitchy. Another slurp. Another handful of nuts; the new diet leaving an avalanche of crumbs down his shirt front.

Harry couldn't resist peeking over to the entrance at regular intervals to see if Susan was coming. The next time he checked he noticed a man loitering outside the front window. The man looked in through the glass briefly. He appeared anxious. The loiterer turned away and began pacing the pavement in a manner that reminded Harry of the polar bear in Belfast Zoo that used to spend its days wandering up and down its enclosure swaying its head to the lonely rhythm of depression.

The loiterer kept glancing at his wristwatch more frequently and faster than the hands could move as if willing the time to pass. Harry recognised the trait.

Curiously, he had a golf club tucked under one arm. It looked like a three or four iron to Harry. Probably a three iron. Out of place in a brasserie or on the high street, in any case.

Judging from his body language Harry assumed that the man was being stood up by his lunch date. From time to time he would try and regain his composure by moving away from the window and leaning against a different item of street furniture: first a bin, then the lamp post, then the pole of the no parking sign; as though his predicament would seem less manifest and be less embarrassing if he kept moving and avoided being seen in the same place for too long, and all the while he glanced at his wristwatch.

Harry turned his attention back to the bar looking for a top-up. The barman was deep in conversation with a group of girls at the far end of the counter who were rewarding his attention with giggles.

"*So he CAN prostitute himself!*" Harry grumbled under his breath.

When he next checked the time it was twelve thirty-five. She was late now. *His* turn to feel anxious. With nowhere to look that didn't involve making eye contact, Harry picked up a flyer from the bar and found himself reading about the benefits of an oven clean:

Only £40! And if you book an oven clean by the end of December, we'll give you a £10 voucher to spend on a manicure. Just think: a clean oven and perfect nails!

Harry looked at his nails. They were far from perfect – well-chewed and raw to the quick. Nibbled away and gorged on.

"*God, she's late!*" he cursed, turning towards the front entrance and then startled by the loiterer who was now looming large in the brasserie window, resting both hands against the glass to shield his eyes so that he could better see into the dining room. The man was scanning the restaurant, analysing each customer in turn. His gaze rested on Harry. For once Harry didn't avert his eyes but stared straight back. The man twisted his head like a confused puppy, held his stare, thinking hard, but then turned away, kicking the roadside bin he'd been leaning on and then lashing out at it with the golf club.

Another drink. Another bowl of nuts. Harry was growing concerned. Twelve forty and still no sign of Susan. He tried sending her a message, but she didn't reply.

She couldn't be coming. Must be standing him up. If she was coming but running late, she would have texted him by now. But there'd been nothing. He'd give her another five minutes and then hobble down the street to the car and drive back to his studio.

Perhaps it would be better if she didn't show up. His conscience would be the clearer for it. No one would get hurt – neither Susan nor her husband. Maybe they would stand a better chance of resolving their marital problems. And why was he doing this anyway? For what benefit? For whom?

Harry stared down at the floor in a trance-like state, willing her to come, only to be brought to his senses by the rising mumbling hubbub of the lunchtime diners and the clatter of cutlery.

Enough. Time was up. A relief really.

"My bill, please?" Harry called, attempting to wrest the barman's attention away from his groupies and keen to escape back to a calmer reality.

"Are we not going to have the pleasure of serving you lunch today, sir?"

What the fuck does it look like, you imbecile? he would have liked to have said but shrugged and offered a weak smile instead.

Harry fished a couple of scrunched up tenners from his trouser pocket, slapped them on the small tray with the bill slip, eased himself off his stool and sidled out of the bar.

He pulled up the collar of his coat as he stepped out onto the pavement and then turned to check the whereabouts of the loiterer with the golf club. The loiterer, who had started to move along the road, spotted Harry emerge, stared back and squinted whilst craning his head forward. Harry smiled briefly, then turned away and shuffled off towards his car.

"HARRY STRING?"

The shout broke a flow of consciousness that had Harry in an imaginary conversation with Susan about why she hadn't turned up and in which he wasn't sure whether to berate her or be understanding.

No. Be cool! he counselled. *Be cool!*

But then he heard his name being shouted again.

"HARRY! HARRY STRING!"

He turned round, hoping against hope that he was going to see the smiling visage of an old friend, but was met with the grimacing face of the man with the golf club moving towards him at speed but still some way off.

"HEY! ARE YOU HARRY STRING?" the man shouted at him in a commanding schoolmasterly kind of voice, which Harry imagined could paralyse a ten-year-old at twenty paces.

Denial the best form of defence, Harry shook his head. But too late. He'd already responded. The game was up. He could see malice in the man's eyes and noticed that his grip on the golf club was tightening to a point where his knuckles were turning white. There was such pulsating hate in the man's expression that Harry thought it time to retreat at haste.

Harry, whose knees were now weak with fear, wobbled away as fast as his mangled pins would allow. He chanced a glance over his shoulder whereupon his worst fears were confirmed when he glimpsed the man closing in on him fast.

Then reality struck: *it's Clive Bloody Heywood! Clive Bloody Heywood!* The moment of revelation accompanied by the realisation that serious harm was headed his way.

All the physiotherapy in the world could not have equipped Harry String with the athleticism required to escape his adversary who, though older, could outwalk Harry even when Harry tried to run. Within a few strides Clive was bearing down on his victim, one who preferred to keep struggling away from his assailant rather than turning around to confront him, as though the act of not looking at Clive Heywood would render him invisible and immune from violence.

Catching up, it was simple for Heywood to hook Harry's right leg from under him with one deft swing of his golf club and send him tumbling to the pavement.

Harry rolled over and then found himself looking up into Clive Heywood's glowering eyes.

"OK, SO WHAT ARE YOU GOING TO DO NOW, YOU FAT BASTARD?" Harry screamed, raising himself up onto his elbows, defiant and counter-attacking with the best insult he could come up with at short notice.

Clive Heywood didn't speak but swung the three iron high above his shoulders and steadied himself for the decisive blow. A *coup de golf*.

Keep your head still, swing with a firm grip and smooth momentum. Maintain club head speed, nice and steady, and remember to follow through whilst keeping your eye on the ... er ... head. Tempo! Tempo!

Clive's golf swing was ingrained. He flexed his spine at the top of his backswing and started a controlled downward stroke, the club head on a collision course with Harry String's right temple.

Bystanders froze, gaped and gasped. Harry closed his eyes and covered his face as best he could with his free hand in preparation for the impact.

My poor brain was his last thought as he rolled up into a ball.

But then nothing. A silent pause. And then a weird sound. A whining noise that appeared to be emanating from the back of Clive Heywood's throat: high-pitched and pained, brief but audible. Sharp. Not unlike the screech of an owl.

Harry had braced his head in his hands, wincing in expectation of the blow and was now wondering why there was a delay in its delivery. Gingerly he opened his left and then his right eye, and in peeping through splayed fingers was relieved to see that Clive was tottering backwards. And although he hadn't released his grip on the golf club, Harry noticed that Clive was now holding the weapon in only one hand; the other clawing at his chest, his face contorted with pain and draining of colour.

And as Harry stirred from the foetal position he had assumed on the pavement, Clive Heywood started to stagger forwards towards him releasing and then dropping the three iron which hit the ground with a *clang*. Clive lifted his other hand till both were raking at his chest, grasping handfuls of navy polyester fleece as he buckled at the knees and started to topple over.

Harry rolled across to try and cushion Clive as he collapsed onto the pavement and just in time to gather his head in both hands as if he were a goalie saving a penalty.

"What's wrong, mate?" Harry asked as they lay side by side.
"*Heart!*" Clive gasped. "*Feet up. Please. Feet up!*"
"What?"
"LIFT MY FUCKING FEET UP!"
"Oh, right, right. Sorry. How's that? Any better?"
But Clive Heywood was past conversation, had blacked out.
"Someone call an ambulance! Hey! You! Yes, you! Call an ambulance. CALL A FUCKING AMBULANCE ... AND CALL IT NOW!" Harry shouted at the nearest pedestrian.

The wail of a siren was not long in coming.

"What have you done to him, you freak!" Susan Heywood screamed at Harry as she ran up and found the two men sprawled across the pavement. Harry recognised her expression: it was Clive Heywood's evil grimace in female form. He glanced over to the three iron, fearing that it might yet come into play. He stood up and clutched Susan by the forearms and steered her away as a paramedic took over at Clive's side, delving into a large bag of gear to retrieve a defibrillator.

Harry ushered Susan into a doorway to create some working space for the paramedic.

"Shit, Harry, what the *fuck's* going on?"

"It seems the strain of attempting to beat me to death with a golf club was too much for his heart, I'm afraid."

"Is he, is he going to—"

"D*ie*? Yes, of course he is. We all do eventually. In the short-term, no. Well, I doubt it. I just hope no one reports him to the police."

"Well you won't be, will you, Harry?"

Harry chose not to respond.

A second paramedic appeared with a stretcher. Harry and Susan stood back and watched the medics work away at Clive and then strap him onto the trolley. As they made their way to the rear of the ambulance Susan followed.

"Is he going to be OK?" she asked, in tears now and tugging at the first paramedic's sleeve.

The paramedic ignored the question but placed a hand on Susan's forearm.

"Are you relatives?" he asked with gravitas, looking from Susan to Harry and back.

"I'm his wife."

"Good. Would you like to accompany him to the hospital?"

The paramedics loaded Clive into the back of the ambulance then beckoned to Susan to join them.

Harry grabbed at Susan's wrist.

"Where were you?"

"Please. Not now."

"You OK? He didn't do any—"

"Leave it, Harry. Just leave it."

Susan wrenched herself free from Harry's grip and climbed aboard. The paramedics looked at one another, exchanged a shrug and then slammed the doors behind them.

"I'll call you later," Harry shouted after her in vain.

The ambulance drove off, lights flashing, siren screaming.

Harry picked up the golf club and set off for his car. The three iron worked well as a walking stick. He'd hang on to it.

Harry glanced back towards the brasserie. The barman was standing in the doorway watching the conclusion of the drama. Harry gave him a nod, but the barman either ignored him or didn't see, turned and went inside, his showbiz smile returning as he made for the counter.

"We won't know for a few days how serious the damage is, Mrs Heywood. The next forty-eight hours are crucial. We've sedated him; we'll get him stable and monitor him carefully. How old is your husband?"

"Fifty-three."

"Good. He's relatively young, then."

The cardiologist standing beside Clive's bed in intensive care was reassuring but businesslike; Susan, in shock.

"He's quite active," Susan added.

"Good."

"He jogs a fair bit and plays golf nearly every day."

"Excellent. Very good."

Susan couldn't help but be distracted by the lines of data on the monitors and tried to decipher meaning from the numbers.

"Look, you've been here for a good while now, Mrs Heywood. You can stay here tonight if you like, but there's not much you can do. As I say, he's sedated and stable. Why not go home, get a good night's sleep and come back in the morning refreshed. We'll phone you straight away if there's any change, but I doubt that that will be the case."

"If you're sure. Really sure."

"Is there anybody you would like us to call to come and take you home?"

"No. I'll get a cab. It's not far."

As Susan left the intensive care unit, she came across Harry String waiting in the corridor outside. Catching sight of Harry brought on tears. She stopped, buried her face in her hands and wept. Harry moved towards her, but was fearful that she might turn on him.

"Hey, it's OK. It's OK."

"Oh, for Christ's sake, Harry! What have I done?"

Harry was relieved when she lent into his arms for a hug.

"It's all right, Susan. I'm sure he'll pull through."

This brought on more and louder weeping.

Harry decided to say as little as possible.

"Come on. I'll drive you home," he whispered, leading Susan to the lifts.

The journey passed in silence. The quiet only broken by Susan's directions: "Next left", "Next right" and "Straight ahead".

"Thank you, Harry," she said coldly, when they pulled up.

"Here, let me," Harry said, prising himself out of the driver's seat to open the passenger door. Susan didn't have the willpower to argue as he guided her through the garden gate.

She let them both into the house and then wandered through the hall to the kitchen where she stopped in front of the sink and gazed out of the window across the thin strip of grass that constituted the garden.

Harry followed then fumbled round the kitchen looking for teabags. He switched on the kettle.

They didn't speak. Harry leaning against the stove; Susan leaning against the sink. She began to cry again.

"I'm making you a brew."

She ignored him. Simply stared out the window, sobbing.

"Susan, he'll be all right."

Susan swung round and gave Harry her fierce face again.

"But don't you see, Harry? That's it, isn't it? There's a part of me that doesn't want him to be all right. Don't you see? In my heart of hearts I'm hoping he's going to die. And how's that for loyalty? The poor man has done nothing but love me, and I'm standing here half-hoping he's going to fucking die. How bloody awful? How bloody awful am I? Are we?"

Harry stepped over and shepherded her to the small kitchen table. They sat down.

"Don't you see, Harry? The terrible thing, the awful, awful truth I now know is ... is that I don't love him at all. Not any more. The poor sod's lying in a hospital bed, could die any minute, and, subconsciously at least, I'm hoping he doesn't make it. I'm *actually* hoping he doesn't make it. What do you make of that, hey? I tell you what I'd say if any of my bloody clients came in and made a confession like that. God, that would be an easy situation to analyse."

"Look, you're in shock, Susan. Don't be so hard on yourself."

"Oh, fuck off, Harry! What the hell would you know about anything? You're not exactly a paragon of virtue and sensible living. Who's ever going to pick you for a bloody mentor?"

"Well—"

"Oh, don't worry, Harry. This has got fuck all to do with you. You're just the bloody eye candy. A cock. Do you really know what the sad thing is though? Do you? Do you know, Harry?"

Harry knew it was safer to keep his mouth shut.

"OK, I'll tell you. When I saw Clive lying in the gutter and you leaning down over him, I was pissed off because I knew *we*, you and me, that is, wouldn't be able to have lunch together as planned. I mean, how callous is that, Harry, eh? How fucking callous is that?"

"You don't mean that, Susan."

"It's not about what I mean or don't mean, Harry. It's what I felt. The instinct. The gut feeling. What I thought. And, it was all about me. Me, me, bloody me. He deserves so much better than that. So much better than me."

They sat and drank their tea in silence.

"I'll call you this evening," Harry murmured after a long pause.

"Battery's down."

"Give me your landline number, then."

Susan scribbled the number on the back of an old envelope.

"I'll call," Harry said, getting up to leave. "And ring me if you need anything. Anything at all. You know, if you need company."

"Sure."

But he knew she wouldn't.

There was a coldness and finality to the conversation that unnerved them both.

22

10.30am. Saturday, 13 December 2008.

"You know, you've never asked me about the crash."
"What?"
"About the car crash. The actual crash. Aren't you even a little bit curious?" Harry asked his father, telephone tucked under his chin, his hands buttering some toast.
"Oh, for Christ's sake, Harry. Please just leave it, son."
"I just want to talk about the crash."
"I know all about the bloody crash, Harry."
"You've never asked *me*, though. *We've* never discussed it."
"Don't be daft. Course we have."
"When?"
"When you were in hospital."
"So, how come we never talk about it now?"
"Because I'd rather forget the whole damn thing!"
"Ironic."
"Maybe, but I don't want to go over it any more."
"Pity."
"Look, are you coming up today?" Harry's father asked, changing the subject and assuming a cheerier tone. He wasn't a great conversationalist at the best of times. Didn't like talking on the phone. Would rather convey his message and be done.

A couple of hours later Harry was cradling a beer and watching the surfers hurtling inshore along the beach below his father's house in Portstewart.
"So, why don't we ever talk about the accident, Dad?"

"Just."

"Just what?"

"Oh, you know."

"But you must see why I want to?"

"It's just—"

"What? Did it scare you that much?"

"*Of course!*" his father snapped. He paused before continuing: "Imagine how awful it would be to see one of *your* kids lying in a hospital bed, Harry. If I lost you, well—"

"But you haven't. Look, I know you don't like to be too open about stuff, but it helps me to talk."

"Well, a lot of the *stuff* you like to talk about, I find a little difficult."

"What do you mean?"

"Well, I've never been divorced and I'm fed up with talking about yours. And then there's your tangled love life."

"What's so tangled about it?" Harry asked, smiling and trying to sound calm.

"Well, after the divorce, when you needed time to yourself, you know, to reflect, you went and bit off more than you could chew with that other girl."

"Who?"

"Don't know her name."

"Martha?"

"Yeah, that's the one."

"Anyway, carry on."

"Must I?"

"Please, Dad."

"Well, as I say, you got through the divorce. You'd had a lot on your plate. Then you decided to start seeing someone else. Not that I was interested. Except, as you know, you were broke. You couldn't afford to buy a loaf of bread let alone take a girl out to dinner. I thought it a bit premature. Didn't think you were ready. That's all."

"Obviously."

"All the same, you were full of it. Tried to talk to me about it. All kinds of soppy rubbish. But, I'm sorry, it wasn't of any interest to me. I cared more about how the kids were coping."

"Of course."

"And, it was around that time that you had your accident. Something happened that made you flip your lid. Something to do with that girl, I thought. I had no idea what it was all about. One day everything was all sweetness and light and the next you were in this big depression. It wasn't like you. I wouldn't have thought something like that would bother you. Let's face it, you've been round the block a few times, Harry."

"Oh, thanks!"

"Anyway, the whole thing with that girl seemed to poleaxe you. And you wouldn't listen to anybody. We all tried. And then you wouldn't shut up about how miserable you were and all that. On and on and on. And then your behaviour became a little odd, to say the least. Next thing we knew you were in hospital having your skull popped open like a tin of sardines."

"You didn't meet Martha, then?"

"No. You kept her to yourself for some reason."

"I imagine I was being cautious, Dad."

"You? Cautious?"

"Yes!"

"So, what happened?"

"Don't know. But I've started to piece bits together. It's coming back to me in fits and starts. It's a pity in a way as, as the saying goes: *what you don't know won't hurt you.*"

"And *curiosity killed the cat.*"

"What?"

"Curiosity ... It could cripple you. I mean it. Tread carefully, son."

"Maybe."

"Look, you're well out of it. Keep well away. You know some relationships aren't ever going to work no matter how hard you try. So just stay away."

"Perhaps, Dad, but I'd like to hear what she's got to say. Get some kind of explanation."

Harry's father grunted, rolled his eyes, thought for a moment and then wandered off to fetch more beer from the fridge.

"By the way, I found this," his father said, brandishing a large Manila envelope as he shuffled back into the room. He tossed it to Harry.

"Huh?"

"It's yours."

"What's in it?"

"A cassette."

"Oh?"

"Yeah, I'd almost forgotten I had it."

"What's on it?"

"Music."

"Right."

"Oh, and you talking a bit."

"What? What about?"

"I don't know. I think it was for her. For Maria. I think you made it for Maria—"

"Martha."

"That's the one. Anyway, it was found in your car after the crash. The police found it in the tape player after the rest of your stuff had been returned."

Harry pulled the cassette out of the envelope.

"Oh my God! How embarrassing. A home-made compilation tape. I haven't seen one of these for years. I must have been keen."

"Mmm, that's my point."

"And here it is ... *Martha Browne*. Her name and address are written here on the side of the tape. Thank goodness you didn't send it to her, Dad."

"Here, let me have a look ... no. Didn't see that. Writing's a bit small. I wouldn't have sent it, anyway. Not whilst you were still ... Well anyway, I didn't."

"And you didn't listen to it?"

"Well, to be honest, I did sneak a brief listen when the cops handed it back. You were in hospital and weren't doing too well at the time. So when I heard you mumbling in a soppy voice, I switched it off PDQ. It was upsetting."

"Bizarre!"

"I think you were a little obsessed with Maria."

"Martha!"

Harry started to play the tape on the drive back to Belfast:

"*Hi, Martha, I put this tape together for you to give you a small taste of our summer ...*"

But, like his dad, Harry switched it off almost immediately, cringing at the sound of his own voice. He thanked the Lord that he'd got it back so he could dispose of it before it caused him any further embarrassment.

Harry spent the rest of the drive deep in thought, wondering how he could have ended up acting so out of character. If the cassette was typical of his behaviour at that time, it wasn't surprising she'd called him a weirdo and ran for the hills. Then he wondered if the tape and his obsessive conduct had something to do with his condition and were a symptom of his aneurysm; a prelude to the haemorrhage.

Back home Harry tried phoning Susan. There was no answer on her landline number and her mobile went straight to voicemail.

"Susan. Harry. Please call. Hope Clive's OK."

But she didn't call back.

On the spur of the moment he punched in the old number he had for Martha Browne. A stranger answered; the number reassigned.

23

3.30pm. Monday, 6 April 2009.

"*I'll have a consonant, please.*"
  "*H.*"
  "*Now a vowel.*"
  "*E.*"
  "*And another vowel.*"
  "*A.*"

Clive Heywood failed to notice the flash of sunlight suddenly turn the lawn lime green from where he was sprawled across the settee. His attention was focused on the TV as he struggled to make a nine-letter word from the letters: H.E.C.I.O.G.N.A.L. One hand slapped his forehead for inspiration as the other pulled at the crotch of his pyjamas to ensure his wedding tackle was well stowed lest anyone should catch him accidentally exposed whilst engrossed in the final round of *Countdown*. Surprise visitors were not uncommon since his return home.

"*Change*," he mumbled at the screen, underwhelmed with his six-letter solution.

Four weeks after being admitted to hospital, Clive was discharged to complete his recuperation at home. He was told that it would be at least another three or four months before he would be fit enough to start back at Supermark. Clive feigned displeasure at this news but was quietly relieved.

Healthwise he felt fine. Diet, rest and gentle exercise had done him a power of good. His stomach was flatter, his clothes looser-fitting and, whilst his confidence had taken a knock, he felt in much better physical condition and looked forward to being able to put his new-found energy to work.

The heart attack had been mild. Thanks to the prompt actions of the paramedics there was little damage to the muscle. In some ways he had been lucky. His consultant told him to think of it as a wake-up call.

It annoyed him, though, when the consultant kept recounting the good deeds of the passer-by outside Bar Zero who had loosened his clothing and made sure he was lying in the recovery position.

Clive intimated gratitude with a smile forced through clenched teeth.

Later, tests revealed that his cholesterol was at an acceptable level, his valves were in working order and his arteries cleared of obstruction.

"Then why the heart attack?" he enquired.

"Pressures of work?"

"Hardly!"

"Stress, then. Something's been bothering you?"

"Possibly," Clive muttered, cursing his wife and her lover.

He was less pleased about the prospects for his golf handicap since golfing was decreed off limits for the time being, along with most other sporting activity. His days were therefore filled with short walks, long telephone conversations, emailing, surfing the net and watching TV. More game shows. More general knowledge.

He had tried to enter the game show *Who Wants to Be a Millionaire* by phoning the number at the bottom of the screen.

"*What is the capital of Australia? Is it: a) Cairns b) Sydney c) Canberra or d) Melbourne?*" was the simple qualifying question posed on the automated phone-in line.

"C. Canberra," he bellowed into the mouthpiece.

"*Congratulations! That is the correct answer. If selected, on which of these two dates would you be able to attend the show? Tuesday, 14th or Wednesday, 15th of April?"* came the automated reply.

"Neither! None! I'm crippled! I can't leave the bloody house!" Clive yelled down the phone when reality bit. He slammed the receiver back onto its base and then smiled to regain his composure and tease his blood pressure down a little.

Susan was keeping out of his way. They hadn't had a long conversation since his return home – certainly hadn't discussed the events leading up to his illness. It was obvious they had a problem to tackle, but both lacked the resolve to tackle it. Clive didn't want to bother himself with arguing with Susan; he was too frail and didn't have the energy for a confrontation and she was worried lest she say or do anything that might induce another heart attack. They both trusted that there would be time to settle matters later.

With Susan out at work all day and getting home late, he had no way of knowing if she was still in contact with String. She had reassured him that she wasn't and wouldn't be. Again – because it raised his hackles to even think about Harry String – he decided not to pursue the matter and took it on trust that she was telling the truth. But still, it worried him that she was being so evasive.

Clive had been told to get as much sleep as possible and, since he took his recuperation seriously, made sure he was in bed by ten. He would announce his departure to the bedroom in the hope that Susan would accompany him, but she always seemed to find an excuse to stay up. A favourite programme to watch. An article to finish reading. A report to write.

If he was awake long enough, he might hear her creeping up the stairs later, trying not to disturb him, and would then be aware of her sliding carefully under the covers lest she might wake him, as if wary that he might roll over and start pestering her.

And Susan wasn't happy. She could sense Clive's resentment, his simmering anger. She didn't like being the guilty party, didn't like that she would have to carry the burden of her misdemeanour for as long as they were together, and knew that the incident was etched on his conscience like an unloved tattoo: out of sight and seldom seen, but there as a permanent reminder. She didn't want to feel like a second-class citizen for much longer and doubted if he would have the generosity of spirit to forgive her any time soon either.

Susan sought the advice of a colleague.

"Susan. I'll be straight with you. What percentage of the couples we see in here where the man or woman has been unfaithful – which, let's face it, is most of them – find a resolution and can move on together as partners?"

Susan struggled to find an answer.

"God, we really do get exposed to the seamier side of life, don't we?" Was the best she could come up with before sighing and shuffling back to her office to try and diffuse another volatile couple.

Susan took to going out most lunchtimes. Wasn't sure why, but had an uneasy feeling that it might be due to a subliminal desire to run into Harry String.

She was in Black's one day when he wandered in. It was about four months after Clive's heart attack. He ignored her at first by busying himself around the counter and taking ages over ordering a drink to make sure she was on her own before sauntering over. As he approached her table he slowed, stopped, smiled and then shrugged.

Impassive, she paused then nodded down towards the empty banquette opposite.

Once seated, Harry looked up and stared into her eyes.

Conversation was slow in coming.

"Clive?"

"Fine."

"You?"

"I'm OK."

They stopped to slurp their coffee.

"And what about you, Harry?" Susan asked to break the lengthy silence.

"My head feels like it's in a vice most of the time. Like I'm paralysed down one side of my face or something. I'm not, but it kind of feels that way. Numb and tingly."

"Have you told anyone?"

"Just you."

"Well, that's pretty stupid, Harry. Tell your doctor."

"Mmm," he mumbled, ignoring her. "Funny, you know, Keira used to say that a lot."

"What?"

"*'That's stupid, Harry.'*"

"Maybe she had a point."

"Towards the end she graduated from saying, *'That's stupid'* to *'You're stupid'*."

"Mmm. Anyway, how are things going with Keira?"

"Improving."

"Good. And your kids?"

"They seem fine."

Another long pause for slurping coffee. The conversation losing impetus. Harry took a deep breath.

"Are you really OK, Susan?"

"Oh ... I ... we ... Oh, I don't know."

"You don't know?"

"No."

"Clive?"

"It's complicated."

"Will he get over you know what?"

"He'll have to. We're married."

"Ah, marriage! The first step on the road to divorce."

"Bravo! I should have that embroidered and framed for my office wall."

"Nice."

"But people can, and do, get over these things, Harry. It's not uncommon."

"Neither's divorce."

"OK, hang on. Is there a reason for your cynicism, or do you just enjoy making everyone else feel as bloody miserable as you are?"

"No. Sorry. Really, good luck to you both."

"Oh, thank you *so* much."

"No, seriously."

"Well, thanks."

"And is *he* going to be OK? Get better, I mean?"

"Yes."

"'Yes'? Just 'yes'?"

"Yes."

"Good."

"So, what are you up to, Harry?"

"Getting better too. Getting mobile. And I'm finally, finally going in for my surgery."

"Soon?"

"The end of this week actually. I'll be in for four or five days."

"Great!"

"Yeah. I'll be sitting at home with my feet up for a while when I'm out if you fancy popping—"

"Can't. I've got to look after Clive now. I've been such a cow; the least I can do is take care of him when he needs me. That and keep out of trouble."

"Is that what I am?"

"You know what I mean."

Another prolonged pause for slurping.

"Don't stay with him if you don't love him."

"That's easy to say, Harry."

"Of course it is, but whatever you do, if you are of a mind to leave him, don't put it off forever. You don't want to find yourself a bedridden eighty-year-old living with someone you have nothing in common with and have become a stranger to."

"Well, that's my business."

"Of course."

"Actually, Harry, maybe *you* should try marriage guidance counselling as a career. I think you'd be good."

"And why not?"

"Look, I've got to go back to work. Where're you headed?"

"Home, I guess."

"HARRY!" A loud voice boomed across the room as Robert Doherty popped up at their table, drizzling coffee down his trousers from an overfilled takeaway cup.

"Jesus, Doherty. You made me jump!" Harry scowled. "Robert. Susan. Susan. Robert."

"Please, have one of these. You never know," Robert said, putting his coffee down and handing Susan his card; Harry frowning beside him.

"Er, nice to meet you, Robert, but I'm afraid I've got to dash," Susan said pocketing the card, shaking his hand and then sliding off the banquette to scurry back to work whilst failing to notice the shadowy figure watching from the park bench across the road.

"You're like a fucking bus, Robert," Harry said with a grin once they were alone.

"I know, that's three times in as many months. Anyway ... Who was that?"

"That's just left? Oh, that's Susan."

"Who's Susan?"

"Don't ask."

"Mmm, interesting."

"No, it's not."

"Attractive, though."

"Let's not go there."

"But more importantly, have you—"

"Have I what, Robert?"

"Seen anything of you know who?"

"Er, Martha? Course not. You told me to stay away."

"I meant to phone you, actually."

"Oh, why?"

"The Bible you gave me. It reminded me—"

"What?"

"She's a Christian. I probably should have told you before."

"Don't worry, I'm not a *total* idiot. I kind of guessed that. Anyway, so what?"

"Oh, nothing."

"No, go on."

"Are you a Christian, Harry?"

"No, not in the strictest sense. Why?"

"She's a born-again."

"A what?"

"A born-again. She takes her religion very seriously, that's all. She's a born-again Christian."

"So?"

"Well, you're not."

"So?"

"Well, think about it, Harry,"

"How do you know all this stuff anyway?"

"Oh, that's my secret," Robert said, starting to make a move to leave.

"Hang on …"

Robert was half out the door.

"Can't, mate. Got a deadline."

Once home, Harry phoned Susan. She was still at work. He phoned her on the hour hoping he might catch her in-between appointments.

"This'd better be important, Harry."

"Need to ask you something, Susan."

"OK, but be quick. I've got a couple waiting outside and they're miserable enough as it is."

"What do you know about born-again Christians?"

"They're fundamentalists. They can be very strict. Well, compared to your average Church of Ireland churchgoer, say. Though there's no reason why you can't be both. But, yeah, they're pretty extreme."

"So, you know all about them, then?"

"Well, a bit. I come across them in my line of work from time to time. As you can imagine, divorce is difficult for those with strong religious convictions. Born-agains in particular. They wouldn't condone or recognise divorce. If it happens at all it's usually something that's being forced on them."

"What about their religious beliefs?"

"What? Do you mean, *what are they?*"

"Yeah."

"Well, they believe the Bible quite literally. For instance, most would be creationists."

"And they ..."

"Believe the Bible word for word. They believe the world is only about six thousand years old—"

"Dinosaurs?"

"Never existed."

"They take their timeline from Genesis. From Adam to Cain and Abel and then on and on and on. But being 'saved' is *the* big thing. They believe that you need to be saved in order to avoid eternal damnation, that is, to be accepted into heaven."

"What, saved from hell?"

"Yes."

"How?"

"By being born again. They believe that we all need to be born again. You know, baptised again in order to accept Christ. In order to achieve salvation: eternal life."

"And what about the rest of us, then?"

"We're all doomed, I'm afraid."

"And what about relationships? Could they have a relationship with someone who isn't a born-again, an agnostic or an atheist, say?"

"I think it would be frowned upon. Not impossible, but frowned upon. Undesirable."

"And marriage to a non-believer?"

"Frowned upon."

"Really?"

"You sound surprised."

"Well, it's all alien to me, but I guess it might explain a thing or two."

"Oh, hang on, don't tell me—"

"Yeah, Martha Browne."

"She's a born-again?"

"Apparently."

"Well, there you go. That explains a lot."

"Maybe. Just makes me want to wash my hands of the whole damn thing."

"Actually, no. No, you don't. You need to find out what really happened to put your mind at rest."

"Do I?"

"Yes."

"Possibly."

"No. Definitely!"

"Oh."

"Do you know where to find her?"

"I think so."

"Well, go and see her. See what's she's got to say. And then, for God's sake, forget that she ever existed!"

24

8.50pm. Thursday, 9 April 2009.

Martha Browne was staring out into the rain through the front door of the shop she managed in Belfast. Lost in thought, she had been cast adrift on a daydream to the rhythm of The Smiths' "How Soon Is Now?" booming from the store's CD player. Her arms were folded across her chest as she waited for a customer to emerge from the last trickle of late-night shoppers.

Bad weather and business was slow, but, no matter, she wasn't selling matches. As she gazed into the black she imagined herself as a mannequin propped up in the shop window of a quiet backstreet boutique. And the mannequin in her daydream was sad, marvelled at the world she watched through the glass but could never join. For she could never be a real girl, just a plastic imitation. She could cry no tears, could express no emotion, would never experience the joy of dancing, eating or drinking; could neither love, nor laugh.

Martha Browne flinched when, for the first time in a long time, her mind wandered onto the subject of Harry String. She could barely remember the days when she had thought of him with any affection and longed for him to call her, meet her, hold her in his arms. When she thought of him now she felt uncomfortable, almost despised him for making her think she had loved him.

And how could she have loved him? So much baggage. A divorcee. An atheist. And so much older, forty-four years to her twenty-eight. Surely she had only *thought* that she loved him? But then ...

No. Enough, enough. She shook her head, closed her eyes, clenched her fists and uttered an impatient grunt to clear her mind of Harry String.

Martha Browne turned her focus onto the shoppers ambling past her door and, like the mannequin in her dream, did not move, was frozen. Then, in the quiet of that moment, she prayed in silence for the passers-by and for the souls of those yet to seek salvation. She chose to omit Harry String from her prayers, however, having decided that it was imperative to shut him out from her thoughts and eradicate him from her memory at the earliest opportunity.

Nine fifteen and the rain was heavy over the city centre. Damp and darkness: a combination guaranteed to lower the spirits.

Harry String was sheltering in a shop doorway on the corner of Upper Queen Street and the lane that ran up to Martha's store. He felt glum, but was at least dry for the moment.

Since there was late-night shopping in Belfast, he remembered that she'd be finishing work at around nine thirty. In any case, he'd wait till nine forty-five. She was sure to pass his way before long; it was her route home. And she walked. Even in bad weather she walked. She was sure to bump into him.

The longer he waited the more awkward Harry felt. He hated to impose on others – never did. But he needed to do this. Needed to talk to her and get some answers. The uncertainty had been driving him mad, had driven him to stand shivering in this shop doorway feeling furtive.

Time dragged. The only entertainment came from the rain drumming on the plastic canopy above and the wind bullying a paper cup as it bobbed on the puddle below.

Maybe she'll be getting a taxi? Surely the shower's too heavy to walk in?

Nine forty passed and still no sign. God, how he hated waiting. But then he heard the rattle of a metal grille. He looked up the alley towards Martha's store where he could now see a woman in silhouette pulling down the front shutter. And then, before it was completely down and padlocked, two more figures ducked under and out onto the pavement. They all huddled together beneath an umbrella, then following a brief conversation went their separate ways. Two turned away up towards the city hall whilst the other headed down the lane towards him. Harry instantly recognised Martha Browne's feline glide.

"Martha!" he said, trying to sound surprised to see her but was then knocked back when he caught her startled expression.

She wouldn't make eye contact with him and started to accelerate past, hunching her shoulders, bowing her head and clasping her umbrella a little tighter to her chest.

"Look. I'm sorry. I really didn't mean to scare you!" he called after her.

Within a few steps she stopped, spun round and glared back at him.

"But you do, Harry! You do! Doesn't that worry you just a little? That I *am* actually scared of you? Is that what you really want?"

"I found this," Harry said, holding up the envelope containing the tape.

"What the hell's that?"

"It's a tape. I recorded it for you."

"What's on it? *The Carpenters Greatest Hits?*"

"Oh, come on—"

"Well, you made a lot of stuff for me, Harry. Then there were the poems and the letters. I got fed up with all your sentimental crap, to be honest. It all got too much."

"I know, I know. I got a little crazy. That's what I'm trying to say. I can see that now. Yes, I got a little crazy. And, I'm sorry—"

"Well, it's a little bit late for that now, I'm afraid."

"I was ill. I really want you to know that. I WAS ILL."

Harry removed the cassette, yanked out a couple of arm

lengths of tape, wound it round and round the cassette and envelope and bundled the lot into the nearest bin.

"There. It's gone. All the crap's gone. I'm better. I've recovered."

"OK. Well done. So what do you want now?"

"Closure."

"And how am I supposed to help you with that?"

"You heard about my memory loss?"

"Who hasn't?"

"Well, I was wondering if you could help fill in some of the gaps. You know, a quick chat."

"So, why didn't you just phone me up?"

"You've changed your number."

"OK. But that's no excuse for making me jump."

"Sorry, it was a spur of the moment thing. I just thought if I bumped into—"

"Well, don't be 'bumping' into me. Ever. In fact, never again. It's creepy."

"Yes, of course. Sorry."

She started to walk away, but then slowed, stopped and turned round again.

"A quick chat, you say? Will you go away and leave me alone then?"

"Yes. Guaranteed."

"You won't come 'bumping' into me?"

"No."

"Alright," she sighed. "I know you've had a rough time, so I'll do this for you, just this once. But you've got to swear you'll stay out of my way from then on, OK?"

"Promise. A couple of questions and I'll be gone. Look, I'm sorry if I scared you."

Martha stared down onto the pavement for a few seconds.

"Right, have you got a car?"

"Yes," he said nodding down the road. "Why, do you want a lift?"

"No thanks, I'm driving."

"I didn't think you drove to work."

"Times change, Harry. And no one would walk to work in this weather."

"Fair enough."

"Anyway, why don't you meet me at Fig 7, the health food bar? Do you remember it? It's on the Lisburn Road at the top of my road."

"Yeah, I think so. Don't worry. If it's on the Lisburn Road it'll be easy enough to find. Will it still be open?"

"Yeah. If we're quick. It shuts at ten. We'll be OK as long as we're inside a few minutes before. But we can't be long, I've got a friend coming round to mine at ten thirty."

"No problem."

"Look, to be honest, I'm not really sure if this is a good idea, but maybe we both need some 'closure'," Martha said in a mocking tone whilst miming quote marks with her fingers.

She turned, dashed off and then darted down an alleyway leading to the entrance of an NCP car park. Harry stepped out into the rain and limped back towards his parking spot; the damp starting to soak into the shoulders of his leather jacket.

Before he'd reached the Volvo, Martha Browne sped past in her MG. He had to hop to one side to avoid being drenched in puddle water.

Yeah. A classic sports car with a radio cassette. Harry could remember driving her somewhere in the little white car. In the short memory clip she was laughing and placed her hand on his knee and gave him an affectionate smile.

Yeah, she's right. Times change, he thought.

The drive over to Martha Browne's neighbourhood was another arrival into daylight from the shadows of the almost forgotten. On the way his memory was prompted by familiar landmarks, and as he arrived he recognised Martha's terraced street; remembered that it backed onto the railway.

Martha was already sipping a peppermint tea when Harry walked into the bar. They were the only customers. She seemed more relaxed and offered him a smile as he approached her table and took a seat. When she deigned to share it, she had a beautiful smile, he thought.

He ordered a coffee.

"Look, as I said earlier, I know you've had a rough time. I felt terrible when I heard about your crash and the extent of your injuries. It must have been awful."

"Crap, eh?"

"Are you better now?"

"Getting there," Harry said coyly, looking down.

"Do you remember this place?"

"Did we come here?"

"Once or twice. You didn't like it much. They don't serve beer and you always complained that they don't do a builder's tea," she said, toying with a teaspoon.

They both fell silent as the conversation lulled – neither of them knowing quite how to behave or what to say.

"OK, what do you want to know?" Martha asked quietly.

"To understand what happened, that's all."

"Understand?"

"You know, what happened with us. You and me. I find the whole thing confusing. My illness, the aneurysm, might well have been exacerbated by stress—"

"Oh, and you blame me for that?"

"No, not at all. That doesn't come into it. I'd just like to know why things didn't work out. That's all. I wonder if I've missed something. I think it'd give me more confidence to move on if I knew the whole story."

"OK."

"I was really worried in case I was abusive or violent. I wasn't, was I?"

"No. Not at all. Look, we broke up. It was just one of those things. It happens."

"But it seems I didn't want it to be 'just one of those things'. From what I've learned it appears we were really close one minute and then, suddenly, not at all the next."

"I don't know. Maybe. But then you did get a bit OTT. It freaked me out."

"Why was that, do you think?"

"Don't know, but the atmosphere changed. You changed. And then there were so many things working against us too."

"Like?"

"Your age. That you're divorced. And then you seemed to lose your nerve."

"What do you mean?"

"Well, you'd always seemed so confident, which was an attractive feature, but then you seemed to grow insecure. Started sending me letters and flowers and presents all the time. And I mean, *all* the time. It got too much. Got to be a bit creepy, to be honest. So I thought it'd be better to finish with you. But then you still wouldn't stop bothering me. And that scared me. It scares me now!"

"*You're scared?* The last time I bumped into you, you know, in Belfast, you were quite scary yourself."

"Well—"

"Actually, and please don't take this the wrong way, I didn't know who the hell you were at the time. Didn't recognise you. Maybe a vague recollection. Then Keira filled me in."

"Keira? Your ex-wife?"

"Yeah. What she said really surprised me. So I checked my old mobile. Came across all the text messages you'd sent me. There's loads. They give the impression that you cared. Really cared. Actually, you've called me a weirdo, but hasn't your behaviour been a little on the odd side too?"

"Look, going out with you ... It was just a bit of fun at first. We were mates. But then when things developed it just didn't feel right. I'm only in my twenties. As I say, there's quite an age gap. I doubt if my parents would have approved. And if it wasn't going to work out long-term, it seemed better to end it sooner rather than later, before anyone got—"

"*Before anyone got hurt.*"

"Well, maybe I didn't appreciate how vulnerable you were after your divorce. If you could have been a bit cooler about the whole thing, things might have turned out differently."

"Sure. But you can't blame me for being sensitive."

"I'm not. I wouldn't. But you got *so* uptight. It's, it's—"

"A weakness?"

"Yes. And unattractive. Suffocating."

"Oh."

"Yeah. A real turn-off. And actually, Harry, I don't understand. If you lost your memory, if all your memories of me were wiped, why does any of this matter to you any more anyway? What does it matter? And, I mean, aren't you just a little bit embarrassed going over all of this?"

"No. Not at all. And as far as the memory loss is concerned, it's not permanent. The thing is, since I've started to regain the memories of the time I spent with you, I've started to have doubts about what really prompted you to end—"

"I've explained that now."

"Yeah, but I'm still not convinced."

"What more can I say?"

"You could tell me why you didn't explain any of this to me at the time. From what I can gather you wouldn't talk to me. I mean, when you told me you were a Christian, I presumed you'd have a strong moral code: be kind and considerate—"

"Just because I'm a Christian, Harry, doesn't make me a saint. I try, but *hey!* What the heck. Look, I was fond of you once, but I'm not now. And maybe I should have explained the situation more clearly to you before. But there you go, I didn't. I'm sorry, but there we are."

"That simple?"

"Yes."

"Mmm."

"Move on, Harry. It's over. Find somebody new."
"That simple, eh?"
"Yes, it's that simple."
"Really?"
"Yes. And I have."
"What? Moved on or met someone?"
"Well, not that it has anything to do with you ... but yes, I've met someone."
"Oh?"
"Yes."

Martha paused. Sat tight-lipped. Annoyed that she'd given away more information than necessary.

"Well, I hope it's going OK for you," Harry mumbled half-heartedly, unsure of what to say next.

"Can you ever really tell?"

"I think I can. I can tell. I can tell when it's serious and when it's just a bit of fun."

"Well, I'm not falling for anyone anytime soon."

"You did once. Don't you remember? '*I love you, Harry. I really love you* ... blah, blah, blah.'"

"I don't remember, and frankly, even if *you* don't, I *do* find this topic embarrassing."

"I don't know, Martha. I get the impression that there's something else. Something you haven't told me."

"No. There's nothing."

They sat in silence for a while, the conversation ebbing.

"Look, maybe you should know, Harry."
"What?"
"The biggest hurdle—"
"Was?"
"Religion."
"Well, I kind of guessed that."

"I mean, one of the first questions I asked you when we met was: *"Are you a Christian?"* And you said no. You were emphatic. And that's a serious issue for me. Insurmountable."

"Well, firstly I didn't know that you were a Christian and secondly I was probably being glib. I got it wrong. These days when most people ask a question like that you kind of imagine that they want you to say no. It was a first date and I read you wrong. I guess it serves me right."

More silence.

"And then there was sex."

"Sex?"

"Yes."

"Oh, because of the religious thing?"

"Absolutely. Things might have been OK if we hadn't—"

"Well, I presume you told me you didn't believe in sex before marriage?"

"Absolutely."

"Er, before or after we'd had sex?"

"Before ... after ... Oh, I don't know."

"Well if it was after, then maybe that was a little late?"

"Maybe. But there we are. Another problem, you see? There were just too many problems."

"I think you gave me up like some people give up smoking, drinking or drugs: you didn't necessarily want to, but felt it was the right thing to do. And the most effective way to give up anything is to cut whatever it is out altogether and right away. Throw all the fags on the fire, pour all the drink down the sink. Get rid of the temptation altogether."

"Your imagination knows no bounds, Harry."

"And your new man. I take it he's a Christian?"

"That's none of your business."

"A born-again?"

"None of your business."

"I'll take that as a yes then."

Martha stared back. Another pause. A longer pause. Martha frozen. Speechless.

Then Harry's eyes lit up. He got to his feet and slapped a hand on his forehead.

"My God, it's so simple, isn't it? It's so bloody simple ... *That's* why you wanted me out of the way."

"What do you mean?"

"You found a new, improved model."

"What?"

"And you didn't, and don't, want him finding out, do you? Of course—"

"What do you mean?"

"You don't want him finding out about me. You don't want him to know that we went out together or that I even exist."

"Wha—"

"That's it, isn't it? If he finds out about me and then about my atheism, he'll be curious. He'll wonder whether we slept together. And then if he finds out that we did – and that it was shortly before you started going out with *him* – he'll wonder why you won't sleep with *him* now. It'll drive him nuts. Either way, he isn't going to be happy about this, is he?"

"Oh, come on! He has a different outlook to you!"

"Poor bloke, he's going to be upset when he finds out about me."

"Maybe he knows about you already. Anyway, a very interesting theory, Harry, but way wide of the mark," Martha replied, her cheeks and throat flushed.

A long silence ensued.

"Martha?"

"What?"

"Did you ever—"

"What?"

"You know—"

"What? Did I ever have feelings for you, do you mean?"

Martha paused. Raised her eyebrows. She had taken to twiddling with her hair and thinking very carefully before answering.

"As I said before, it all got a bit creepy. It all got too much. Then, shortly after we split up, I spotted you in Lisburn. You looked dreadful. I thought you'd followed me. Thought you were stalking me."

"Hang on. Was this around the time of my accident?"

"Possibly."

"Actually, I remember. I was walking back to my car. I'd been to a wine tasting. Bumping into you was a coincidence."

"Well, at the time I didn't think so. When we spoke on the street I told you I'd call you, but that was just to get rid of you. Then, a while later, maybe a couple of weeks, I got an angry email from you saying you were cutting off all communication. Boy, was I glad. And then, shortly after that, I heard about the crash."

"How did that make you feel?"

"Confused. Confused and upset. In some small way I felt responsible. I felt I had played my part. A small part. Oh, you know ... was partly responsible."

"And you didn't come to visit me in hospital?"

"No. I didn't think I should. I didn't want to upset your family. It seemed kinder to stay away."

"Fair enough."

"Look, Harry, there's obviously been a fair amount of misunderstanding, but there's not a lot I can do now."

They fell into a protracted silence as words became harder to find; the long pause suggesting that they'd reached a dead end.

"Is that it, Harry? Have you heard enough?"

"I guess," he said slowly. "There's not a lot more I can think of to ask about."

"Look, Harry, this has to be it. There's nothing more I can tell you. Do you think you can get over this now and leave me alone?"

"Sure. And don't worry, I won't say anything to your male friend should I meet him. I don't know who he is anyway."

Martha shrugged and looked down.

They sat in silence, shuffling their feet and shifting uneasily, waiting for another topic to fill the void. Nothing came.

Martha stood up, smiled and walked over to the till to pay.

"Look, thanks," Harry said as they left the health food bar. "Do you think we could ever be friends?"

"No, Harry. Too complicated. It's better if we move on. Keep to separate paths."

Harry looked into Martha's eyes, searching for some kind of familiarity or fondness. There was none. Martha looked away, embarrassed. Harry turned and stepped out onto the street.

"By the way, Martha. Belfast's a small city. If I do bump into you again, please don't have hysterics. It happens."

Martha smiled briefly, nodded and then set off down the road for home.

Harry clambered into the Volvo, let his head slump forwards onto the steering wheel, sighed, sat up, arched his back, turned the key and accelerated away.

25

7.30am. Friday, 10 April 2009.

The day of admission for what Harry String hoped would be his final surgical procedure. He arrived at St George's half an hour early and was asked to wait in a reception area before his first appointment. To kill time he mulled over the events of the previous evening.

As soon as Harry had got home from the health food bar he rounded up everything he could find associated with Martha Browne. The whole lot was dropped into a large black bin bag, double-knotted and then dumped in the wheelie bin at the front of the house.

The previous weekend had been Harry's turn to take Emily and Danny. He was delighted; relished their company and wanted to spend time with them before going into hospital. Having them about the place was a great antidote to his ongoing preoccupation with self-analysis.

Keira dropped them off early on the Friday evening.

"So, what do you fancy?" Harry asked, resurfacing from hugs and kisses and thinking fish and chips or burgers.

"Line dancing!"

"Er, what?"

"Line dancing!"

"Are you serious?"

"Yes!"

"Oh, OK. And where—"

"Killyleagh. Mum and James want us to go."

"Aha. So the line-dancing king of Killyleagh has granted us an audience."

"But they do, Dad. They really want us to go. And they really want you to come too."

"Are you—"

"They do, they do. They both do. 'Bring your dad'. They both said it," Emily enthused.

"Don't worry, we'll look after you," Danny added.

"Can you really see me line dancing?"

"No. But you can sit and watch from the bar—"

"Steady!"

"Seriously, you'll love it."

"And do you wear all the gear? Does Mum wear the gear?"

"No. And it doesn't matter. It's just something to do. And it's fun!"

"James wears all the gear," Danny chipped in.

"I'm sure he does. I'm sure he looks very fetching."

"*Steady!*" both kids said, mimicking Harry's voice and giggling.

"And does it go on for hours and hours?"

"No. Only about an hour and a half."

"And where is it in Killyleagh?"

"The Duck."

"The Duck? I didn't know there was one."

"Oh, come on, Dad!"

"What time?"

"It usually starts at about seven."

The Duck and Goose was an ivy-clad country pub off the main road to Downpatrick whose walls and ceilings had been slowly tanned in layers of nicotine and vegetable fat. It smelled better full than empty, the general aroma more acrid since the implementation of the smoking ban a couple of years before. The carpet was red, patterned and thick enough to soak up any spillage, dark enough to hide any stain.

The niches in its stone walls housed a collection of stuffed animals, cobwebs and fluff. The taxidermy on show included a brace of snarling foxes, a dog-sized pike frozen in mid-air on fishing wire, multiple birds of prey and a stag's head whose expression suggested ignorance of its decapitation.

Tonight the ambience was electrified by the raw energy emanating from the latest round-up of cowboys and cowgirls resplendent in rhinestone studded shirts and fringed skirts and jeans. The majority appeared middle-aged. Middle-aged and over-excited. There was a buzz that gave life to the old bar, a frisson of excitement fuelled by drink and driven on by the promise of the entertainment to come.

Harry, too, felt a scintilla of nervousness at the night in prospect, never mind that it was cultural anathema to him.

The three of them stood in the wide expanse of carpeted no man's land between the front of the bar and the dance floor, overawed by the colourful panto playing out before them.

"Harry!"

Keira was calling from the far side of the room. James Johnston was standing beside her, head-to-toe in Johnny Cash black with grey fringing. His ensemble was topped and tailed with a Stetson and cowboy boots. Harry noticed that Johnston wasn't wearing his specs. Quite a transformation, he felt. In fact, he hated to admit it, but Johnston looked quite dashing.

"Keira! James!"

"Hi, Harry, I'm so glad you brought the kids."

"Yes, thanks for coming, Harry."

Harry was heartened by their friendliness. Maybe he'd underestimated James Johnston. But glasses or no glasses, his Belfast accent still didn't quite sit right with a cowboy suit.

James busied himself talking to Emily and Danny whilst Keira and Harry stood side by side, stunned into silence.

Harry leant over and whispered: "See what I mean? Better without the glasses."

"I know. I think you got that right. I had a word. Contact lenses," Keira whispered back and smiled.

"You don't dance at these dos, do you, Keira?"

"Maybe a token effort at the end. It's not really my scene. But the kids love it. It's just a bit of fun."

"I'm sure they'll grow out of it."

"Now, don't be getting all snobby on us, Harry."

James turned to them:

"How are you with country and western, Harry?"

"I've always been a bit of a Tammy Wynette fan, myself."

"Don't tell me … 'D-I-V-O-R-C-E'."

"You got it, James."

"Now, can I get you folks a drink?" James asked, before striding over to the crowded bar with the order.

"You're not going to hit him, are you, Dad?"

"*Adults* don't fight, Danny."

"They do on my Xbox."

"As I say, Danny, adults don't fight."

Harry was happy to sit the night out perched at the bar sipping a couple of pints whilst watching the line dancers stomp through their repertoire. Much to his surprise, he didn't feel out of place and was reassured by the welcome afforded to strangers.

The regular line dancers at The Duck came in all shapes and sizes, but seemed to share a common joie de vivre promoted by the inclusive nature of the dancing. It looked fun. They looked fun. They were having fun. Harry felt loathe to criticise. It also amused him to watch his kids joining in. They stood to the back so they could follow the moves of the regulars at the front. They weren't adept, but were keen and grinning from ear-to-ear.

Further into the evening Harry spotted Keira stepping out of the front entrance; he presumed she was taking a fag break and slipped out after her.

"It's good to see you happy, Keira."

"I hope you mean that, Harry."
"James's all right."
"You don't say?"
"Love of your life?"
"Doesn't need to be. And don't go there."

Harry smiled, paused, kissed her forehead and went back inside to the bar.

Harry got a cab to St George's on the morning of his operation. He was hungry and thirsty, but 'nil by mouth' was the only instruction to observe before the procedure and was a small sacrifice. His dad had offered to drive him in and keep him company, but Harry decided it would be easier to maintain a calm demeanour if he went alone and without having to cope with his father's anxiety.

Before he was admitted onto the ward he was directed to Mr Patterson's office for a consultation. A final neurological once-over. That done, he was taken across to the appropriate department to be prepped for the main event.

Lying on the hospital bed brought back memories of his long-term recovery. The smell of antiseptic, the hustle and bustle of the staff's daily routine and the ebb and flow of visitors reminded him of the unique qualities of the clinical environment.

As he succumbed to the anaesthetic flowing through his system, Harry was last conscious of a slow-motion replay of his kids line dancing and the broad smiles on the faces of his ex-wife and her new man.

26

1.20pm. Friday, 10 April 2009.

Harry regained consciousness just after lunch on the Friday. He slept fitfully all afternoon, feeling drowsy at best when awake. Concentration and communication were pretty much beyond him. Before the anaesthetic wore off he was put on a morphine drip. When he looked down to check Mr Bannister's work, he was relieved to find that his legs were still a pair. They felt sore regardless of the medication, however, and there wasn't much to see, just a vague outline beneath the sheets.

His father was there when he came round. Billy String had brought the daily papers and a bag of tangerines purchased from the shop in the hospital foyer. He stayed an hour. They didn't talk much as Harry dozed for most of that time.

The next time he woke, Harry became aware of a fuzzy vision of Susan Heywood. Even in a blur her dark hair and full, red lips were unmistakable. Except for his dad he'd had no other visitors, not that he would have been aware of them anyway. Though he had sent Susan a text to give her details of his admission, it surprised him that she had come and wondered if it was out of a sense of duty or just pity.

It was hard to entertain her, too. For the most part she simply held his hand without attempting conversation.

"I'll not stay long. I can see you're knackered. Didn't want you to be alone. The nurses say the operation went well."

Harry grunted. It was all he could do to tap her forearm with the fingers of the hand she was holding before falling back to sleep.

He got another surprise when Keira brought the kids in to see him after school, but he was still too weak to respond with much more than a smile, a gentle wave and a nod.

As it grew dark, and after his supper tray had been collected, he envisaged a long, peaceful sleep; glad that he had a single room, at least for his first night. The thought of sleeping on a ward with other patients didn't appeal, especially if there was a snorer or a moaner amongst them as had been his previous experience.

At eight o'clock, and following the end of evening visiting, the accommodation and corridors of St George's grew quiet save for the occasional bleeps and squeaks of the various monitoring equipment, the subdued babble of TVs and the groans and moans of the elderly and demented. All was mostly calm.

Harry felt too drowsy to read or watch and slept. A deep sleep full of vivid dreams. Pleasant dreams of his youth, of being at home with his parents; walks along the Causeway Coast with his mother, collecting shells in White Park Bay; going to watch Coleraine FC with his dad; visiting Belfast Zoo with Keira and the kids when they were tots.

Then the dreams grew more sinister and gothic. Dreams of beasts hounding him through trees and thickets, and then of dark, hooded characters following him down alleyways and corridors, stalking him across desolate wastelands and chasing him through the rubble of ruined buildings.

In a nightmare he became aware of a figure, a man, sitting in the shadows across from his bed. Immobile, the figure breathed deep, slow breaths and looked over towards him with menace. He was tall and dark, and as Harry raised his head for a better view the man rose to his feet and shuffled closer, stood beside the bed and stared. Before long, within a minute or two, he bent down till his lips were almost touching Harry's right ear, close enough that Harry could feel the man's breath on his cheek.

"Good evening, Mr String. I don't imagine you were expecting me," the dark figure whispered.

"Who ... Who are you?" Harry croaked.

"Clive. Clive Heywood. I don't think we've been formally introduced."

Harry decided he'd prefer the dream to end but could neither think of, nor find, an escape.

Clive Heywood soon realised it would have been better to have formulated a plan of action before rushing out of the house on impulse following the tense supper he'd just shared with his wife. The meal had left them both hoarse from shouting and tearful. He knew that clarity of thought would be necessary if he were to accomplish anything useful at the hospital and avoid shooting himself in the foot. But a red mist had descended. He'd only meant to give Harry a fright, scare him off, but once he was at Harry String's bedside the urge to commit an assault, or worse, was growing irresistible. Like anyone Christmas shopping without a list of what to buy and for whom, Clive's head was in a spin and he didn't know what to do next.

Gaining access to Harry String's ward had been simple. Having stalked Susan to the hospital earlier on, following her up onto the ward at a discreet distance and locating Harry String's private room, it was easy enough to ingratiate himself with the nursing staff once he'd watched Susan leave: *"Hi! I'm Mr String's cousin ..."* And Clive was quick-witted enough to ensure that his presence was well enough noted before he left the ward in the afternoon so that his would be a familiar face when he returned later that night.

Clive also took the precaution of wearing his Supermark boiler suit, confident in the belief that the presence of a boiler-suited tradesman would likely go unchallenged almost anywhere in a building where maintenance work is constant.

"I believe my wife was visiting you earlier today." Clive hissed at Harry String, spitting out the words in a fine spray, unable to conceal his mounting anger.

He leant in a little closer, counterbalancing his weight by placing his right forearm across Harry's chest.

Harry had no sensible answer.

"What do you want?" Harry rasped after a short pause, his breathing hampered by Clive's weight.

Clive just stared.

"How did you know I was here?" Harry croaked.

"I followed her, you idiot. And, it would seem, for good reason," Clive spat venomously.

"Jealous, Clive?"

"*Vindicatio, dulce!* Henry."

"What?"

"It's Latin, little man. Look it up."

At this point Harry took the precaution of making a surreptitious search for the emergency call button above his head and tried to calculate the likelihood of being able to reach it if he made a sudden lunge.

Clive Heywood placed his free hand on Harry String's throat and started to squeeze. Harry couldn't help but notice that in order to mask his forensics Clive had taken the precaution of wearing a golf glove.

"Pleeeagh!" Harry screeched. But Clive's grip on his windpipe was too restrictive. Not so firm as to be life-threatening, but firm enough to prevent clear speech and enough to be uncomfortable and, despite the morphine drip, painful. But Harry, at this point, could detect the lack of a killer instinct in Clive's grip. An encouraging sign, and a weakness of character Harry thought typical of the professional classes.

Though Clive Heywood had had no intention of making a physical assault, coming face-to-face with Harry String for a second time brought home the reality of his wife's infidelity and betrayal. An image of this wretched cripple lying naked and coupled with his wife came to mind, the two of them writhing on *his* bed in *his* home; String running his shrew-like hands over her breasts and gyrating his hips against her loins. Faster and faster and then frantic and furious till exploding inside her, the two of them screaming with passion then kissing wildly. A blind rage followed in a flash as Clive lost control, tightening his grip whilst bringing his other hand to bear on his victim's neck. Now he wanted this over. Wanted this man gone. And who would know?

Harry immediately sensed the increased threat. There was breath in his lungs, but breathing seemed near impossible now. And as his lungs started to tighten and burn, starved of fresh air, he began to flay his free arm searching for something, anything, to grab and with which to fight off his assailant. But his fingers found nothing.

Beginning to panic he thrashed both arms, his right pulling away from the morphine drip, tugging on the tube till it tipped the stand over and sent it crashing to the floor.

Breath was so short. Unconsciousness loomed.

"You're not smiling now, are you, you cunt?" Clive taunted in a deep, slow whisper.

The desperate, groping fingers on Harry's right hand moved faster and ever more frantically. And, just as they were starting to become numb and lose feeling, the tips touched something solid. Round and solid. The tangerines! The plastic bag of tangerines! In a final effort his fingers grasped at the bag and finally got a grip.

Such was Clive Heywood's concentration on the madness at hand that he didn't notice the tangerines as they rolled off the bed and bounced past him. Neither did he notice that Harry was still gripping the plastic bag from which they'd fallen loose. But Clive soon became aware of the carrier as Harry scooped it over his head like a hood and twisted it behind Clive's neck till the transparent plastic was stretched taut across his brow, nose, lips and chin; Harry pulling with all the force he could muster.

And as Clive slowly released his grip on Harry's throat, so as to tear at the suffocating film, Harry was able to take deep gulps of air to relieve the burning in his chest.

Clive's face now bore the open-mouthed incredulity of a gargoyle; a horrified gurn distorted by Harry's polythene tourniquet.

"*Te pedicabo, vermiculum,*" Harry croaked at his adversary whilst firing him a defiant wink.

Clive stared back, bemused.

"Colloquial Latin, Clive," Harry whispered with a wry smile.

"*Bugger off, little worm?*"

"Exactly."

And as Clive backed away, tugging himself free of Harry's grip, Harry had a last view of him lurching out of the room in panic, his hands to his head, snatching at the plastic bag, and then turning and running off down the corridor.

The commotion had attracted the attention of the night staff who were gossiping round the reception desk. Caught unawares, there was little they could do to stop the madman as he sprinted past.

Harry, meanwhile, had blacked out; the temporary lack of oxygen combined with the strain of the struggle compromising his ability to stay conscious. The commotion and Clive's frantic departure gave the night staff cause to dash to Harry's room. The scene of scattered furniture, spilled oranges, toppled drip and an unconscious Harry String was alarming. Security was called immediately.

Clive Heywood was desperate to get out of the hospital, away and home to Susan. He needed to talk to Susan. Must talk to Susan. Needed Susan. He took the stairs rather than the lift for fear of being trapped or cornered, sprinting as fast as his legs would carry him; surprised by the perspiration dripping down his face and into his eyes. His lungs were pumping, tightening, and then a sharp pain started to drill deep to the core of his chest. His ears, alert for the sound of pursuers, became aware of the sound of feet clattering on the stairs above him, maybe a floor or two up. There was more than one person, two, maybe three, and they were descending fast and getting nearer.

Clive looked up and was spotted by a security guard who was leaning over the handrail of the floor above.

"*Oi! Security! Stop right there!*"

But there was no way that Clive was going to stop now.

The survival instinct kicked in, his legs flailing as fast as he could move them down the stairs; moving so quickly that he almost ran into the facing wall at the bottom of each flight. One flight, then the next, then another, the floors merging into one indistinguishable blur. And voices shouting after him. Angry voices. Barking voices. Voices of men who would restrain him. Stop him from leaving. Stop him from seeing Susan. Beat him. Hurt him. And they were getting louder and nearer. Angry voices. Barking voices.

Then the stairs stopped as the ground stretched away from him towards the hospital foyer.

Looking ahead he could see no obstacle between him and the exit, and so sprinted for the sliding doors and escape. But then he heard the men running across the floor behind him. Closing. Getting nearer. He could almost hear their breathing and feel their breath. And halfway to the doors the pain in his chest intensified, became chronic. Unbearable. And then there was a bursting in his chest so sudden and so painful it made him wince then scream. And then he couldn't breathe. Couldn't draw breath into his lungs. His eyes could see, but his limbs no longer moved. Stopped responding. Ceased. And with gears mashing, Clive felt himself stagger, then trip into a stumble and then tumble. And, as if in slow motion, his arms stretched out to break his fall and then crumpled like a collapsing undercarriage as he fell face first onto the concrete floor.

Clive's consultant had advised gentle exercise. That and rest and recuperation. Sprinting up and down stairs and attempted murder were not on the agenda, however. Clive Heywood lay face down and motionless in the middle of the entrance hall.

Dead, stone dead. He would not now be making it home to Susan till the night before his funeral, and only then in a box.

Meanwhile, Harry was tended to by the gaggle of nurses from reception who dashed in, reconnected his drip and checked his vital signs. He was then rushed up into intensive care; the bruising to his neck, his shallow breathing, high blood pressure and dilated pupils were of grave concern.

27

11.10am. Sunday, 12 April 2009.

Harry String first became aware of the daylight as his eyelids strained to open; the muscles fired by a sudden impulse, a small spark, as life returned to nerves and neurons and his brain function reactivated.

The eyes became half-open, still dark and near lifeless, the eyeballs barely visible. And slowly, slowly they received sight. Vision: a dim sparkle, and they could see as if looking out onto the dawn of a first day. Yawning. A birth or rebirth; the senses raw and numb and jerking and sensitive, growing aware of what is and wondering what is to come. No past or future, just a confused and awkward NOW.

Now is, and now starts.

And the eyes scanned the room seeing only soft edges and fuzzy shapes without focus. A chair, a television, a lamp, blinds and a trolley: all forms oscillating like the view along a long road through the heat haze in summer; undulating bands of steel and charcoal; everything vacillating in a wavy monochrome. And all that could be seen was blurred as if observed through frosted glass.

And a first thought comes: a wish that the light be brighter to lend sharper definition to the monochrome. But even where there is light, like the dull glow from the windows, it pains the eyes to see.

And there is no recognition. No recognition of the room or understanding of its function. Its contours do not register. With distorted vision the eyes see a grey and intimidating world.

The eyes look down. They see a body. Their body. It must be. Stretched out and prone, lying on a bed. This bed. Then they follow the line of the torso. Following along the outline of the legs and feet the eyes arrive at the toes. They are bare, a hint of incapacity. And then the eyes spot a bowl of tangerines on a tray and they stop. They focus. The tangerines register. They have significance. Their age? How old?

"Daddy? Daddy?"

Ah! So the eyes have ears. I can hear!

It's a gentle voice. A female voice.

And the someone who is calling is in the room and is bending over the body. My body.

"Daddy? Look, Mum! He's responding. Quick, come and see. His eyes are moving."

"Harry? Harry? Can you hear me, Harry?"

This voice is soothing and kind.

The first instinct is to communicate and so he makes a stab at replying, but can only produce a raw and unintelligible grunt.

"Look, Mum! He's trying to talk again. Daddy? Daddy?"

"It's OK, Harry. Sssh ..."

Through the gloom, Harry String watched the woman put a finger to her lips. His eyes strained to focus, but the effort of recognition was enough to edge him back into the deepest of sleeps.

The next time Harry's eyes opened the woman and the girl were still sitting with him – the woman holding his hand. And his eyes started to bring a sharper definition to his surroundings. Less grey. More colour.

And in full colour the room felt less hostile. But looking down the bed he could still see bare toes.

"Hello, Harry. How are you feeling?" The woman was talking as if he were a small child, a baby even, annunciating with great care as if he might be deaf or from Mars.

Harry tried a sound that he guessed might work:

"Whoo ... whoo ... whoo?"

"He's talking, Emily!"

Harry felt inspired by the woman's reaction and would have tried to say more, but his lips couldn't keep pace with his brain.

"It's Keira, Harry."

"Key ... Key ..."

"Yes, Keira, Harry. And here's Emily."

Frustrated at not being able to make more or faster progress, Harry shut his mouth and let his eyes carry the burden of learning and communication. But every eye movement, every thought and every observation exhausted him. And though he fought the temptation, he could not help but feel drowsy, so drowsy, and couldn't keep his eyes alert, or open, and couldn't help but slip in and out of consciousness.

When he next woke, the eyes opened wider and his vision was sharper. He could feel more movement in the muscles around his eyes. They were moving more rapidly and beginning to dart. Harry needed to shut them intermittently to slow the movement. And then he became aware of some feeling in his limbs and along his extremities: his fingers, his toes, his lips. He found he could turn his head and when he did he saw Keira curled up on the easy chair beside his bed.

"Key ... Key ..."

Harry tried to alert her, but his voice lacked volume. He resorted to a grunt. This he found more effective. Within seconds Keira looked up, sat up and leaned over to him. She looked transformed. New hair colour, tanned, different scent and much taller.

"Thank God, Harry!"

She seemed emotional. Grasped his hand to her lips.

"Key ... Key ..."

"No, Harry. It's not Keira. It's me, Susan. Keira's gone home. Do you know where you are?"

Obviously, the hospital. Harry had a vague recollection of the place, but no more. The new woman, Susan, was smiling, but he could see tears in her eyes.

It confused Harry at first that Keira had left. She was all he had known in this new incarnation, but she was gone.

"Key ... Key ..."

"Oh, don't worry, I'm sure she'll be back. I met her earlier. She told me she comes with your kids every now and then."

Harry looked around the room. A hospital room. That's it, it's a hospital room like any other. And the tangerines were gone. He checked the colour scheme. Saw blues and light greens. At least they were neutral; he could put up with that.

Susan kept talking. Wasn't sure if Harry could understand, but had been advised to chat away to him anyway and so talked non-stop.

Then something clicked.

"Susan?"

"Harry?"

A pause as he pulled his head clear of the pillows to get a better view.

"What happened, Susan?" he croaked.

"Jesus, Harry! You had us worried there for a while."

28

11am. Monday, 6 July 2009.

Coffee time. Harry String was the first to arrive as usual. In the three months since his final round of surgery he had become a regular at Black's on the Stranmillis Road. It was now his favourite haunt. It had been refurbished in the spring, whenever Harry was in hospital. Gone the minimalist late nineties brown and beige and in with the mid-noughties boudoir effect. An interior festooned with velvet drapes, splashes of gold, Victorian chintz and a flock wallpaper that reminded Harry of his favourite Indian in Brick Lane. Not his taste, but what the hell? Anyway, it had become a home from home: the old staff still worked there, the coffee was as good as ever and there was plenty of parking nearby.

Parking had become less of a priority for Harry, though. The procedure to straighten his legs had been as successful as he had wished for and the medics had hoped. He wasn't sprinting personal bests, but his limp had diminished and become barely noticeable. The positive change in his physical condition had boosted his confidence and lifted his mood. He was far less self-obsessed and now tended to look forward rather than back.

Harry nabbed his favourite window table and sat facing out onto the street. There was just enough light to read his paper by. He kept an eye on his watch. Bloody Robert Doherty. Fifteen minutes late already. Strange considering how urgent he had been about meeting up when he had phoned that morning.

Another glance and when he looked up Robert was there, perspiring a little and panting a lot.

"Want a top-up, Harry?"

"No, I'm OK. So, what's so bloody urgent, Roberto?"

"Hang on, I'll tell you in a minute ..."

Harry turned and watched Doherty amble over to the counter and followed his interaction with the staff. He couldn't hear, but was entertained by the guffawing that ensued. It interested him that a character like Doherty could be so bright, creative and competent on the one hand and such a complete buffoon on the other.

"OK. So, what's up?"

"Look, I can't stay long, but I wanted to tell you face-to-face. I've just landed us a cracker of a job, Harry."

"Really?"

"Really."

"What?"

"A book."

"What kind?"

"Food book of course."

"Happy days! Who for?"

"Who's the nation's favourite celebrity chef right now?"

"Erm, not the blonde on the Channel 4 show on Saturdays? Saturday something or other? Rebecca Thingy?"

"That's the one. Rebecca Thingy."

"Nice one!"

"She's everywhere right now. Hot. Anyway, the publishing company wants us to do her next cookbook. *Seafood from Spain* or something. They want you to take the pictures. Liked your seaweed thing. They're really, really enthusiastic. It'll be a two, maybe three-week shoot in Spain around the southern coast and the Balearics. Fancy it?"

"What do you think, Doc?"

Work was hit and miss for Harry. Busy one moment, slow the next; lucrative when busy, nothing coming in when not. Therefore he'd always taken the precaution of keeping his overheads low. The studio room cost buttons, he was mortgage-free and conservative in his spending. In short, he could survive the weeks when there wasn't work, the financial famines, and, as long as he didn't go too mad, could pay off most, if not all, of his accumulated debt when a lucrative job came in.

"Look, I'm really sorry but I've got to dash," Doherty said, finishing off his espresso in one gulp.

"What's new? Oh, hang on, Robert, haven't you forgotten something?"

"Eh?"

"Your latest business card?"

"No time, H."

"No card?"

"Nope."

"Oh."

"Look, I've forwarded you the email from the publishers, Harry. Have a careful read and get back to me pronto. We'll set up a meeting. They're really keen to get you on board. I mean, they'll pay your full rate plus expenses."

"Excellent."

Robert Doherty put his cup down and stood up to go.

"Er, Harry ..."

"What?"

"Don't look behind you, but—"

"*What?*"

"Oh nothing, nothing. Look, got to go. We'll speak soon."

And with that he was gone.

Harry shook his fists under the table in celebration. A book and some foreign travel were just what he needed to counter the lethargy starting to set in.

After a slurp of coffee to regain his composure, he glanced over his shoulder. There was nothing in particular to see except a group of loud women nattering through lunch a few tables back. Then, just as he was turning away, he caught a glimpse of Susan Heywood in the middle of them; preoccupied with the chatter, animated, hands karate-chopping the air and oblivious to her surroundings. She looked as radiant as ever.

Harry froze for a second or two not knowing quite what to do next. He would have loved to have gone over, to have made contact, hear her voice, feel her touch, but decided to slip away quietly.

Back on the street he took a deep breath to get his bearings and was about to walk off when he felt a tug on his sleeve.

"Hey! You not even going to say hello, then?"

"I'm sorry, you looked busy. I didn't want to bother you."

"It's OK. They're old friends. Ladies who lunch. Fancy a coffee, Harry?"

"Are you sure?"

"Of course. Why not?"

"Here?"

"No. Let's go somewhere quieter. There's a bar just up the road."

"What, Bar Zero? Really?"

"Oh, it'll do."

Harry nodded and then followed Susan as she turned to go.

It was only a short walk up Stranmillis. The bar was busy with lunchtime diners. They were shown to a booth at the back of the dining room and ordered a couple of coffees.

Harry could feel himself blushing. Didn't feel confidant.

'I'm sorry about—"

"Clive? There's not much you can say, really, Harry. Well, especially you, I suppose."

"Still. I'm ... I'm ... Sorry for your loss."

"Thank you. And I know you mean it."

"I remember seeing you at the hospital, Susan. I was in a bit of a state. I was glad you came though."

"Well, it was difficult. I would have come again, but it was just impossible really. I couldn't. It didn't seem right. Obviously there was a lot for me to cope with round that

241

time. You know, the funeral and then, after ... Well, I had to deal with Clive's family and things were a little—"

"Complicated."

"Yep."

"And now?"

"Better. Got a new job. Sold the house. Got an apartment by the river."

"What's the job?"

"Do I have to tell you?"

"Yes."

"Really?"

"Yes."

"Don't laugh, but I'm working in a funeral parlour."

"An undertakers?"

"That's the one."

"How come?"

"You won't believe this, but I met them through Clive."

"As you do."

"They handled his funeral. I met them when I went to their offices to discuss the arrangements. They liked my manner—"

"Naturally."

"They asked what I did and all that, and then a week or two later they offered me a job. Just like that! So I work for them, front of house, dealing with their customers, the bereaved. I am very empathetic. And I like to think I'm good at it. My counselling experience has come in handy, at last."

"Hence the dark outfit?"

"Exactly."

"It suits you."

"Thank you," Susan said, looking coy.

"What about you, Harry?"

"This and that. Work's been a bit up and down. I'm much better physically though and no long-lasting problems from my most recent setback—"

"Let's not go there."

"No. And it looks like I've got a book coming up. Robert was just filling me in."

"Good for you."

"Yeah, it's a food book with a celebrity chef. It's got massive potential or so Robert says."

"Nice."

The energy and enthusiasm with which they had started the conversation as old friends began to stall, neither of them able to keep up the pretence of relaxed charm for long. Following a brief pause the mood changed.

"You know, I would have called you, Harry, but—"

"Look, I understand, Susan. It's OK. It's not been easy for either of us.""

He reached across the table for her hand and held it. It was warm. She didn't resist.

Susan looked up into Harry's eyes.

"I've thought about you often, Harry. I've nearly called you on a number of occasions. Loads of times, actually. But then I didn't know how you'd take it and then I felt bad about Clive too. Oh, you know ... It just always seemed too soon and too complicated. And then I thought maybe I should just leave things. Well, you know ... Just leave it to fate."

"That's OK. As I say, I understand."

"Really?"

"Really. And are you alright?" he asked gently.

"Getting there."

The conversation lulled again. They smiled politely, which felt unnecessary and false.

"Did you ever catch up with Martha?"

"Yes, I did actually."

"And?"

"What a disaster! A complete waste of time."

"Oh."

"Well, I guess I got a few answers. Laid a ghost, I suppose."

"Well maybe not a complete waste of time then."

"Yeah, probably."

"Mmm."

Harry frowned. Could feel the rhythm of the conversation dying as another drawn-out pause threatened a stall.

And so Harry took a punt.

"Hey, look, there's no way of doing this subtly. And you may well tell me to go to hell. And I don't know if you'll want to anyway. And I don't know if I should really be asking, but—"

"Oh, just spit it out, Harry!"

"Would you like to come to Spain with me, you know, get the hell out of here?"

"*What?*"

"You once told me you wanted to run away to Spain on the back of a tomato lorry—"

"No. That was your idea, you *eejit*."

"Well, do you want to come to Spain with me? Just clear off and go?"

"What, for a holiday?"

"Well, it's work actually, but you'd enjoy it. It would be an adventure."

"Sounds dangerous."

"Would the funeral parlour let you go for two or three weeks?"

"What's the job?"

"Well, I'll be needing an assistant on the book I'm doing with Robert. We're shooting in the south of Spain."

"Oh."

"I'll need a bag carrier. You know, someone to pass me this and that. It's only an excuse to get you out there, really. It'll be easy. It'll be a really creative atmosphere. No one's going to object or anything. It'll be fun."

"Not too professional, then?"

"Sod that. They need me. I'm going on my terms. Anyway, you'd be great. You did it in Portaferry."

"It was Strangford, Harry."

"And you'd get paid, of course. It'd be a great escape!"

"And will there be any ..."

"Any what, Susan?"

"You know ... unprofessional behaviour?"

"What do you think?"

"I reckon there's a distinct possibility."

"So, do you fancy it?"

"Well, it's a lovely idea, Harry, and a flattering offer ... And I'm sure we'd have a great time in Spain, but I'm afraid, just at the moment, I like my job. And I've only started. And it's a commitment. Having accepted the job, I feel I owe them."

"Oh. So that's a no, then, I take it?"

"But you'll be coming back, Harry."

"Yes."

"Well, I'm not going anywhere. I'll be here. *And*, you've got my number."

"True."

"But then again, you'll probably meet some drop-dead gorgeous señorita once you get to Spain."

"I won't. I'll only have eyes for seafood and sangria."

"Really? A man with your reputation."

"Very funny. I'm serious."

"You? Serious?"

"I can be."

"Really?"

"Really. Tell you what, take this," Harry said reaching down the neck of his shirt.

"What is it?"

"Well, you see ... Apart from my kids, a clapped-out Volvo, a few books and some CDs, it's all I have. It's the only thing I possess that means anything to me."

"Really?"

"Yes. Think of it as a kind of deposit. A token. I'll be back for it."

He stood, leaned across the table, kissed Susan briefly on the lips, placed his mother's locket into her hands and left before she could return it.

When Harry got back to his studio he read Robert Doherty's email and gave him a quick call on the landline.

"Where are you, Doc?"

"Can't speak. I'm working, Harry."

"What?"

"I'm on a shoot, you plonker."

"What?"

"A cover shoot. You know, for the *Telegraph's* travel supplement. It's the one the tourist board sponsor every year. We're in the grounds of the Clandeboye Estate for a couple of days. Today we're shooting an effing male deer—"

"A stag—"

"Yeah ... a giant red stag, whatever ... rising out of the lake like Excalibur. Anyway, whatever it is, it's bloody huge."

"Bit of a cliché though?"

"You said it. It's someone else's idea of creativity, not mine."

"Hey! You couldn't lend it to me for a while, could you?"

"A stag? Piss off! Are you mad? If you want a pet, come round and take my bloody dog for a walk."

"Seriously, though, Doc. I was wondering: is there enough in the budget for me to hire an assistant on the Spanish shoot?"

"I'll check. Anything else you require? A valet? Smoking jacket? Cocktails?"

Harry put the receiver down.

29

7pm. Monday, 6 July 2009.

Robert Doherty arrived straight from work. Martha Browne's shop was only a stone's throw across the city centre. It was convenient that they were both working late – he picture editing for the travel supplement, she completing a stocktake.

"Are we walking, then?" Robert enquired with a broad grin, sidling up to Martha Browne just as she was pulling the front shutter down.

"Why not?" she replied, her voice barely audible over the loud clang of metal on concrete.

They linked arms, turned and headed off at a jaunty pace, quickly settling into a bouncy rhythm reminiscent of Dorothy and the scarecrow following the Yellow Brick Road. A few blocks later Martha leaned over and delivered a playful peck on Robert's cheek. Then another and, giggling now, another in quick succession.

"Enough!" Doherty said, struggling to fend her off, then, holding her at arm's-length, fighting back with tickles. Getting the upper hand he swung her up and over his shoulder and started to spin round on the spot once, then twice and then three times till she shouted: "Stop! Stop!" And, since he sensed he had unbalanced her and that she was giddy, set her carefully back onto her feet facing him, locked her in his arms and kissed her square on the lips, briefly but firmly.

They both pulled back. He winked at her, then she at him. And then they continued on their way.

"So, where are you off to with Harry, Robert?"

"Spain. We're starting off in Valencia."
"When?"
"In a couple of weeks."
"That's short notice."
"Yeah. But it's a great opportunity and too good to miss."
"And how long will you be away for?"
"About three weeks."
"Are you going to tell him, then?"
"Nah."
"Good."
"Why? Do you think he needs to know, Martha?"
"Maybe. Sometime. But maybe not just yet. Not now."
"Well, I guess that's your call. Just let me know."
"Yeah, OK."

They strode on in silence until Robert slowed the pace from a yomp to a stroll. Then stopped altogether as he felt the mood change. Turning towards her he clasped her hands.

"By the way, I've finally worked it out, you know," he said in a soft voice.

"What?"

"I've broken the code."

"Oh, well done, Mr Turing. And what code might that be?"

"The Bible reference. You know, in Harry's Bible."

"What?"

"The Bible you gave Harry, Martha. Your inscription. I've worked out the meaning of the Bible reference."

"Er ... How do you know about that?"

"He gave me the Bible. He didn't understand what it meant. The reference, I mean. Asked me to take a peek."

"Hey! You weren't supposed to see that. Nobody was supposed to see that!"

"Look, it's OK, it's OK, I can give it back to him – though I don't suppose he really cares."

"It was very personal at the time—"

"Look, don't worry about it. *He* doesn't understand the

significance and I won't tell him. Actually, Martha, how come you've never given me a Bible?"

"Because you've got one."

"Anyway. The Bible reference ... Chronicles—"

"What about it?"

"I've worked it out."

"Worked what out?"

"The reference. What it means. It's obvious, really."

"Oh, congratulations."

"I'm not a hundred per cent sure what you were trying to tell him, but I think I understand the implication."

"Yes, well—"

"*And they entered into a covenant to seek the Lord God, blah, blah, blah* ... It's obvious really."

Robert paused, looked her straight in the eye to gauge her response, then continued when none was forthcoming.

"A covenant. A pact. I think you made a pact with God."

"What?"

"You made a pact with God. You did, didn't you?"

There was a lengthy pause before she replied.

"Look, he was ill. Very ill. He'd been having bad headaches. Then they diagnosed the aneurysm. Things weren't looking too good for him. I didn't know what to do or who to turn to. Didn't know who could help. Well—"

"So you made a pact with God?"

Martha shrugged. She looked tearful.

"It was a sacrifice I thought I had to make."

"So, the deal is ... You give him up and God saves him?"

"Kind of. I thought that maybe later we could be friends. But then he had the crash. I thought he was going to die then, anyway," she said in a quiet voice.

"And ..."

"Well, I thought maybe the car crash was a warning to keep away. So I decided to cut off *all* contact with him."

"So, that's why you stayed away from the hospital?"

"Pretty much. What do you think?"

"It's not for me to say, Martha. I'm sure you did what seemed right at the time. It's not for me to judge."

As the conversation stalled they strolled on again holding hands, then within a few yards picked up the pace when it started to rain.

"You're not going to say anything to him, are you?"

"No. Certainly not. It's not my place to. But will you?"

"No. I think it's best forgotten."

"Yeah. Agreed."

They paused as they crossed the Lisburn Road.

"Do you still have feelings for him, Martha?"

Doherty gave her hand a reassuring squeeze.

"Mostly, I think not. Then again, sometimes, I think maybe just a little, but gradually, less and less."

"And is that OK?"

"Yes. The way things have worked out it's probably for the best anyway."

"And what about us?"

"Look, we're fine. Yeah, we're really fine. Relax."

"Good."

"So please don't go worrying yourself, Robert."

"No, I won't."

Robert stopped and turned to face her again.

"So, when do you think I should tell him about us?"

"One day. Not yet. There's no rush. Anyway he probably doesn't, or soon, won't care. I'll just stay out of his way. You know, till he finds his feet. Meets someone."

"Actually, I think he has."

"Oh, good. Good. I'm glad."

"So, you're OK, Martha?"

"Yeah. It is what it is."

"Agreed."

They arrived at Fig 7, sat beside one another on a banquette and ordered green tea.

30

5.50am. Tuesday, 7 July 2009.

Keira String and James Johnston were asleep. Church Park Road, Holywood. It was not long after dawn; the sun just starting to tease the bedroom blinds.

"What time is it?" James Johnston asked, his gravelly voice crackling across the silence as he lifted his head.

"It's early. Too bloody early, JJ."

"I'm going to pop out for the papers and get some croissants as soon as the shops are open."

"Whatever," Keira groaned, rolling over to go back to sleep. "Just don't wake me or the kids."

But James was wide awake now, and, tempted by the promise of the warm yellow light leaking in round the sides of the blackout blind, dawdled round the bed to take a peep at the day.

"Holy shit!"

"*James, James!* Not now. Please, not this early," Keira pleaded when she'd checked the time on her mobile again and saw the figures five-something.

"Jesus. No. No, Keira. You have *got* to come and look at this."

"James!"

"You have got to look at what's in the bloody garden."

"James! For fuck's ..."

But too late. Keira's curiosity had been pricked. Irritated, she leaned forwards and sat on her haunches at the end of the bed huffing and rubbing her eyes with one hand whilst flapping the other in James' direction to encourage him to unveil whatever was beyond the blind.

"Bloody hell. Bloody, bloody hell. Beautiful. So, so beautiful," Keira sighed, grinning such a wide, joyous smile that her lips rolled back to expose her perfectly aligned and brilliant-white teeth.

On the lawn beyond their window stood a large, fully-grown and exquisitely marked stag. The sunlight bringing a richness to its chestnut coat and highlighting in silhouette the broad sweep of its antlers.

A thin film of early morning mist still hung over the grass to add a surreal air of theatricality to the scene.

And the stag had its head raised as if in defiance, so that when it turned to meet their gaze it seemed that it was staring back at them. It also appeared that its stare – with dark eyes glistening in the light, both rebellious and triumphant – was just for them. It's eyelashes flapping to add a coyness to its demeanour enhanced by the steamy breath meandering from its nostrils.

Keira and James exchanged glances then laughed.

"How—"

"Harry String?" James muttered.

"God! Probably."

"Maybe he still loves you, Keira."

"Oh, let's hope not."

"What about you?"

She thought for a moment. A brief moment.

"Sometimes. Rarely. But sometimes."

She lay down, pulled the covers over her head and went back to sleep without noticing the large horsebox abandoned in the lane at the back of the garden with the message: *Jesus loves you!* hand-painted on its side in worn and weathered characters.

31

11.05am. Thursday, 23 July 2009.

When jetting off from Belfast to any destination where sunshine is the norm you can almost be guaranteed that, on the day of departure, the sun, for once, will come out and send you on your way worrying about the weather you'll be missing at home. (However, it will also be sure to be raining on the day of your return.) It was no surprise to Robert Doherty, therefore, that when he arrived in Holywood twenty minutes early to pick up Harry String and his camera equipment en route to the airport, he found him sitting in his small front garden, head back and eyes shut, basking in the gentle mid-morning sun.

"Have we time for a cuppa, Doc?" Harry asked tentatively.
"Are you packed and ready?"
"Naturally."
"Then I guess so. But a quick one, mind."
Tea made. They both headed for the suntrap out front.

"Have you got your shooting schedule there, Harry?"
"Of course. Let's see ... First, we meet up with Rebecca in Málaga, this evening, right?"
"Yeah. One night at the Molina Lario on arrival then we all move out to the first location which is—"
"Up the coast. We're heading east."
"Valencia."
"So, why are we flying into bloody Málaga?"
"It's easier to get flights there at short notice and cheaper."
"Is it going to be an economy trip the whole way?"

"No. Rebecca wouldn't stand for that and the publisher's pretty sympathetic to her needs. They have to be. I mean, you know, Rebecca's last book went global. A bestseller."

"So what happened to the team she worked with on that one?"

"Don't know. They were due to do this book. You'll have to ask Rebecca."

"Fancy another cup?"

"OK, but a very quick one."

Harry ducked inside and stood over the kettle willing it to boil. He smiled at the thought of the work in hand and although it would be no holiday, he had an open and creative brief and loved the region.

As the kettle came to the boil he thought he heard voices over the bubbling water.

"Hey, Harry ... There's someone here to see you," Robert called from the hall. "Er, please go through, he's in the kitchen."

Odd, Harry thought. He wasn't expecting anyone and had already said his goodbyes to the kids when his dad picked them up earlier.

At first he couldn't make out who was approaching as, with the strong sun behind, they could only be seen in silhouette.

"You still looking for an assistant, Mr String?" Susan Heywood said, strolling into the kitchen and smiling.

"Bloody hell!"

"Does your offer still stand?"

"It's a bit bloody late. I was going to recruit someone locally in Spain—"

"You sure you really want to do that?"

"OK. But what about the flight?"

"Do you mean the fourteen forty-five to Málaga arriving at seventeen hundred hours this afternoon?" Susan said producing a printout from her bag and waving it in front of Harry's face.

"How—"

"After our last conversation I was curious. Called your friend, Mr Doherty, here. He filled me in. He was very encouraging."

"And how did—"

"Belfast's a small town, Harry. And, anyway, I have his number."

"Don't tell me—"

"Yep, I've got one of his cards."

"Ah. Should have known. Cheeky sod."

"Who? Him or me?"

"Him, of course."

"So, do you want me to come or what?"

"What about your job?"

"I've quit. Had enough of funerals. It was kind of cathartic at first, but not so much now."

"Just like that?"

"Well, thanks to a little downsizing, plus Clive's pension and life insurance policy I'm a woman of independent means. I can afford to come and go as I please."

"Impressive."

"One thing, though. If we do happen to get on in Spain, if we survive the trip and arrive home together and we're still talking, that is. If we're together. If we're going to stay together ..."

"What?"

"You're moving into my place."

"Eh? That's a bit forward."

"Well, I can't be doing with any more hanging about and, to be honest, I can't stand it here."

"But really? Move in? Are you sure?"

"Yeah, and why not?"

"Fair enough. I should warn you, though—"

"What?"

"I'm not easy to live with."

"But can you handle me? Have you got the balls?"

Harry just smiled.

"You'll do then."

"Are you being romantic, Susan?"

"Romance is overrated, Harry."

"Maybe. But let's not kill it off altogether."

"By the way. Talking of romance. Your mate, Robert here. I'd ask him about your woman, Martha Browne, if I were you."

"Eh? How do—"

"I bumped into them the other night frolicking on the Lisburn Road. They're an item it would appear."

"An item?"

"You know ... dating."

"How did you—"

"*Know it was her?* From the snapshot in your wallet. So, anything to say, Robert? Harry? Is this going to be a problem?" Susan asked abruptly.

Robert looked at Harry and shrugged.

"Harry?"

Harry shrugged, shook his head and then raised his hands high and wide in surrender to the situation.

"Good. Right then, boys. If we don't want to be late, I'd suggest we'd better get going."

32

10.30pm. Tuesday, 20 May 2008.

The last bars of Andy Williams singing "Music to Watch Girls By" faded and were followed by a hissing on the cassette loud enough to attract the attention of the old man still standing beside the upturned Volvo with his collie. He was growing cold and impatient for the emergency services to arrive.

The old man tutted. He'd drawn solace from the Andy Williams. It had brought a little home comfort to the bleak and boggy field.

All the while the old man had been popping his head through the windscreen to monitor the driver who was still suspended upside down with blood oozing from the cut above his eye.

"It's OK, son. They'll be here soon," he would reassure.

The few seconds of tape hiss on the radio cassette were then interrupted by a deep and mellifluous voice. It seemed to be a commentary of sorts in what the old man considered an educated accent:

"By the time you hear this, Martha, I guess they'll probably have found me and you'll be wondering what happened. Well ... I imagine it's quite obvious by now. Anyway, I just wanted to say sorry. And I am sorry. Truly sorry. It's just that things have got a bit out of hand lately. Shame, but there you go.

And anyway ... in a manner of speaking, this ... all of it ... doesn't really matter, you know. None of it. Not really.

Let's face it, life's a pretty strange affliction. Unavoidable I suppose ... An incurable disease ... and usually fatal.

Gets us all in the—"

As the car's battery ran out of charge, the tape clicked to a stop.

The old man looked down to his collie and smiled, "Radio play, Alfie – just a radio play. Pity, sounded interesting."

He looked up again when he heard the sirens of the emergency services wailing down the main road from Enniskillen and then watched their lights sweep across the hedgerows as they drew near in the lane.

As the lead vehicle pulled up at the field's gate and the wreck was illuminated in the glare of its headlights, the old man turned and headed for home, dragging his collie behind him.

If you liked this, try these:

Jake's Eulogy

Charlie Clarke has been asked to give a eulogy at the funeral of an old college friend, Jake McCullough. Problem: they have had no contact for years and Clarke has nothing to say. In researching his friend's recent past Clarke discovers that Jake has been living a double life ...

Jake's Eulogy is a black comedy – a chaotic journey which starts on the south coast of England and follows a winding path to Northern Ireland and back. Along the way come the distractions of lust, hard-drinking and dark secrets – all mixed with a cocktail of confusion, mayhem and madness.

'Everybody should read this book before they die ...'
Dylan Jones, GQ Magazine

On the Island

Driving home from work, Dillon Jenkins finds a man sprawled across a traffic island in the middle of nowhere. His offer of help leads to a partnership with sometimes comic, often dramatic, results ... a journey that sees the two men pass through an underworld inhabited by drug barons, terrorists and the law.

Set in and around Belfast during the early 1990s, *On the Island* has an eclectic cast of characters whose paths cross in surprising circumstances.

Mystery, suspense, romance and redemption are the ingredients which make *On the Island* a rich feast of adventure.

"A thought-provoking and pacey read filled with memorable characters ..."
Tara Craig, Go Belfast Magazine

available at indiego.co.uk